UNWANTED FATE

A. GORMAN

Books by A. Gorman

Their Sins Series

Rules of Her Sins

Blackmailed

Standalone

Love, With All My Heart

Coming soon

A Gentle Touch (novella)

Unwanted Love

The Weekend

To Delisa Lynn, thank you for not giving up on my words when I wanted to delete them all.

To everyone else, be the change the world needs. —A.

CHAPTER ONE

Emily

*R*AIN DRIPS OFF THE CANOPY I'M STANDING UNDER IN A STEADY staccato rhythm, and my mother's quiet weeping breaks my heart piece by piece. I don't know if it will ever heal from the pain that I'm feeling at this moment. The American flag on the large dark oak casket gently ripples in the humid breeze, and in the brief moment of silence, I swear I hear his laughter in the wind.

"Attention. Standby. Ready," yells the officer in charge of the members of the Honor Guard. I can hear their rifles click into the loaded position. "Ready. Aim. Fire."

Rifle shots echo through the cemetery, vibrating the air around us. A light haze of smoke makes its way into the canopy, surrounding us. "Ready. Aim. Fire." Seven more shots ring out, making me jump into my mother, and the final seven rounds blast out, leaving my already frazzled nerves raw.

"Present arms," the officer calls out as the last echoes of the shots fade out, and a lone trumpeter begins mournfully playing "Taps". My mother's unable to stand up by herself anymore, and I grab her around the waist, pulling her into me, holding her up until the minister tells us to take our seats. The song concludes, and I can't stop the chills running down my spine or the goose bumps rising on my exposed skin.

"Order arms. Port arms. Right face forward march," bellows out the officer again and the men, except for one, march away from the canopy, and go behind us where I can't see them.

"You may be seated," the graying older gentleman tells everyone.

Mom falls into the padded folding chair, but I don't let go of her because I don't know if she is capable of sitting up on her own. The six officers move into place, picking up the flag that's rippling in the wind and initiate their tedious job of folding the flag with precision.

I look away, willing myself to stay strong for my mother, but I see my brother standing under a weeping willow in the distance. I wipe my eyes, allowing them to focus, and I look again. The man standing there is older than he first appeared, and sadly, is not my brother. Although by just glancing at the man, he would easily pass as a relative of mine.

The stranger looks up right as I'm about to return my focus on the flag folding and our eyes meet. Something familiar about him clicks in my mind. Have I met him before? Surely not, because why is he standing over there and not here?

I look at my mom who is still in my right arm and start to say something, but all thoughts of the man under the tree fade from my mind as an officer bends down on his knee in front of my mother. With meticulousness, he presents the flag from Nate's casket to her. Mom's hands shake with grief and isn't able to hold on to the flag, and I take it from her. I hold it close to my heart while still supporting her with my other arm as the officers' march off.

"That concludes the service," the older gentleman speaks out to everyone in attendance.

We want some private time to say good-bye to Nate before they put him in his final resting place and as soon as everyone has said their good-byes, we will too.

The condolences and kind words seem to be never ending, but soon it's the chaplain, the funeral director, Mom, and me left by the gravesite. I don't know if I'm prepared to do this. I don't know if I can ever say good-bye to my best friend, my protector, my twin brother.

Mom seems to have calmed herself and is beside Nate's casket telling him everything she thinks he needs to know. A strong gust of wind blows through the canopy, threatening to blow it over, and I see my mother is lying over the casket with tears running down her face as she softly strokes the wood. I can't leave her up there anymore.

"Mom. It's time." I have to force the words out of my mouth.

"I can't. No parent should have to bury their child," she weeps.

"I know, but Nate wouldn't want us to mourn for him like this." I pull her into my arms, and the gentlemen from the cemetery lower the casket into its final resting place.

My mom looks up at me, and trembles out, "Emily, I hope know how much I love you and your brother."

"I know, Mom. And I'm sure Nate knew too." She pulls me into a tight hug as the casket reaches the bottom of the grave.

"I don't know why it had to be him."

"Me either, but he died doing what he wanted to do."

"I wish he never would have reenlisted."

"I know, but we can't change the past. We can only honor his memory, his heroic sacrifice, his love for our country…his job of keeping us safe."

She doesn't answer me, but she bends down, picks up some dirt from the previously hidden pile, and throws it on the casket. I do the same, mirroring her gesture of saying good-bye. As if they were waiting on me, the workers cover the casket with the remaining dirt.

"Ladies, are you ready?" the younger funeral director asks.

"Yes, Mr. Hanes," I reply, needing to get Mom settled in at home.

I look at the willow tree, hoping the man would still be standing there, but he is no longer there. Wonder if he was attending Nate's funeral, or if he was just paying his respects since it was a military funeral? I don't remember him walking through the calling line at the funeral home. If he was attending, why was he so far away? He could have come to the grave site, but it was almost as if he was trying to stay out of the public eye.

There was a familiarity about him. Maybe I've briefly met him at a family reunion—I'm sure that's it.

"Emily," my mom asks, pulling my attention to her. "Are you staying with me?"

"Yes, I'll stay with you. I don't have to return to work until Monday."

"Good. I have enough food to last me a month, and I need help eating it," she says with composure in her voice.

"I'll help you store it so it won't go bad."

She nods. "I need to help going through Nate's belongings."

I don't say anything as I'm at a loss for words. We make our way to the funeral home's black Lincoln, climb inside, and Mr. Hanes shuts the door.

Taking a deep, calming breath, I slowly let it out.

"Are you sure you want to do that so soon?"

"If I wait, I'll never part with his belongings. I don't want you to have to be stuck with his things and mine when I pass on."

"Fine. If you don't mind, I'll take his clothes to the community center. I'm sure some of the boys could use some newer clothes."

"Sounds like a good plan. I'm glad they will be put to good use," she says as she looks out the car's window.

"Me too, Mom, me too," I whisper out as I think about what life is going to be like without Nate.

The ride from the cemetery to the funeral home seems to take forever as the unforgiving Reno sun has made an appearance after the rain clouds dried up. Even though the windows are tinted, the heat from the sun is making the backseat unbearably hot. Once we arrive at the funeral home, my mom collects the things that we brought, and we are quickly on our way to her two-story home in Silver Springs, near the Lahontan State Recreation Area.

I pull into the driveway and the house never looked so small, and I help Mom get her things out of the car and my overnight bag and carry them to the front door. She fumbles with her keys and unlocks the deadbolt on the old white door, the smell of Nate's cologne consumes me, and I'm no longer able to be strong. I fall to my knees, crying. I've lost the other half of my heart, my brother. My mom pulls me into her lap, and we sit in the doorway sobbing, letting the grief overtake our bodies.

This day, I'll never forget, the day I buried part of my heart.

I don't know how long Mom and I've been sitting on the floor, but our tears are dry and our bodies no longer quiver with sobs, and we know it's time to move past our grief. Moving on would be what Nate would want us to do, and I think smelling his cologne was his way of letting us know that he's watching over us. Until his death, he hadn't been in the house since Thanksgiving, and that was five months ago.

"Hungry?" Mom asks as we pick up our bags and shut the front door.

"A little." Not really, but if I don't eat, she will be upset.

"Let's work on the kitchen, then we will work on Nate's things," she says as she puts her bag on the couch.

I nod and follow her into the kitchen, and try to prepare

myself for what is to come after we eat a late lunch.

After eating a late lunch, we get to work transferring food that friends have brought over from their dishes to plastic storage containers and freezer bags. I thought Mom was exaggerating about the amount of food she received, but I think it was an understatement. By the time we finish, it's almost evening time.

"Mom, can we go through Nate's things in the morning? I think it would be a good idea if we try to get some rest tonight."

"That's fine."

"Why don't you go and take a hot shower while I finish this up? I'll put the remaining dishes in the dishwasher and we can be finished with the food."

"That might help me relax." She smiles softly at me while she pats my right cheek with her right hand. "I love you, Emily."

"I love you too, Mom."

She takes a small breath and turns to head upstairs. A few minutes pass and I hear the water turn on in her bathroom. I return to the task at hand so I can take a shower myself before I go to the room I occupied for almost nineteen years.

Patrick

"KRISTIN! PLEASE GET ME THE REPORT ON DONATIONS AND grants for this quarter," I yell into the intercom

"Yes, sir. I'll send it to you and bring you a hard copy as

well," she replies, pleasantly, ignoring my gruffness.

"Thank you."

"You're welcome." The intercom clicks off.

I know Kristin will take a few minutes to bring in the reports I need, so I turn on the TV to check out the local news and weather. I'm supposed to shoot eighteen holes tomorrow if the weather cooperates.

"In local news, twenty-three year old fallen hero and Reno native Nathan Janes was laid to rest today in Our Lady of Peace Cemetery. The governor and first lady paid their respects to the soldier's family…"

My phone rings, and I miss the rest the news report on the local hero.

"Yes, Kristin?"

"Mr. Nichols called and was hoping you are available next Friday to present a check to a community center on the southwest side of town. He has to go out of town."

"Yes, please clear my schedule for the day. I'll spend a few hours there," I say and instantly regret the words the moment they came out of my mouth. "Will do, sir. I'll be in a moment."

"Thanks."

I hang up the phone in time to catch the tail end of the weather. "…tomorrow will be sunny and a high of eighty-two."

"Perfect weather for a game of golf," I say as I sit back in my chair, thinking about my life.

You're worthless, boy, my father's voice echoes through my mind. His voice pushes me to better myself daily, but I find myself failing when I drown out his words in a bottle of bourbon.

Ten years ago, I'd never thought I'd be in a position like this: playing golf for work, sitting in an office that's larger than my college dorm room, and over-looking Reno. I worked at a grocery store in high school, barely sleeping enough to stay alive, but after five years with CU Gold Company, my life has changed. I'm the CFO and in charge of donations and grants. Along with making sure CUGC follows proper accounting practices, I make sure organizations have the money to provide those less fortunate with food, water, clothing, and other necessities.

I pull my mind from my thoughts and flip the channel to CNN, trying to catch the latest stock numbers and any world news that would affect the gold market. Lost in the mindless rhetoric of the news show host, I don't hear Kristin knock or enter my office until she's in front of my desk.

"Thank you," I say and sit forward in my chair as she places the sheets of paper on my desk.

She nods, and adds, "I included the projections for the next two quarters as well."

"Perfect. Just a reminder, I'll be on the golf course with Sanders tomorrow. If anything pressing arises, please call."

"Yes, sir. Will you be in the office Saturday?"

"Yes, but you don't need to come in."

"Okay. I will make sure to leave you a detailed list of anything that needs to be handled before Monday."

"I love your organization, Kristin. I appreciate all you do."

"Thank you, Patrick."

"You're welcome. I'm going to grab lunch; do you want me to pick you up anything?"

"No, I'm fine. Thank you. I might head out early today and will grab something then."

"Okay. Call me if you change your mind."

"Thank you. Will do."

She walks out of my office and softly shuts the door. The kind, *mature* woman keeps my temper in check and keeps me sane. I pick up the reports she placed on my desk and lean back in my chair and my mind returns to the funeral of the fallen soldier.

I know soldier deaths are sadly almost a daily occurrence, but there was something about him. Probably because we're close to the same age or it's because he's from here? I'm not sure, but refocus my attention to the reports and get the information I need for a meeting this afternoon.

At a quarter till three, I'm finished with the write up I need for my meeting with Kane Nichols, President of CU Gold Company. I arrange my desk so I know what I need to work on when I come into the office on Saturday, but knowing how my overactive mind works, I'll return after I run my errands today.

Since I sleep here more than I do at home, I have a couch that turns into a bed as well. Up two levels is a full service fitness center, so I can shower up there, so no one but Kristin knows that I stay overnight. She makes sure I have several clean suits and other changes of clothes for me. I think of Kristin more of a mother figure than an assistant most of the time.

My office clock chimes three and I turn off the screen on my computer. I stand and walk over to grab my jacket that hangs on the back of the black leather chair facing my desk, and pick up the documents I need for my meeting with Kane. Approval from this meeting will free up a million dollars to donate to veteran services around the city. I open my office door, I see Kristin typing away at her computer, and I flip the lock on the door and pull it shut.

"Kristin, I'll be in Kane's office for a meeting and then I'm heading out."

"Good luck, and have a good evening, Patrick."

"You too."

I confidently walk to the other side of the office building and up one floor of the massive structure, which houses main corporate workers. Each level houses a chief officer and their department. My department and I are on the eighteenth floor.

Aneesa Rose, Kane's assistant is sitting at her desk, filing her nails. I swear the only reason he keeps her around is to look at her body. She has to be fresh out of high school. The common sense of a gnat, but she has impressive assets, not that I stare at them, much.

"Aneesa, Kane's expecting me."

"I'll let him know you're here, Mr. Matheson," she says in between chomps of her bubble gum. She puts the nail file down and picks up the phone.

I step away from the desk so I don't have to hear her talk and chomp gum.

"Mr. Matheson, Mr. Nichols said go on in."

"Thank you, Aneesa."

She nods her head and resumes filing her nails. I shake my head as I walk by her desk and enter Kane's office. I close the door behind me and think to myself, *I'm going to nail this proposal.*

"Patrick, good seeing you, what can I do for you?"

"Well," I begin, "I found a few non-for-profits that could really use some help…" I laid out the plan in front of him, knocking the presentation out of the park.

"Sounds like you've done the figures. I'll run it by the board, but I'm sure that they won't have a problem, especially since a few of the guys are retired military."

"Great. I have copies of these numbers in my office, so I'll leave everything with you."

"I'll let you know tomorrow after we meet," Kane says, putting the file in his portfolio.

"That works. I will be out of the office. I'm playing a round of golf with Sanders tomorrow."

"Ah, so you're the poor SOB that got roped into that." He shakes his head, feeling slightly sorry for me.

"Have to keep the man happy." I smirk.

"He has a killer swing after a few beers. Keep him sober if you want to win." He chuckles.

"Thanks for the heads up," I say with a laugh. "Have a good evening."

"You too, Patrick. We'll be in touch tomorrow."

"Thanks." I walk out of the office and see Aneesa is still doing her nails. I chuckle to myself, as I walk down the stairs to the parking garage to retrieve my car. Time to grab an early dinner and a few drinks at the tavern down the road, because tonight I'll be here working on other financial reports that need to be turned in next week.

CHAPTER TWO

Emily

$\mathcal{I}$AWAKE A FEW MOMENTS BEFORE MY ALARM IS SET TO GO OFF, and at five thirty, "Sister" by The Nixons fills the room. Tears stream down my face and onto my pillow. This was Nate's song for me. He would sing it to me each time we spoke on Skype, and our last video chat plays over in my mind. My brother was so happy to be coming home in a few months, but instead, he came a few weeks ago.

My eyes burn with tears that haven't fallen yet, my chest aches with the grief I feel, and my body feels like it weighs a thousand pounds. Reaching over to where my alarm sets on the nightstand, I turn the blaring thing off. Silence fills the room and for a brief moment, I wish I hadn't turned off the music.

I allow myself to mourn and pull myself together to get up and get ready for work. Most people aren't happy to return to work on Monday's, but I love my job. I love the people I work with, the kids at the center, and I love helping people better themselves or making sure they have the necessities to survive.

Returning to work will help me also get my mind off Nate's death by returning to my much needed routine. Oh, Nate, why did you have to leave us so soon? I don't know if I'll ever understand the why, but at least I have almost twenty-four years of amazing memories with him.

When he enlisted in the Navy, it was the first time we had been a part for more than one night. Growing up, it was just Mom, him, and me. Nate and I had the super-twin bond, and we always knew when one of us was thinking about the other and within minutes of that thought, we would get a text or a phone call. When he died, the feeling was there but faded, going from a warm, fuzzy feeling to a bitterly cold emptiness, a void that I'd never felt. I knew something had happened to my brother, but I never thought that he had died until my mom had called me when the officers made their appearance on her doorstep.

The tears threaten to return, but I will them not to fall. I roll out of bed and get to my typical morning routine, shower, dress, and eat. If this were a typical day, I would have a minimal hair and makeup routine, but I need to address the dark circles under my eyes before I eat breakfast.

Since I took longer than normal putting makeup on, I have to rush through breakfast to make it to work on time, and run out the door. I don't have to be in my office until eight since my position is the Community Outreach Director, but I like to get there around seven to see the children before they go to school to make sure they are doing well and have full bellies.

I pull into the Project Hope Community Center parking lot at five till seven, and I check myself in the rearview mirror, making sure I look decent. Even though the center is full of children, my position consists of meeting with people who need assistance. When I'm not busy with clients, I often play basketball in the gym with the children.

I've always loved children, and I'd planned on working as a school counselor after graduating with a degree in social work. When I saw this position online, I instantly applied for it, although I doubted I would get it due to my lack of experience. However, since I did community service through AmeriCorps giving me experience in the non-profit sector, had "phenomenal" references, my boss's words, and she liked me from the moment we met, she offered me the position the day following my interview.

As I walk to the door of the community center, I think about the two and a half years I've been here. I feel like I've made a difference in the community, or at least I hope I have. This position is rewarding in so many ways I've lost count. I feel at home here. I won't say that what I do is a piece of cake, because it's not. There are children here with abusive pasts, children that go hungry at night, children that have one or no parents, children from every walk of life that attend the center.

I try to be their friend, someone they can confide to, and some days, the replay of the events that have happened in their life away from the center and school has my stomach rolling.

Even though I try to be here for them, they still get lost along the way and run away from their problems. A few of the girls from the center have gone missing, three in the past few months. Eight girls have vanished without a trace since I've been here—that's eight too many.

Other stories fill me with joy as they tell me that their parents got a new job, they got a bed to sleep in, or things that I take for granted. Sometimes I get to meet their parents as they see me for assistance, and I try my best to help those that really need the help.

Opening the heavy glass door, the familiar mustiness of the center hits my senses and comforts me. My heels click on the concrete floor as I walk to the main office that sits to the right of the entrance. I am the first of the office staff to arrive, so I have to juggle my purse and briefcase in my arms to find my keys I absent mindedly threw in my purse. Finally finding them, I unlock the deadbolt on the door, and walk through the threshold, turning the lights on as I go to my office to unlock the door.

I feel relieved as I get back into my normal routine as I push my door open and place a stopper under the bottom to prop it open, and turn on the lamp that sits on my desk. The light instantly shines on the picture of my brother, mom, and me at my brother's boot camp graduation. I bite my lip to keep it from quivering. Maybe I shouldn't have returned to work yet, I don't know if I'm able to be here, but I know that Nate would be upset with me for putting life on hold.

Picking up the framed picture, I sit down in my black ergonomic office chair, and run my fingers over my brother. "Oh, Nate, I miss you so much…" I say to the picture of us.

A knock at my door interrupts my thoughts and I look up to see who is at my door, Victor Avro.

"Hey, Victor," I say as I set the photo on my desk and try to compose myself. "How are you this morning?"

"Hi, how are you… I'm mean…that was silly of me to ask," Victor says, fumbling with the files in his hands.

"You're fine, thank you for asking." I offer him a small smile. "I'm doing okay. I still can't believe he's gone."

"I'm sorry. If there is anything you need, please let me know."

"Thank you…" I remember I have Nate's clothing in the rear of my Rogue. "Are you busy right now?"

"No, I was getting ready to make some copies of these files," he says as he holds up the files he was fumbling with moments ago.

"Do you mind helping me carry in some bags of clothes? I think we can get them all in one trip."

"Yes, of course. Let me place these files in my mailbox and I'll be back to help." He turns and walks out of my office.

While he goes to the mailboxes, I turn on my computer and lock up my purse and briefcase in my desk drawer. With my keys in hand, I walk out to the main office door and wait for Victor to return. A few moments later, he meets me at the door.

"All set?"

"Yes. Are these clothes for the kids or for the Place Hope Closet?" he asks as I lock the main office door.

"I thought I could split them between the two. I didn't realize how much clothing my brother had. There are things with the tags on them still that I thought could go to the Closet. I'm sure someone would enjoy getting something brand new."

He nods and we walk outside to my SUV in silence. I click the unlock button on the key fob and open the back door to get the bags of clothes out. There are four shopping bags full of clothes. Mom refused to put them in trash bags as she said, "Your brother's clothes aren't trash," and she dug out large bags used for Christmas time purchases.

"Do you think we can get them all in one trip?"

"Yes, I think I can get them all."

"Oh, no. I can carry a couple."

"Okay, can you hand them to me so you can shut the door and lock it?"

I nod and I pull out each bag one by one, handing them to Victor. I pull out the last one and don't hand it to him. He scrunches up his nose in frustration, but I can carry at least one bag.

"I got this one. Let's take the bags to my office and I can sort them."

"Sounds like a plan."

"I'll get the doors since your hands are full."

He laughs and shakes his head at me, as if he doesn't know

what to say.

We get the bags in my office and the smell of my brother fills my small office. I smile, knowing that a little bit of him is here, and I look up at the clock on my wall and notice it's seven thirty. A few of my favorite kids should be here and I walk toward the brightly painted cafeteria, and can hear the sound of children laughing and talking filtering down the hallway. I put a smile on my face as I walk in the double doors and see the children. They are exactly why I need to be here today.

Patrick

Seven forty-five. Ten minutes after Kristin found me in a drunken haze at my desk, I'm running like a thoroughbred on the treadmill, trying to sweat the alcohol out of my system. After gaining some clarity and running eight miles, I go sit in the sauna to finish pulling the residual alcohol from my body.

I stumble out of sauna as I head to the locker room to shower and dress. I'm glad I don't have any meetings until one o'clock today, because I need to get my head on straight. Before stepping into the shower, I check my phone to make sure I didn't miss anything while I was sobering up.

Looking at the messages and phone call log, I notice my sister called about twenty minutes ago, and I know she's probably heading to class, so I don't call her. I put my phone up, retrieve my shower bag from the locker, and head to the bank of showers around the corner.

Twenty minutes later, I dress in a crisp blue and white striped suit with a royal blue tie, and I'm ready to face the day. On the way down to my office, I notice my sister has called again, and still didn't leave a message. I wonder if she's accidently dialing me? Who knows. I'll call her around lunch time, so I don't bother her.

I make it to my office, and Kristin has cleaned and organized everything to make it look like an office, not my living space. A cup of coffee and a breakfast sandwich sit next to the keyboard. I unbutton my jacket, sit down in my oversized black leather chair, and flip my computer screen on. While it flickers to life, I take a sip of the black coffee in front of me, and it is the perfect temperature. As the smell of the sandwich hits my nose, my stomach growls, reminding me I've not eaten since brunch at the country club yesterday.

The new email notification pops up on the screen, so I click the notification box and read the email. I check the other messages while I drink my coffee and eat. A phone call should have been placed instead of sending me multiple emails on the same topic. I push my empty cup off to the side and pick up my office phone to call the financial analyst under me to address the pressing issue that is sitting in my email.

"Good morning, Patrick," Neil Rodhe says after the second ring.

"Neil. My email is blowing up this morning with reports of no growth for this quarter. We were projected to have at least five percent growth." The line goes silent. "Neil?"

He clears his throat. "This is the first I've heard of this. Let me see what I can find out—"

"You should have been the first to know about the potential shortcomings. You're the manager of the department. Be in my office at noon and tell me what the hell is going on."

"Will do, talk then—" I slam down the phone, not waiting to hear any more of the BS excuses from his mouth.

I press the button on the intercom for Kristin. "Yes, Patrick?"

"Neil Rodhe will be here at noon for a meeting. Cancel my 1 pm appointment, clear my schedule for the rest of the day, and have lunch delivered in. Thank you for the coffee and sandwich this morning."

"You're welcome. Do you need anything for the meeting?"

"Yes, please get me the projected growth reports for this quarter and the actual growth year to date reports."

"Will do."

"Thank you." I remove my finger from the button and get to work figuring out what the hell has happened to our projection numbers.

Kristin knocking on the door and entering my office pulls me away from the reports I've been looking at since she brought them to me this morning.

"Lunch is here."

"Place it on the sideboard, please. Neil should be here in a few—" He walks in before I can get the rest of the sentence out. "Kristin, please hold my calls."

"Yes, sir. Mr. Rodhe." He nods as she walks out the door.

"We can sit over here so we can eat lunch while discussing the numbers. I hope there is an explanation behind the emails I received." I look him in the eyes, he quickly darts his eyes to a folder in his hands and places it on the table. "Drink?" I ask as I hold up a bottle of water and a Coke.

"Water is fine. I ran the numbers myself, Patrick. And whoever had entered the projections last week made a huge error," he says, rummaging through the stack of papers. "The projection is on track for five percent. The analyst completely left out India's number. They are the driving force right now."

I place the water and his lunch on the table and I do the same with mine. Taking a drink of water, I let it flow over my tongue, hydrating my mouth. "Do you know who would forget such an important piece of information?" I'm concerned because neglect like this can cause people to lose their positions.

"A newer employee, I've reprimanded her," he says, but it sounds like he is making excuses to me. His lack of eye contact makes me wonder if there is something else going on that he isn't telling. I'll let it go for now.

"Sounds like she might need to be retrained, please make sure that she is," I say between bites of lunch.

"Good idea. I'll get on that when I return to my office." He crosses his legs and uncrosses them, trying to get comfortable.

"While you're here, we will go over all the financial reports of every department so we can address any other issues."

"Okay," he says with a slight look of disgust on his face.

"You have time, right?"

"Yes, of course." He sits rigidly in the chair.

"Good. Let's get underway," I say with a slight smile and a nod.

Three hours later, we've gone over every line of the twenty-six page report. I've highlighted some areas that are showing in the red and I'll address those numbers with the corresponding department.

"Thank you, Neil, for getting this straightened out."

"You're welcome."

"Make sure that your employees follow the correct protocol next time."

"I'll make sure it is addressed when I get to my office."

"Please copy me on the memo."

"Will do. Anything else?"

"I think we are done for now."

"Okay, if you think of anything else, give me a call. I'll be in the office the rest of the day."

"Thanks, Neil." He stands up and I stand with him, offering him my hand. He hesitantly shakes it, and he seems slightly aloof. I'll have to ask Kristin if she's heard any rumors about him.

I walk to the door and open it for Neil, and at the sound of the door opening, Kristin turns to face me.

"Mr. Matheson, you have a few messages. Also, your sister called and said it's important that you call her as soon as you can," she says as she walks over to me, handing me the messages.

"Thank you, Kristin," I walk to my office, closing the door behind me, pick up my cell phone off my desk, and sit in my chair. I wonder what is so important that Addison couldn't leave a voicemail for?

I search through my contacts, looking for her number and press send when her name appears on the screen. The phone rings and rings, and I think it's about going to voice mail and I hear her voice.

"Patrick...it's Dad," she hoarsely answers.

"What happened?" I ask without emotion in my voice.

"He had a stroke. It's not looking good."

"Where is he?" I couldn't care less about my father, but I won't tell my sister that. She doesn't know anything that I lived through with him. *You're worthless.* I was seven when she was born, and she only saw the good of Dad. To her, he is the best father ever, but she didn't have to live through his abuse, both mentally and physically. Honestly, what the SOB gets is what he deserves.

"He's in the CCU at University of Nevada Reno Hospital. I'm staying with him right now. He's still unconscious, but all of the tests show that he still has brain activity so that's good."

"Okay, if anything else happens, let me know. I can't leave

work right now," I lie. I don't want to be in the same room as the man, unconscious or not.

"Are you sure?" she says in between sniffles.

"Yes, but if you need anything call me okay. I'll have my phone on me." I feel a little guilty for lying.

"Alright, Patrick. I love you."

"I love you too, sis," I say truthfully.

I press end button, and I hope that I don't have to make an appearance at the hospital anytime soon.

CHAPTER THREE

Emily

$\mathcal{T}$HE CENTER IS BUSTLING WITH ACTIVITY WHEN I PULL INTO the parking lot. Today is our community celebration, and it's drawing the attention of the media and city officials because we are receiving a grant from CU Gold Company. The center director and I applied for it over six months ago, and we were afraid that we didn't get the grant until the company contacted us a few weeks ago. The celebration is the perfect opportunity to accept the grant for the community.

This morning I put in a little more effort in choosing my attire, a light blue skirt business suit with a white blouse, because I have a feeling that my boss Kelly Lui will have me be the one in front of the camera accepting the check. I want to make sure I make a good impression for the center.

As I walk to the entrance, I see Victor decorating the entrance with brightly colored balloons and streamers in various hues of orange and yellow.

"Good morning, Victor," I say with a big smile.

"Hey, Emily. It's a mad house in there. Kelly is running around, going crazy. Maybe once she sees you're here she'll calm down," he says with a chuckle.

"She's here?" She normally doesn't arrive until eight or eight thirty. Some days it's nine in the morning. She stays later in the evening, though.

"Yes, and so is most of the office staff."

"Sounds like I might want to get in there. Talk to you later."

"Good luck." He shakes his head as he laughs.

I hurry through the open entrance doors and pick up my pace to the main office, and I hope I didn't miss a memo stating I needed to be here earlier. The office door is closed, and I peek in the glass before I make it to the door, seeing Kelly pacing.

"Good morning, everyone," I say as I walk in the door and head to my office.

"Emily! Great, you're here," she says as she pulls me in the opposite direction to her office.

"Um, was I supposed to be here earlier?" I say a little worried.

"No, but I was worried you wouldn't be here," the frazzled older lady rushes out.

"I wouldn't miss today for anything…" The statement dies on the last word. They know the kind of week I've had, and they know that a few members of the military will be attending today. "I know how important today is. I'm glad to be here," I say with a smile.

"Good. The presentation will be at eleven, after they present the check, you will need to do a small photo op and a short interview with the CBS affiliate." Say what?

"Are you sure you don't want to do it. What if I fumble with my words, what if I forget what to say? What if—"

"You'll do just fine. I have faith in you. You're the Community Outreach Director, and it's time for all of Reno to meet you and know who you are."

"Do I look okay? Oh my. I'm nervous."

"You look delightful as usual. Just be yourself and everything will flow out naturally."

"Thank you. That is kind of you to say." I smile at her compliments.

"Just the truth. Emily. I'm going to get out there and make sure that everything is organized and set up for the community day. I'll see you in a bit." She rushes out of her office, leaving me behind.

I giggle and smile at her craziness as I head to my office to unlock the door, and as I open the door, the scent of Nate greets me. While going through his clothes on Monday, I decided I couldn't part with his Navy sweatshirts, T-shirts, and sweats. I took most of them home, leaving a couple of each here. Kids can be messy at times and I end up wearing their creations. I smile at the thought and get to my morning routine—feeling off because I'm running behind. I turn on my computer and lock away my belongings, and I try not to think about today's activities because I'll make myself nervous thinking about everything. Ah. I'll be on TV. I'd better call my mom.

Picking up my office phone, I quickly dial her number. She's a transcriptionist so she doesn't always answer the phone, but I don't think she's returned to work yet. I'm about to hang up the phone when I hear her say, "Hello."

"Good morning, Mom. Did I wake you?"

"No, darling. I was out on the deck enjoying a cup of tea. I didn't hear my phone ring until I came in to fix another cup. How's your morning?"

"Good, I think. I'm going to be on TV."

"Oh?" she says, wanting me to go on.

"The center is receiving a grant and Kelly wants me to do all the publicity shots."

"That's magnificent, Emily. I can't wait to tell your—"She stops midsentence, breathless. "My friends," she says, trying to recover.

"It's okay, Mom. We can still talk to him," I say as a lone tear falls down my cheek.

"He would be so proud of you, Em."

"I hope so. Um, as soon as I know what time they will air the segment, I'll text you."

"That sounds good. Are you coming home tonight for the weekend?" she hesitantly asks.

"I can. I don't have any plans," I reply as I absent-mindedly organize my desk.

"Then we can watch your interview together, hopefully,"

Mom replies, happiness returning in her voice.

"I'll bring dinner. Think about what sounds good and when I text you later we can decide."

"Okay, darling. I probably should let you go. I love you, Emily."

"I love you too, Mom." She ends the call, and I put down the phone and open my email to see what I can do before I need to head out to the celebration.

"Emily, it's time," Kelly shouts from the main office's entrance. I look up at the clock on my wall and see it's a quarter till eleven. The morning flew by with all the emails and phone calls that I needed to make. I'm rather bummed I didn't get out to the celebration sooner.

"Coming, Kelly." I grab my keys and head outside, meeting Kelly at the threshold of the office, and we walk toward the exit.

"It's wild out there. I think there is triple the amount of people from last year. I don't even know if we have enough food for the closing celebration."

"Possibly send someone to get punch and cookies from the grocery up the road?" I stop, so we can quickly brainstorm before we are outside of the center.

"See, this is why I have you here. You think outside the box." I smile at her. "I'll send Victor. I think he would be able to get in and out of the store quickly."

"Sounds like the perfect idea." She nods at her statement, and we resumed walking.

We make it outside and the weather is spectacular. The sunny sky is clear and the temperature is in the low 80s, making it perfect to be outside. A bounce house with children lining up to bounce inside, games to win small little prizes, and picnic tables fill the grounds around the center. On the other side of the bounce house is a stark white canopy with a stage and camera tripods set up underneath it. I'm guessing that is where I need to go.

I walk under the canopy and wait for Kelly to place me where I she wants me. After five minutes of waiting, she comes under the canopy with three people I haven't met before in tow.

"Emily, this is Patrick Matheson the CFO of CU Gold Company, and he will be presenting the center with the check." I shake his hand and his touch causes goose pimples to appear on my skin, and I smile when he holds onto my hand longer than normal. Usually, I freak out with the prolonged hold, but I don't want to let go of his hand.

"Nice to meet you, Ms. Janes. Kelly has told me so much about you and your work in the community." His voice is sexy, like a smooth drink of whiskey. I grin and nod like a love struck fool at him.

Kelly continues, "This is the new area director of the Community Centers of Reno, Samantha Devine."

"Nice to meet you, Ms. Devine." I quickly shake her hand. Her quick, cold glance snaps me out of my daze. As fast as she looked at me, her eyes are back on Patrick.

"And this is Maven Shade, Ms. Devine's assistant."

"My pleasure, Ms. Shade," I say as I shake her hand and smile.

"Likewise," she says quietly, with a blush in her cheeks. She must be new too.

"This is how I would like everything to go..." Kelly tells everyone where we need to go and how she wants this presented to the media. She's picked a few kids to be in the photos and on TV, a few children that have touched her life, with Patrick, the mayor, and myself. Samantha and Maven are here to field questions, per Kelly. I love her blunt, *I take no shit* personality. "Any questions?" she asks us.

We all shake our heads.

"Good. Time to get this rolling. Emily, Patrick, let's head to the stage. I think I saw the mayor arrive a few moments ago with a few military personnel." She's off to find him before anyone can say another word, and within moments, she returns to the stage area with Mayor Jim Grove and the four children she picked.

She taps on the mic, "Ladies and Gentlemen of the Place Hope family and our honored guests, welcome to our community celebration. I hope you're having fun today..." Her speech is to the point and has several tears in the eyes of the people in the audience. When she's finished, Patrick takes the podium, gives a remarkable presentation of the grant, and says wonderful things about the center. After everyone finished talking, I'm ushered to the front of the stage to say a few words and accept the check on behalf of the center.

After a mirage of flashes and adjusting my pose several times, I'm standing in front of several TV cameras answering questions from news reporters. I try to not the let the nervousness come through in my voice, but I'm sure people will be able to tell I'm scared shitless. After a few more questions, I'm able to go and enjoy the rest of the celebration. I'd love a Jack and Coke right now to calm my nerves.

"You looked like a natural up there answering their questions," Patrick Matheson says after I walk out from under the canopy, startling me because I wasn't paying attention to who was around.

"Oh, Mr. Matheson, thank you," I say with a timid smile. The man is striking, very sexy. I can see why Samantha couldn't keep her eyes off him. His blond hair and blue eyes remind me of a surfer, and the way his suit fits, I'm sure he probably could surf.

"First time?" he asks as he lightly brushes up against me. The brief contact sends a jolt of electricity through my body, rendering me a little speechless.

"Y-yes. Normally, Kelly is in all the press ops, but for some reason she wanted me to do it today," I rush out, trying to collect my thoughts.

"Well, it's nice to have the opportunity to meet you, Ms. Janes." He winks. Holy hell. Is he flirting with me? Surely not. "So you're the Community Outreach Director," he asks, engaging me in the conversation.

"Yes, I try to make sure everyone who comes in here receives the help they need."

"Impressive," he says with a million dollar smile.

"And with CU Gold's grant, I'll be able to help a lot more people," I say with a huge smile, trying not to suck up. Wait. Yes, I am, and flirt right back.

"I am glad we get to be part of what you are doing for the community." He smiles more natural, and dimples appear on his cheeks.

"Me too, I—oof!" is all I get out as I hit the ground and watch Patrick's face fill with horror.

"Emily! Are you okay?" Patrick asks, as he helps me from ground. I look down, and I'm covered in dirt. Damn it, that's going to be a bitch to get out of my skirt.

"Ms. Emily! We're sorry. We were playing football and the ball got away from us," Ty, one of the big kids at the center, says as he helps brush me off. Then he runs over to the boys and continues to play.

"I'm okay. Thank you for helping me up, Mr. Matheson. I'm going to head inside and freshen up," I say shaking and embarrassed

"Sure you're okay?" he asks with concern, and I notice he hasn't taken his hand off my arm as heat radiates from the contact.

"Positive. I'll be right back." I smile and turn to head into the building.

I'm glad I have Nate's clothes here and a few other things

especially tennis shoes. *I'd look a little strange in heels and shorts.* I chuckle as I walk to my office. This is just a typical day at the community center.

Patrick

I COMPLETELY FROZE AS EMILY HIT THE GROUND, BUT I honestly didn't see the kid coming until it was too late. After a boy almost twice her size plowed her to the ground, she got up and walked it off as if nothing had happed. What can I say about Ms. Janes? She's very enchanting, a natural beauty, someone who makes doing activities outside of work enticing, and I can tell she's impassioned when it comes to her work. Her eyes sparkled when she was talking about helping people in the community.

So many organizations are after money, but instead of using it where we thought they were going to, they used it for their salaries. Seeing this type of involvement in the community makes me glad to be here, CUGC here. Excellent opportunity for the company, and I hope this partnership is something we can make permanent.

I walk around and talk the people who make up this community. No one has had a negative thing to say about the center and its staff. They've talked about all the programs they offer, and the center's website that I researched only listed half of what's really going on here. I make my rounds and bullshit for a few moments with Mayor Grove. We play golf together and a little friendly bull shitting is necessary when I see him.

When I excuse myself from talking to him, I see Emily come out in shorts and a Navy T-shirt. I wonder if she was in the Navy? I guess I could ask.

"You were in the Navy," I ask.

"It is…was my brother's shirt," she says with a slight frown.

"Oh, I'm sorry." I feel like shit that I said something.

"Thank you. He was killed a few weeks ago. We were finally able to lay him to rest last week." She bites her cheek, willing herself not to show emotion.

"Thursday, Nathan Janes?" I ask immediately.

"Yes, how did you know?" She's shocked that I know.

"I saw the segment on the news. Again, I'm sorry for your loss."

She gives me a smile and changes the subject.

"Are you staying the rest of the celebration or do you need to get back to the office?"

"I had planned on staying." *Especially with her here.*

"Good. A few of the children stopped me to ask. They enjoy talking to someone new." The compliments completely make my day.

"I enjoy meeting them and learning about their community. We didn't have anything like this when I grew up, and it's nice to see an effort to bring the community together."

"Your statement is so accurate. Project Hope brings the *hope* into this community."

She smiles at me and her affectionate nature warms my cold soul. Kane is normally the one that comes out in the community, but I deal with the public when it benefits the company or myself, especially myself. I have to prove myself to someone I'm not worthless, me, and I don't want a child growing up like I did, hungry and abused. That might make me a bit of a selfish asshole, but I do it to quiet the voice in my head.

I look at Emily and her vibrancy makes me think she might be able to help me with my newest project.

"I have a question, you can tell me *no* since you're still grieving, but I have a project coming up involving organizations that handle veteran affairs… I would love to have your insight on how best to help soldiers and their families."

She bites her bottom lip for a few moments, and I can tell she is thinking what to say. I know she's going to say no.

"What's your timeline?" she asks as she tries to mask the pain of her lost brother.

"I have approval for the money and the organizations researched, I just want to know where would be best to allocate the funds."

"Can we meet next week to discuss your thoughts?"

"Yes, that works." I put my hands in my pocket and grab my metal card holder. I pull out one of my business cards and hand it to her. "Call my assistant, Kristin, with the day and time that works for you."

"Will do."

"Thank you, Emily."

"You're welcome. Would you like to meet more people that the grant will be helping?"

"Yes, lead the way."

She smiles and walks over to the kids and adults surrounding a large table of drinks and cookies. When we arrive at the small group of people off to the side, she introduces me to several families who tell me their history. Many of their stories have similarities of the physical and verbal abuse I lived with, and in this moment, I've never been more grateful for the Carlino's support when I was a teen.

After several hours at the community center, I'm hot, sweaty, and I want to get out of this suit and shower. I'm glad that I was part of this presentation. If I hadn't been, I wouldn't have met Emily. I think her insight will be a huge asset to my next project. As I walk to my car, I hear, "See you later, Mr. Patrick."… "Bye, Mr. Patrick."… "Bye."… I smile and wave as I walk by.

I make it to my car and remove my jacket before I get in, and I turn the AC on full blast as soon as I turn the ignition on. While waiting for the AC to cool the interior of the car and me, I think about the best way to get to my house south of the city. I hit the home button on the GPS and have Siri worry about getting me there in the shortest time.

For the first time in a while, I think I might actually stay at home and sleep in my bed. There's a calmness over me I haven't felt in years. Maybe the kids wore me out with tossing the football around and playing a few games of hoops. I told the boys I let Emily win, but she smoked me, twice. I guess I'm a little rusty. Mmm. The way our bodies touched, the smell of her perfume; I won't soon forget Emily Janes.

Pulling onto the road that runs in front of the center, I head toward the interstate. As the familiar scenes of the city fade away, I know I'll be home in under twenty minutes. I can't wait to get these shoes off, they aren't meant to play basketball in.

CHAPTER FOUR

Emily

$\mathcal{A}$FTER THE HOUR DRIVE TO MOM'S LAST NIGHT, I CRASHED after dinner. The celebration was superb, and I'm excited that we had such a huge turnout. However, it made for a very busy and long day. Mom and I have an appointment at the spa this morning. We've only visited the spa a few times and she said this was something we needed to do; we need to take care of ourselves.

We arrive early, and the receptionist asks us to take a seat until they are ready for us. There's a side table full of magazines and I pick one from the stack, not paying attention to which one I grab.

Flipping through the pages of the magazine, none of the stories grab my attention, and I'm about to shut the magazine when a picture of a familiar face catches my attention. I open the magazine to view the full article about CU Gold Company's New CFO Patrick H. Matheson.

I read the article, and I see he's single to my surprise, he's a graduate of the University of Nevada Reno and interned at CUGC—so that's how he got into the company? Skimming through the fluffiness of the piece, the mention of losing his mom has me backing up to reread word for word the rest of the article.

Wow, his mom passed away from a heart attack when he was seventeen. Sounds like he lost his main supporter, but found comfort from the Carlino's, the owners of the store where he worked as a teen. He credits them for him being where he is today. Reading the last couple of paragraphs, he wants to put CUGC on the map for their effort to help end childhood hunger and poverty.

The article floors me, could this be the same guy I was spending time with less than twenty-four hours ago? I met the self-assured and well composed business man yesterday, but this article describes a complex, compassionate, and in a way, a quixotic man who wants to change the world.

I put the magazine down and replay the conversations I had with Patrick, and—

"Are you okay," my mom asks from the other side of the side table.

"Yes, just thinking about this guy I met yesterday," I say, thinking of Patrick's drool worthy suit clad body.

"Oh?" Her curiosity is piqued.

"The man who presented me with the check yesterday at the celebration, the magazine I was reading had an article about him, and the way they painted him seemed different from the man I met yesterday."

"Which one do you think is really him?" She raises her eyebrow at me.

"Possibly a little of both. I think he was out of his comfort zone yesterday, but after reading the article, it's possible the center hit too close to home." I sigh, wondering if made a fool of myself by flirting with him.

"You're normally a good judge of character, I'm sure you'll figure it out if you see him again." She reaches across the table that separates us and pats my hand.

"Not if…I have to schedule a meeting with him next week to discuss a project of his."

"I'm sure that will be closer to the real him when you see him again. One on one is a lot different than in the public eye."

"True. I—"

"Cassandra and Emily?" a spa employee calls out.

"Yes?" my mother says.

"This way, please."

We follow her into the changing room of sorts in the spa. The room offers soft lightening and the cream colored large room has hidden changing areas, showers and restrooms, and lockers around the perimeter of the area.

"Please remove all your clothing and jewelry and dress in the robe provided. You can place all of your belongings in the lockers behind you. There is a safety pin on the key to fasten the key to the inside of the robe pocket." She lists out what we need to do while setting out everything we need.

"I'll leave you two to get undressed and prepare your massage tables."

"Thank you," I say as I smile. I so need this massage.

We go behind the curtain and change into our robes, and put our belongings in the lockers. The anticipation of her returning has me feeling giddy because it's been a while since I've had a full body massage, without expecting to exchange it for sex.

"I scheduled facials too," my mom says.

I giggle, as I was just thinking about sex when she says facials. "Sounds good," is all I can get out.

A few moments later, the spa employee returns and leads us into a room with two tables. Candles are sitting on the shelves around the room to light the area, and the sounds of relaxing water music plays softly around us.

"Natalie and Ragan will be your masseuses today and will be with you in a few moments. Please let them know if there are certain areas you want them to focus on today. I'll leave you to get comfortable on your table. Enjoy your massage, ladies," she says politely with a smile and walks out the door.

"I hope I don't snore," my mom says while she's finagling with the sheets and her robe.

"I'm sure you wouldn't be the first person. Do you need any help over there?"

She is yanking and pulling on the sheet, and I think she might fall off the bed she is pulling so hard.

"Finally! Nope, got it," she says breathlessly. I was able to get my sheet up and my robe off without any trouble.

There's a quiet knock at the door as I'm about to say something, and in walk two ladies in pink scrubs with the spa's logo on the left side of their chests.

"Hello, I'm Natalie and this is Ragan. We're glad you're here today. Are you ready?"

"Yes," we say at the same time with too much excitement.

"Fantastic. Since I've worked with you before," she points to mom, "I'll work with you again. Emily, Ragan is amazing, and I'm sure you'll be impressed." I nod my head, because I don't care as long as they know what they are doing.

The ladies get in position and start with the massages. Ragan's hands feel wondrous and I feel myself drifting to sleep. She grasps my glutes, and I jerk up in bed. What the hell was that.

"Sorry, Ms. Emily. Did you hurt your buttocks area recently? It feels bruised."

"I fell yesterday. I guess I didn't realize that it was tender because it doesn't bother me while sitting."

"I'll put some Arnica on it. Let me finish the other side, and I'll place warm towels on you. While you're resting, I'll mix up the Arnica in coconut oil and apply it. I'll send the rest home with you. It's great for bruises and helps with swelling," she says in a whisper, trying not to interrupt my mom's massage.

"Thank you," I murmur, trying to re-relax face down on the table.

My mind revisits yesterday and replays all the events that happened at the celebration, especially the moments with Patrick. There's something about him, he's very charming, but I can't help to wonder if it's a façade? I hope that it's not, but I have a feeling I'm going to find out—I want to find out.

Our time at the spa is over before I want it to be, but it's time to return to reality. I think I'm going to talk Mom into doing this monthly or at least every other month. Even though it felt like Ragan was ripping my butt cheek from my body, the ointment she put on after soothed away the ache in my rump.

We stop at a deli on our way to Mom's to grab a late lunch and it's the perfect way to complete our morning out together.

"Nate's headstone should be in place now," my mom randomly blurts out while we are eating. Not exactly what I'm expecting her to talk about.

"Do you want to check and see? To make sure it's how you want it?" I know if I don't offer, she will go by herself.

"If you don't mind, we can head over after we eat."

"That's fine. I don't think we have anything else planned."

"No, I didn't know if you were staying the whole weekend or not."

"I guess I thought you would know I'd be here until Sunday afternoon."

"I know that now; do you want to go to mass with me in the morning?" Church. Blah.

"Early mass?"

"Yes, of course."

"That's fine. Mind if I borrow a dress." She just looks at me.

"I don't know if I have anything long enough. They all will be short on you."

"That's the point."

"Smartass." She shakes her head and resumes eating her lunch. I'm sure I just got out of going to mass with her, and I smile to myself and finish my sandwich in a comfortable silence.

The sun at this time of day is blistering hot, unlike the last time I was here. What a difference a week makes in a cemetery. I don't know exactly where I'm going and I hope she does.

"Go around the bend and take a right. Drive out a little ways. He's in a row almost by himself. There are four empty plots around him…" she trails off.

Four? What is she talking about? I guess we will have to talk about this later. I'm too busy trying to concentrate on where I'm going and keeping the tears at bay.

"Slow down. See that tree? Park right there." She looks out the window. "It's there," she says, pointing her finger out the window.

I pull under the tree and turn off the car. I lick my lips and take a slow, deep breath.

"Yes." She gets out and I quickly follow behind her. I look around on my way to Nate's resting place, and I see the willow tree where I saw the man under during the funeral. I continue to walk but I'm not paying attention to where I'm walking and run right into my mom.

"Um. Sorry. I guess I wasn't paying attention." Oops.

"You're fine. Well, what do you think?"

I look at it, and our family picture is in the center of the headstone. *Nathanial Kendrick Reed Janes, 23 years of age. He gave all serving his country...* I can't read anymore as my eyes fill with tears, but my eyes advert to the name. Why is there *Reed* on there?

"Mom? Did they mess up Nate's name?"

"No." She doesn't explain herself any further.

"Okay." I notice there are fresh cut flowers on his headstone and I wonder if she brought them recently. "Pretty flowers you brought here."

"Those aren't from me. I haven't been here since the funeral, because I haven't been able to bring myself here."

"You should have called; I would have picked you up."

"It's okay, sweet girl. I can make it here now. The grief is still here," she puts her hand on her chest, "but it's getting better." She smiles through her tears.

"Oh, Mom." I pull her into a hug and I swear I can feel Nate's arms around us. *I love you too, Nate.*

Patrick

"*P*ATRICK, IT'S ADDISON. PLEASE CALL ME. DAD'S AWAKE. LOVE

you." *Message two.* "Patrick. Please call me. I love you." *Message three.* "Patrick Harrold Matheson! Call me." *End of messages.*

Ugh. She's upset with me. I hate it when Addison's mad at me—the one person who used to protect her. I throw my phone down on my desk and push myself into my chair. Shit. I don't even know what time it is. Or what day it is for that matter. Squinting my right eye, I look at the clock with my left and see it's nine.

I pick my phone back up to see the day, Sunday. Well, that's good. At least I didn't drink this day away too. I look at the empty bourbon bottle and glass on my desk and rake my hands through my short hair. I'll have Kristin pick up more Monday.

I put my phone down, but I decide to call Addison now instead of later.

"About damn time you called me," she answers without the phone even ringing.

"Hi." I don't even know what to say.

"Dad's awake. I thought you should know. You really should come see him."

"I…I don't know about that."

"Please, Patrick? I'm sure it will mean a lot to him," she begs.

I chuckle. "I'm not so sure about that."

"Well, visit him for me then," she pouts.

"Okay, fine. Give me an hour or so. I need to finish some things here and I'll be there."

"Thank you, Patrick! I'm sure you'll be surprised."

Yeah, I don't think it will be me. "See you shortly. Love you,

Addison."

"Love you too."

I put my phone in my suit pocket and get my belongings together to go upstairs. I need to give Kristin a case of wine or two for always making sure I have everything I need, even when she isn't here. I pull a clean suit out of the coat closet, pick up the small gym bag from the floor, and head to the showers.

The drive to the hospital takes thirty minutes. For a Sunday afternoon, traffic is heavy. I pull into the large concrete parking garage attached to the hospital, and drive around as if I'm really looking for a parking spot. I drive to the top of the structure and park in a spot near the elevators.

I hate elevators, especially hospital elevators. The last time my father raised his hand to me was at the hospital after my mother died. The next time I got in one, I relived the pain I felt that night. I try to avoid riding in them, but they are usually close to the stairs. I get out, lock up my car, and proceed to the stairs to exit the garage. Step by step, my feet feel like they are getting heavier and heavier. I'm not afraid to see my father; I just know what it's going to be like when I see him. Stroke or not. The man hates me.

After what seems like hours, I finally make it to the front of the hospital, and walk inside to the help desk.

"Hello, how can I help you?" a younger looking woman who's wearing a volunteer badge asks.

"Hi. I need the room number for Harrold Matheson."

"Are you family?"

"Yes, ma'am." She blushes at the use of ma'am.

"Okay, sir. He's in room 308 in Critical Care. Take this bank of elevators to the third floor and take a right. His room will be the last room on the right," she says with a smile.

"Thank you." I nod as I shove my hands in my suit jacket and walk to the elevators.

All the elevators are on other floors and I look around for the stairs. I finally see a door with the stairs symbol a few feet from the elevators, and I take them to the third floor. I hope I run into Addison so I don't have to go into my father's room.

The CCU is hectic with activity when I arrive, and I walk around for a few moments looking to see if Addison is outside of my dad's room. I don't see her anywhere so I'm hoping she's in his room.

I find the room labeled 308 and softly knock on the door.

"Come in," a garbled voice replies from the other side.

I walk in through the door and there lies my father in his bed, completely alone in the room. I should have called before I came in. Too late now.

"Father," I say clipped as I walk into his room.

"Patrick. I take it Addison called you." Seems like his memory is intact.

"Yes. She wanted me to come and see you."

"Well, you're here. You can leave now," he raises his voice.

"Gladly. I didn't come here for you anyways."

"You always thought you were too good for us. You're sadly mistaken, boy."

"That's where you're wrong. I never thought that. I was worried about keeping Addison and Mom safe from your hands."

"I never abused you."

"Maybe the stroke did affect your memory. I often went to school with bruises on my face where you thought I needed to be taught a lesson."

"You did. You were worthless growing up and a smartass. You needed to be knocked down a notch or two."

"I worked and kept straight A's, and while you were at the bar, drinking your check away or screwing bar flies, I made sure Mom and Addy were taken care of. I did a hell a lot more for them than you ever did."

"You selfish son of a bitch, get the hell out of here. I don't want to see your face ever again, you worthless piece of—"

"Enough! Both of you. I could hear you yelling down the hall. The nurses were calling security when I walked by. I told them I would handle it," Addison says as she rushes into the room.

"I was just leaving, Addison." I grab the door she just came through.

"I'll walk you out," she says as she grabs my hand.

I walk out the open door and apologize to the nurses standing outside of the door.

"Patrick, I had no idea…" Addison says, lost for words.

"I know. I tried to keep it from you. I know how much you love him."

"He's never spoken to me like that or even said anything negative about you to me. Actually, he doesn't even bring you up," she says as she wipes a tear from her cheek.

I pull her into an open conference room and hug her.

"It's not your fault. Don't worry about it, okay?"

"But…he used to hit you?" The hurt shows in her face and I don't want her to worry about what went on between my father and me.

"All in the past."

"I don't understand any of this." Tears streak her face.

"Do me a favor. Make sure he's taken care of, okay?" I lift her chin so she looks me in the eyes.

"Yes." She sniffles.

"Good. Do you need anything? Hungry or thirsty?"

"No, I just ate."

"Are you sure?"

"Yes, Patrick."

"Are you okay here by yourself?"

"Yes, our neighbor lady stays with him while I'm in class." How did she grow up so fast?

"If you, not Dad, you need anything, call me, okay." I look her in the eyes so she knows I'm being serious.

"I will. Thank you for coming."

"Anything for you, Addison." I hug her tightly and let her

go. "Call me."

"I promise," she says, sniffling.

"I love you."

"Love you too."

We walk out of the room, and I head straight for the stairs, going down them as fast as I can. I need to get out of this stairwell, out of the hospital. I feel like I could hit something, anything, as the words *you're worthless* keep running through my mind. He has always thought I was nothing. Like I was a huge mistake in his life and that's exactly why I strive to be the best I can be. To prove him wrong. I'm not worthless—I'm worth millions.

Once I'm in my car, I rev the engine and speed toward the exit. I want to be away from here as fast as I can. I head to the one place that I can get lost in what I'm doing, and only one person there who knows about the kind of relationship I have with my father or how I grew up, my office.

You're worthless...echoes through my mind as I climb the stairs to the eighteen floor.

You'll be nothing when you grow up...plays in my ears as I sit behind my desk.

You hear me, boy? You're insignificant...booms in my head as I look at my credentials and awards on the credenza.

His words play on a constant loop in my head and they haven't stopped since I left the hospital, and working hasn't snuffed them either. My father will not break me—I refuse to let it happen. I look up at the clock on the wall; it's a quarter till midnight, I'm sober, and I have been since I left here earlier today. I should have gone home to drown out his voice, but I didn't. Instead of pouring a drink, I poured myself into work.

The veteran's project is looking like it will help a lot more people than I originally thought after running the numbers most of the evening. I think I can work out partnerships too, making the money go even further. With Emily's input, I'll know for sure.

Emily Janes… She's the drink I need.

The young beauty has to be right out of college. She doesn't look like she's had to face the harshness of the real world, other than her brother's death. Probably grew up in a two parent home in the suburbs. She seems dear and innocent but someone I could see writhing under me in pleasure. Emily Janes would never have someone like me.

I would be too demanding of her.

I'd take away her enchantment, the light in her eyes…and scare her away.

CHAPTER FIVE

Emily

$\mathcal{T}$HE FEELING OF WHEN YOU KNOW SOMETHING IS GOING TO happen, but you don't know what it is so you have no way to stop it, comes over me as soon as I sit down at my desk. Dread fills my stomach.

Yesterday was a fantastic day, because the bank called and confirmed the deposit of the grant from CUGC, which allowed us to move forward with our plans for the money. Last week the board approved our ideal allocation of the funds. While a majority of the funds will stay in the community center and help with programs, sports, meals, and the kids, the remaining money is going to community outreach, stocking the food pantry, electric assistance, rent assistance, or anything else that might come up.

I try to my best to help anyone that comes through my door that actually needs help. I've had a few people try to slide into here and get free food or assistance, but I quickly caught on to their game. I find it so upsetting that people lie to receive free help. Anything to get something for free.

However, the icky feeling is still there. I look up and see it's close to lunch time. Instead of sitting here worrying about what might go wrong, I kick off my heels and grab my tennis shoes. The kids will be in the gym playing basketball and I think a game of basketball will do my soul good.

Hollers and giggles of the children reach my ears as I get closer to the heavy gray metal doors of the gymnasium. I open the doors with a loud squeak and everyone looks to me, and a few of the children wave. I look around and see Victor talking with a few of the older boys on the other side of the gym, and I head in their direction.

Victor looks up as I'm half way to where he's standing and his caramel colored eyes watch every step I make, with a grin on his face. He's very attractive and looks good in gym shorts and a T-shirt, but I made it a rule of mine to not get involved with someone from work, especially after I dated my AmeriCorps team leader. That didn't end so well.

"Hey, guys. How's it going?" I ask, trying to avoid Victor's stare.

"Good, Ms. E.," a few of the boy's reply.

"What brings you to the gym," Victor asks.

"I was feeling a little restless and thought I would shoot some hoops," I say in my best macho male accent, making everyone laugh.

"Here's a ball, have at it," Victor bounces the ball to me and

I catch it.

"Thanks!" I reply with a little too much enthusiasm.

The dimpled ball feels good in my hands as I bounce it around the half court. I pull up and shoot a jump shot, swoosh. A round of hoots ring out behind me and I turn see Victor and the boys are watching me.

I shake my head and let my body sync with the rhythmic sound of the ball hitting the gym floor. Basketball has always been relaxing to me. Nate and I both played in high school and we would often practice together. Being on the court makes me feel closer to him.

I bounce the ball a few more times and shoot again, this time hitting it off the rim. I jog to retrieve the wild ball and grab it before it goes under the bleachers. I dribble to the goal and opt for a lay-up this time, and the ball kisses the backboard right in the middle of the box and goes straight in.

More hoots and hollers ring out and I feel better.

"Thank you, thank you," I bow in front of them, making them laugh even harder.

"Ms. Emily, can you teach me to play basketball?" Tasha, a fifth grader, runs up to me and asks.

"Of course. First, you need to learn to dribble, okay? You do it like this," I dribble the ball with my fingertips. Her eyes are wide with excitement. "Try to use your fingers," I wiggle my fingers at her, "when you dribble. Your turn."

She takes the ball and slaps at it. I gently grasp her hand

within mine and gently push the ball down to the floor. "There you go. You got it." I move my hand and she is bouncing the ball by herself.

She laughs in delight.

"Keep working on that and the next time I'll teach you how to shoot, okay?"

"Yes. Thank you, Ms. Emily. See you later," she says as she rushes off to her friends on the side of the court.

"You're really good with kids," Victor says from behind me, a little closer than I'd like, especially being around the kids.

"Thanks," I say uncomfortably turning around, taking a step backwards.

"You should think about working with the kid's full time instead of the office with all that paperwork." He winks at me.

"If I didn't enjoy my position so much, I would give it thought, but I really like working with everyone in the community, not just the kids," I answer him truthfully

"I thought I would try. It would be nice to see you more," he says as he reaches out and places his hand on my arm.

"Um. Thanks. I, um, need to get going, lunch time and all. See you later." I try not to run from the gym, but my feet want to sprint.

I hope I read that wrong, but I'm sure he was coming on to me. No way, mister. As soon as I'm through the gym doors, my pace slows down. I walk into the main office and head straight to our restroom—I need to freshen up before I go pick up lunch.

The sense of doom has left my gut and hunger has taken its place. I think I'll ask the ladies if they want me to pick up their lunch too.

After picking up Chinese for everyone from the restaurant fifteen minutes away, I'm able to sit down and eat before my one thirty appointment arrives. The mail arrived while I was gone and I sort through it in between bites of my sesame chicken.

When I reach the bottom of the pile of the mail, there's a letter I've been waiting for, or check I should say. A local masonic lodge donates to us yearly and their grant feeds fifty families a month. I take a few more bites of chicken before I push the container off to the side.

I rip the end off the envelope and pull out the inside, and I open the tri-folded sheet of paper and there isn't a check inside. I read the letter included. "No no no. This can't be happening," I say out loud.

I knew I shouldn't have planned to receive the grant, but it was a done deal or at least I thought it was. Even though I have CUGC's grant, without the additional grant, I won't be able to help as many families. There has to be a solution.

I drum my fingers on my desk and that's when I my eyes catch a glimpse of a business card. Patrick. I was supposed to call his assistant to schedule a meeting to discuss the veteran's project, but it completely escaped my mind until now.

I pick up the card and run my fingers along the numbers; would he be able to help me? Or am I chasing the impossible? I guess there's only one way to find out.

Patrick

THIS DAY CAN GO TO HELL. IF ONE MORE THING HAPPENS, I'M going to punch something. The projected numbers are fucked up, again. Someone is going to lose their job, beginning with Neil. Kristin told me she heard rumors he's looking for a new position elsewhere, but she couldn't confirm if they were true or not. I guess I could help him out by firing him. One more strike and he won't have to worry about having a job here.

I quickly send an email to Kane, letting him know about the problems that I'm having with Neil. I want to make sure that they everything is documented to cover my ass in case he tries to pull something if I have to fire him.

After sending out the emails, I'm going over the numbers again. I employ people to do this. Why are they even working here if this can't get this done correctly?

"Patrick, line one," Kristin's voice calls out from my office door.

I look up from the stack of papers that surround me and see she's popped her head in my office. "Thank you, Kristin."

I pick up the phone, wondering who the nameless caller is.

"Patrick Matheson."

"Patrick…"

"Did something happen, Addison?"

"Dad had another stroke, and it caused irreversible damage this time. They want to transport him to hospice to live out his final days there. I...I can't make these decisions by myself."

"Do you know if he has a will?" Probably not, I cradle the phone between my shoulder and ear and rub my temples. My headache is going to be a migraine by the end of this call.

"I think he does. If he does, it will be in his office."

I take a deep breath...she can't do all of this on her own.

"Tell them to keep him there for at least another forty-eight hours. If it's a problem with insurance, I'll cover it."

"What? Why? Especially after all he said," she asks, baffled.

"I'm not doing it for him, remember? I'm doing it for you. Tomorrow, meet me at the house and I'll help you go through his office. Hopefully we can find a will or something stating what he wants."

"Thank you, Patrick."

"You're welcome. I'll talk to you tomorrow."

"Okay, love you."

"I love you too," I say, hanging up the phone.

"Argh," I scream out, throwing my water bottle that was sitting on my desk at the door.

There's a knock at the door and Kristin walks into my office. "Everything okay?"

"Yeah. No. I don't know. I have a lot of things to sort out. That was Addison, and our father is pretty much brain dead. We have to figure out how he wants to live out his final days."

"Oh, Patrick. I'm so sorry. I know your father and you aren't on good terms…"

"Thanks, Kristin. I'll get it worked out."

"I'm going to lunch. Do you want me to pick you up anything?"

"No, I'm okay. Thank you."

"Call if you change your mind."

"Will do."

She closes the door quietly behind her.

The silence of the room is almost deafening. The guilt of how I treated my father the last time I saw him consumes me, darkening my mood. My jaw clenches as the pain he'd inflicted on me causes my temperature to rise, making me sweat. I take a shuddering breath, trying break the rage that has a hold on me. Eyeing the liquor on the sideboard, I start to stand up, but I don't.

Taking a deep breath in, I hold it, and let it out. Deep breath in… As I soothe my temper, I realize I shouldn't feel guilt for my actions. My father treated me like shit. He hit me; he screamed at me; he called me names. He wasn't a father. He wasn't even a friend. He definitely wasn't a man. Even if he apologized for everything he has done to me, I don't think I'd ever forgive him.

Why should I?

You're worthless, Patrick. Worthless.

Why did he treat me like he did? Why did he have to take out all of his frustration out on me, his son, his child? I tried to be the best I could, and did everything I could to make him proud. Everything I did never felt good enough for him. I always had to prove myself, my worth.

I take another deep breath and reflect on everything I have today, everything I've accomplished and in all conscience, he's why I am where I am today. His words, actions, lack of involvement fuels the rage that tries to consume me every second of the day. Instead of letting it take over the rage, the hate has driven me to be successful because I have to prove to myself daily that I'm nothing like he says I am. I'm not some insignificant, worthless, child. I'm a man, a very successful man.

The rages calms down, but the silence still begs for his voice to replay in my mind and my body still craves a drink. I won't allow it. There's no room in my head for his words, for him, and I shouldn't let alcohol consume me like his words. I need to get out of this office for a few moments. I need fresh air. I get out of my chair with haste, pushing it backwards so hard that it hits the window with a reverberating thud.

I open the door and see that Kristin hasn't returned yet, and I walk out of my office, shutting the door behind me. As I walk passed Kristin's desk, the phone rings. I look down and see it's my line. I pick up the receiver and push the button to answer the call.

"Patrick Matheson."

"Um, hi, Mr. Matheson. It's Emily Janes from Project Hope."

"Hello, how can I help you?" All thoughts of my father vanish.

"I was calling to schedule a meeting with Kristin, but I guess I dialed you by accident?" she says, sounding embarrassed.

"No, you dialed the right number. I was by her desk and answered the phone."

"Oh. Well, I was hoping to talk to you anyways."

"Give me a few moments. Let me go into my office."

"Okay." Her reply is almost a whisper.

I put the call on hold and walk into my office, closing the door behind me. The silence has left the room, no longer toying with me.

"Ms. Janes?" I ask after picking up my phone.

"Yes."

"What would you like to discuss?"

"Well, how serious were you about donating more money to the center?" she asks hesitantly.

"I don't offer money just to be kind, Ms. Janes. I do it because I'm in a position that I'm able to help. So to answer your question, Yes, I was very serious." That comes out a little harsh.

"Oh. I guess I'll cut to the chase then. A grant we've received every year for the past five years has dried up. We are getting zero from it after being told we would receive a hundred thousand." Oh, that's all she needs

"So you need a hundred grand?"

"Yes."

"Give me two hours and I'll be over to discuss details."

"You don't have to do that. We can schedule a time."

"I did. I'll see you around three."

"Ah, well. Okay. Thank you, Mr. Matheson."

"Welcome, Ms. Janes."

I hang up the phone and prepare to leave for the afternoon. Maybe this day will be better after all.

CHAPTER SIX
Patrick

"Kristin?" I bark through the intercom, hoping she's at her desk.

"Yes, I just got to my desk," Kristin's caring voice replies.

"Clear my schedule. I'm going to meet with Emily Janes at Project Hope at three."

"Done. Will you be in this evening?"

"No, I'll head home after my meeting."

"Have a good night, Patrick. And please try to get some rest."

"Will do. You too, Kristin."

I pull out my briefcase, put all my working files in the matte black leather case, and close it with a click. I turn off the screen on my computer and before I head out the door, I glance at the clock again, and I have two hours to get to the southwest side of Reno.

The community center today looks completely different from the community center I was at on Friday when I pull into the parking lot. All the décor, extra tables and chairs, games, and canopy are gone, and in their place is bare ground with sparse grass.

I park off to the side of the building and wait a few moments before getting out. I'm almost an hour early—I hope she doesn't mind. I check my email, trying to kill a few more minutes, but I run out of time consuming tasks so I turn off my car and head in the building.

My eyes take a few moments to adjust to the dimly lit hallway void of light from the bright sun. I walk into the main office and don't see anyone that screams *I'm the receptionist*. A lady in her mid-forties looks up from the computer screen and smiles.

"Can I help you, sir?"

"Yes, I'm here to meet with Emily Janes."

"She's with a client right now, if you would like to have a seat in a chair behind you, she'll be with you as soon as she can."

"Thank you." I turn to find the seats behind me are semi-broken down. They look like that might be from an era before I was born. I sit down and pull out my phone. Reading the emails, I didn't read out in the car. I glance up and see the lady eyeing me under her lashes. I chuckle to myself and resume reading my mail.

Ten minutes later, I hear a door open and I hear Emily's voice.

"I'll let you know for sure, Mrs. Smith. I'll be in touch soon," she says kindly. Then I see the woman she was talking to, she has to be in her late sixties or older.

"Thank you, dear. Have a good one," she says as she hobbles

out the door.

I look at Emily, and she looks radiant. She's wearing a charcoal gray shirt with a matching jacket and a white blouse under the it. Her three inch heels put a dent in our height difference.

"Mr. Matheson, you're early." She looks surprised to see me here already.

"Traffic wasn't that bad." I give her a small smile.

"That's good. Would you like anything to drink: coffee, water or soda?"

"Sure. Coke or Pepsi?"

"Coke products."

"A Coke is fine."

She smiles. "I'll be right back."

She walks down a hallway opposite from the direction she came and is gone a few moments before reappearing with two Cokes.

"This way, please." She stands a few feet from me, waiting for me to stand up and follow her. She turns and I follow her nice ass all the way into her office. "Please have a seat," she says as she sets the Cokes on her desk and shuts the door behind me.

"Thank you for the drink."

"No problem. Thank you for coming over today."

"I'm hoping you have time to help me out too."

"Of course."

"Outstanding. So I'm sure you have the plans for what you would use the grant for?"

"Yes, Mr. Matheson—"

"Ms. Janes, I think we are beyond the formalities. Please, call me Patrick." She blushes.

"Okay, Patrick. Yes, I have all of the details worked out and they have the preapproval of the board too, pending we get a grant."

"Without going into line by line by line of the document, where is the money going?"

"Feeding the community. We get an average of fifty families a month that have to use our food pantry in order to have at least one nutritious meal a day. Honestly, that is still too low for me. I try to give families two to three meals a day…" She continues with her plan on feeding the people in the Project Hope community.

Her passion radiates from her body as she talks about giving to those less fortunate. This vibrant woman entrances me. She could be at home grieving for her loss, but instead, she's working through her own problems to make sure people have something to eat. Perhaps I was completely wrong about her. She wears her pain differently than I do, and she hasn't let it make her cold.

I'll run this grant by Kane, I don't think it will be a problem, but in case there's an issue, I'll set up funding from me as well. I notice she's staring at me, not talking.

"I think it sounds like you know exactly what you want to do with the money. I don't think there will be an issue getting you the money. I have to write it up and submit it to the board for their approval. *If* something happens and they deny it, I have a backup plan. Don't worry, okay?"

"Thank you," she says with excitement.

"My assistant might need to call you for specific details; can I get your number?" She opens her desk drawer and digs through the stuff. She finds what she is looking for and pulls out a business card.

"Both my office and cell phone numbers are on here." She hands me the card and our fingers touch. So soft, so warm. She shivers in her chair as if it's cold in here. Do I affect her? Hmm.

"Thank you. If you don't mind, I only have a few questions about the grant I'm working on."

"Okay, what do you need?"

"What should I focus on? An organization that provides a number of services or should I do individual organizations that provide one service?" I'm sure I have the answer, but I want her thoughts since she's experienced.

"I volunteer with an organization that all of the services they provide are done in-house. They provide housing, employment and training for positions in the community, food services, and family support services... everything that a soldier and their family need to get acclimated to civilian life again."

"They help the family too?" That is an interesting concept.

"Yes, because they need to learn how to help their veteran return to family life verse military life. PTSD is very common and their family members need to know the signs so if they see them, they can help the veteran get the help that they need quickly."

"That's impressive. Do you still volunteer there?"

"I…I haven't since Nate died. They did call to check on Mom and me, though. It's a very tight-knit community."

"Sounds like a good place to start with. I'll get their information from you before I leave… How are you doing?"

She looks confused that I'd asked a personal question, and she looks like she's at a loss for words.

Emily

ℋOW AM I DOING? HE DID ASK AND I MIGHT AS WELL BE HONEST.

"I'm trying not to cry right now. But I think I'm doing okay. I miss Nate so much. He was my twin brother, and he's never been more than a phone call or email away until now. I miss everything about him." A tear runs down my face and he hands me his handkerchief from his breast pocket. "Thank you." I smile and wipe my face.

"I know I need to move pass his death and live life. If I don't, I'll go crazy missing him. I still have a few voicemails and listen to them when grief overcomes me. He loved me and that's what keeps me moving forward," I say as more tears run down my cheeks.

"Sounds like you had an amazing brother." He gives me a sympathetic smile.

"He was more than a brother. He was the only male in the house so he was my protector, brother, best friend all wrapped up into one."

"I'm sorry, I didn't know." He places his hand on mine, offering me comfort, and the warmth of his hand wraps around my body, cocooning me.

"Oh, you're fine. I never met my father. My mom said he moved on to his next life before we were born."

"It was only you, your mom and brother?"

"Yes, and now it's just Mom and me."

"Are you close?"

"Yes, very much so, especially after Nate left for basic training. I'd moved away from home to go to college, but I came home every weekend to spend time with her. We were able to talk to Nate too."

"I'm glad you have each other," he says sincerely, but he looks a little uncomfortable.

"How's your family? I have to be honest; I read your interview in Reno Business Monthly."

He freezes and stares at me. Did I say something wrong? I mean he did ask me about my family. Was it not right for me to ask about his? I need to apologize.

"I am...sorry"

"My father is dying," he rushes out.

"Oh, Patrick. I am so sorry. I shouldn't have asked. I feel like an ass now," I say, embarrassed.

"Please don't, because I don't even know how to feel about it." He looks conflicted.

I don't know what to say, so I chew on my lip, hoping he will continue talking.

He takes a deep breath and licks his lips, and hesitates for a moment. "Not many people know this, but I grew up in the hands of an abusive father. It was nothing for me to go to school with black eyes, bruised jowls, or bruises elsewhere on my body. I took his beatings so my mom and sister wouldn't have to. To him, I was worthless and weak since I just stood there and took what he dished out. I was only a burden to him."

He pauses for a moment, and continues, "I worked throughout high school at a small grocery store. The Carlino's took me in under their wings. They helped me get into college and paid for it since my father refused to help me with anything. That's when I decided I had to prove to myself that I could be something if I put my mind to it, had the support to do it." I sit here in shock. I had no idea this man, this beautiful, charismatic man, was so broken.

"Please don't feel sorry for me," he says, looking at me.

"I don't. I...uh..." He nods at me and stares at me for a few moments as if he's debating if he should say more.

"If you read the article, you know that my mom died when I was seventeen. Her death really took a toll on me, and I was reckless after her death. Drinking, staying out late, missing work, and not even going home. Mr. Carlino found me one night sleeping in the breakroom at the grocery store, took me to his home, and told me that I needed to get my head on straight. I had a sister that I needed to look after. That scared me straight. I didn't want her to have to live through the pain I did, and she didn't have to. My dad never touched her because he changed after my mom died." He rubs his eyes, trying to regain his composure.

"And even more after I left for college. He was the father I'd always dreamt of having. I'm glad Addison experienced that. She needed that foundation of a good parent. Now the bastard is dying. He can't apologize for anything he's said over the years." He laughs. "I went to see him in the hospital Sunday because Addison wanted me to, and he made sure to tell me what he thought of me, always worthless in his eyes. I guess it's too late for an apology."

My heart is breaking for him. I don't even know what to say except sorry.

"I'm—"

"I'm embarrassed. I'm sorry that I've taken all of your time with my family drama. I better get going," he rushes out as he cuts me off.

"Please, Patrick. Don't be. You haven't taken all my time. If you need a friend to talk to or anything, please call me. I'm always available." I smile even though my heart hurts for him.

"I wouldn't want to bother you."

"It wouldn't be a bother. You have my number now; please call it if you need a friendly voice. I might have to tell you one of my bad jokes."

"You tell jokes?"

"Not just any jokes, but really bad jokes."

He chuckles. "I might have to call just for a joke."

"That's fine with me."

"Good. I do need to get going though. Thank you for the information and for listening."

"Anytime."

"We'll talk soon."

"Sounds good. Have a good evening, Patrick." I want to hug him, comfort him.

"You too, Emily." He opens my office door and walks out. I'm standing here in confusion, trying to put together what in the hell just happened.

I shake my head and sit down at my desk, organizing my papers while trying to wrap my head around Patrick and his life. I push my thoughts out of my mind to focus on work so I can get out of here.

*H*OT STEAM RISES ALL AROUND ME. I HAVEN'T HAD A RELAXING bath in a while and today is the perfect day for one. Birdy's *Beautiful Lies* album is playing though the Bluetooth speaker in my bathroom, while I lie back in the tub, sipping on a glass of wine.

The events of the day replay slowly in my mind, and I still

can't believe that Patrick opened up to me like that. Everything I felt for him before has multiplied by a hundred percent. Not because I feel sorry for him, but because he chose to shine in adversity, when he could have easily given up. Instead, he became determined to go for what he wanted out of life.

In his moment of rawness, the least I could do was offer to be a friend. Someone he could talk to, vent to, someone who wouldn't judge him. Someone he could call a friend because something tells me he doesn't have many close friends.

I inhale deeply, hoping the steam will help relax me, but my mind goes right to Patrick. There's just something about him that makes me want to help him. I'm very attracted to him. Not just his looks, they are a bonus, but his personality, friendliness, kindness… I could go on and on about what I find in him. I think some of those qualities are a cover-up, because he doesn't want to let anyone too close to find out who the real Patrick Matheson is—the one that was abused by his father.

Willing myself not to think about him anymore, I think about my mom. I haven't talked to her since yesterday and probably should give her a call before I go to bed. I spend a few more minutes in the tub before I pull the plug on the drain and shower.

Twenty minutes, I'm out of the shower and ready for bed. I clean up my mess from the bathroom and put the dirty clothes in the hamper and the empty wine glass in the dishwasher. I grab the remote of the Bluetooth speaker and turn it off so I can call my mom.

I pick up my phone and hit send when I see her picture pop up on the screen. Her phone rings two times and on the third, she picks up.

"Hello, Ems. How are you?"

"I'm doing okay. I hadn't talked to you today and I thought I would call and check on you."

"I got out today and ran a few errands. It felt good to get out," she says, but I can hear someone talking in the background.

"Is someone there?"

"It's just the TV. I was watching a show and I kind of want to see all of it. Can I call you later?"

"Um…okay. Sure. I'll talk to you later. I love you, Mom."

"I love you too, darling." She quickly hangs up.

When did my mom get into TV shows? Who knows? I put the phone on the charger to charge and get into bed. I hope sleep comes quickly; it was a crazy day.

CHAPTER SEVEN
Patrick

Why would I expose myself to her like that. I think as I sit here at my desk, reliving my telling Emily about my shit childhood, my dad, my mom… She's so easy to talk to, so easy to get lost in, and I find myself wanting to tell her things I've never wanted to tell anyone else. As soon as I got in my car, I put her number in my phone. I'm sure it would be a surprise to her, and to myself, if I do call her. I want to call her…

True to my word to Kristin, I came home after I met with Emily. I find it odd to be home in the daylight twice in less than a week since I'm normally at the office all hours of the night, and when I am home, I leave before sunrise.

I've been in my home office doing some work since I came through the door. The information that Emily gave me has me making a second check of the research I'd done on these veteran's organizations. I want to try to have this done before I shower and attempt to sleep, but the numbers aren't holding my attention as I look around my office, trying to figure out what is missing from here, from my life.

When I first bought this house, I loved it. I was able to afford it on my first salary with CUGC. As I quickly moved up the ranks in the company, I doubled and tripled payments and three years later, I paid it off.

I loved the office as it has a view of the open land, and I put my desk where I could look outside at any time. My degree and awards hang on the walls, with a few pictures of my mom and sister. Where there are personal touches in this room, the rest of the house has the art décor that came with the house. I haven't decorated it with anything of mine, because I don't have anyone that comes over to impress, so I left it as it was when I moved in.

One day I'll slow down and decide what I want to do, but I don't see that happening anytime soon with the crazy stock market. I wonder if Addison would help me touch it up to something a little more modern—I need to call Addison to see what time she has class tomorrow. Then we can go to the house during the day instead of the evening.

I grab my phone and dial Addison's number.

"Hey, Patrick," she says without the phone ringing, again.

"Hey, yourself. I was calling to see what time you have class tomorrow."

"I have class until one, why?"

"Want to meet at the house around one thirty then?"

"That's fine."

"Great. So…any change?"

"None. They keep asking me what we want to do."

"Seriously? Do I need to come to the hospital?"

"No, I will get them to chill until tomorrow evening. I told them we were trying to find his will."

"If they get too pushy, let me know."

"I will."

"If anything changes between now and tomorrow, call me, okay? If not, I'll see you tomorrow at one thirty."

"All right. Night Patrick. Love you."

"Love you too, squirt." She laughs at my childhood nickname for her and hangs up the phone.

I go to the files I have open and check the numbers I have, because I want to be able to give everything to Kristin in the morning to make the finalized file.

My growling stomach interrupts my thoughts and I decide to call it quits for the night. I go to the kitchen and try to find something to eat. When was the last time I actually went to the grocery store? Last month, maybe it was two months ago. Looks like I need to pick up a few things and at least get food for the freezer. I find a can of Campbell's Chicken Noodle Soup in the cabinet and look for a bowl to put it in to heat up in the microwave.

I sit at the bar, eating my chicken noodles, and think about how good it's going to be to actually sleep in bed, again. My eyes are drooping by the time I finish the soup, and I decide not to even bother with a shower. I strip my clothes as I make my way to the bedroom and fall into bed, thinking about Emily as my head hits the pillow, and I drift to sleep.

W HO'S SHINING THAT LIGHT IN MY EYES? I OPEN ONE EYE TO
see where the light is coming from and see that it's not someone,
but something. The sun. How did I not know that it shines in
here? Why hadn't I noticed that before? Because I've never slept
in here that long. Shit! What time is it? I rummage around in
the bedsheets, feeling for my cell phone, and I find it. I put it up
to my face to see that it's a quarter after seven and my phone is
almost dead. Damn it.

I look for a charger and send Kristin a text that I will be in
after nine, which is almost a never for me. There's no sense of
rushing. I would be rushing to sit in rush hour traffic. I stretch
my body, and I feel rested. I can't remember the last time I slept
through the night without waking up at five in the morning or
without the sleep being from being drunk.

What was I thinking about when I went to sleep last night?
Emily Janes. What is it about her? The newness of her is pulling
me in. No. There is something else. She calms me. The rage is
quiet when she's near, and I can be me around her. The guy no
one sees except Addison.

I go to the closet and grab jeans, a dress shirt and a
sports coat, and place them on the clothes rack outside of the
bathroom. When I go over to my father's house, I don't want
to be uncomfortable. I walk in the bathroom and turn on the

shower, and jump in the shower, hurrying.

Almost two hours later, I'm walking up the flights of stairs to my office. I make it to the floor and I'm almost to Kristin's desk when she sees me. Her face lights up in a smile.

"I see you got some rest?"

"I did. Thank you. I have the files we've been working on ready, and I have a new one for you too. When you can, come into my office and we will get to the paperwork."

"I'll be in a few moments. Do you want coffee?"

"Please. Thank you." I walk into my office, leaving the door open.

Before I can get my computer screen on, Kristin is in my office with coffee and a notepad, ready to write down what I need her to do. I'm so glad she's *my* assistant.

"First off, I'm leaving around one. I'm going to help Addison look through our father's papers to hopefully find a will or something."

"Okay, will you be gone all afternoon?"

"I'm not sure, but if Kane or someone else needs me, call me please and I'll come in. I think several people are on vacation this week, so it's been quiet."

"Will do."

"Second, I reran some figures and I think I've narrowed it down to two organizations I want to work with." I open my briefcase and hand her the file. "All of my notes are in there, please make the adjustments to the permanent file, and send it to Kane."

"Okay, I'll double check all the figures too, and if I see any issue, I'll let you know."

"Perfect. This new file, we already have a file on the center, but this is specifically for their outreach program. I need to see if there is going to be a problem since we've already made a larger grant to them if we make a smaller grant as well." I go over the details of new grant paperwork and whom the grant will be benefiting, and I talk about the center and Emily.

I look at Kristin and notice she's looking at me strangely.

"Did I spill coffee on me?" I look down and make sure I didn't carelessly spill it on me while I was talking.

"No. I've never seen that look on your face when talking about a woman."

"Um. What look?"

"The look of you might like her."

"I do like her. She's an inspiration to be around."

"Not that kind of like, Patrick."

"Oh."

"Speechless? I do think you're smitten with Ms. Janes. And if she can put a smile on your face, I'm all for it." She smiles. "Anything else I need to do?"

"No, that's all for now."

"I'll be at my desk if you need anything further."

"Thank you, Kristin."

"You're welcome." She smiles and exits the office, closing the door behind her, and her statement makes me question myself.

Does Emily besot me? I have my answer instantly, without a doubt. She's someone who I find fully engaging, someone who I enjoy having a conversation with, someone who I'd want to be around more than just for sex.

I chuckle at the last thought, because it's been a while for sex or anything sexually stimulating. The last time I had a steady girlfriend was college…five or six years ago, I think. This company became everything, my life, and honestly, I wouldn't change it. If I would do a better job of balancing my personal life and business life, then maybe I could have a steady relationship, a relationship with someone like Emily.

She seems like the type of person that would understand that it takes hard work and long hours to accomplish goals in the business world. Several of the women I dated in college where high maintenance. I mean I enjoy looking at a woman who takes pride in their appearance, but when they call or text every ten minutes or expect gifts all the time, it's too much. Way too much for me.

I'm sure that's partly because of the way I grew up. I don't ever remember my father getting my mom anything, but he isn't the best example to use of how a man should treat a woman… Enough of thinking about women, my father, and life. I need to get things completed so I can leave in a few hours.

*T*HE HOUSE I SPENT THE FIRST EIGHTEEN YEARS OF MY LIFE still looks the same as I pull up in front of the dilapidated structure. The sage colored paint is fading and the roof needs to be replaced. The house hasn't changed at all in nine years. I haven't been back since I left. As I sit in my car waiting for Addison to arrive, I review the files that Kristin emailed me to review.

She's finished the file for Project Hope Outreach Program and it's flawless. There shouldn't be an issue getting it approved by the board. I check a few other emails, nothing that needs an immediate reply and I can address them tomorrow.

I push the power button, turning the screen off on my phone and look in my rearview mirror to see Addison pulling in behind me. Perfect timing. I get out of my car and wait for her by the rear of my car.

"Hey, sis. How was class," I ask as we walk toward the house.

"Easy day. Math and English." She grins. "You know that stuff you don't know." She sticks her tongue out at me.

"Don't call me when you can't figure out how to use the quadratic equation," I deadpan.

"The quadi what?" she says, confused because she's not a math person at all.

"I suggest you refer to me the math king."

"Yeah, yeah. I could call you Paddycakes and you'd still

help me." I laugh because when she was little she called me her Paddycakes because I used to sing the nursery rhyme to her.

"You're probably right." I gently bump into her while walking to the front of the house.

"Are you okay being here?" She looks a little worried when we reach the door.

"Yes, I'm fine. Let's get inside so I can get in and get out of here.

"Okay." She unlocks the door and the familiar mustiness of the old house hits my nose. The smell is one I'll never forget.

"Everything in the same place?" I ask before I head to the right.

"Yes, nothing has changed. Even your room is still the same. I'll begin in his bedroom. He keeps things in there too." I nod and head to his office.

When the man was sober, he was meticulous and brilliant with numbers, and kept everything organized in his office. I'm sure he's where I get my love of math from, but I think that's all. He loved women and alcohol more than his family, actually I think just me because Addison said he's fatherly to her. I'd still like to know what I did to him to get him to hate me so much.

The room smells like stale cigarettes as I enter—this is the only room he smokes in. *You're worthless,* echoes in my head as I look around, and everything has a thin coating of sticky tar. I can't wait to get out of here, away from the voice. Around the room are bankers boxes and each one is labeled with a year, some boxes have multiple years.

I don't remember seeing these boxes in here, but this room was off limits to my sister and me unless we were in here with dad, and I could have easily missed them. Sitting down in the old brown leather chair at the desk, I swivel the chair around and open the box closest to me, a box from six years ago.

As I look into the box and look through the papers, I see they aren't what I am looking for. Instead, the box holds newspaper clipping from when I was college and what looks like to be letters. I pull one out of the envelope and read it…it's a letter from the Carlino's to my father, letting him know how I was doing.

They kept in touch with my father? How did I not know? I don't know if I should be angry or happy right now. I return everything to the box and put the lid back on. I grab another box, the year I graduated from high school. The contents are the same as the first box. I put it down and go to another box, but the year is labeled with an A. Inside the box is Addison's school work and accomplishments.

He saved everything? I don't understand. He kept track of me even though he hated me? I'm at a loss right now.

"Addison?" I yell for her. A few moment pass and I can hear her running down the stairs.

"You yelled?"

"Yeah. Have you looked through these boxes?"

"Nooo. I didn't even know they were in here." She tilts her head to the side with a *what the hell* expression on her face.

"So they are new?" I question.

"New to me." She shakes her head, trying to come up with an explanation.

"Each one is labeled with a year, and has mementos from that year for either you or me. It's like a scrapbook in a box."

"You're kidding me."

"No. It's crazy. Why would he keep track of me? The man hates me. Why would he keep my memories around?"

"I don't know. I wish I did. Like I said, he never said anything about you at all. Basically, he made sure I had whatever I needed and worked."

"Nothing makes sense… I don't know what to think. Any ways, did you find anything upstairs?"

"No. Anything down here yet?"

"Nothing. Do you see any boxes without years on them? Maybe that's where we should start?"

"Let me look…" She walks around the room looking at each box. "No. Did you try the desk?"

I'm an idiot. "Not yet." I turn the chair around, swiveling it back to the desk. In the middle drawer, I see only a few pens and paper clips, and a set of keys. I open the top drawer on the right side and it's full of note cards. I try the second drawer, locked, and I try the third, locked as well. I pick up the keys out of the middle drawer and try them in the lock. Bingo.

The second drawer pops open once the lock is unfastened. Expecting to find papers, I find photos instead, and pull them out. Photos of Mom, me, Mom and me, and Dad and me, and they have to be twenty-five years old. I don't remember them. Everyone looks happy, even Dad. I put them on top of the desk, and Addison picks them up and smiles.

I open the third drawer and I think it finally has what I'm looking for. A thick warn manila packet with *Important Financial Documents* written in red ink on the front. I grab the dense file and untie the red string holding it closed. I pull out the papers inside and two smaller envelopes fall out into my lap, and I place the papers on the desk and pick up what fell.

I turn them over and notice that our names written on the front of the envelopes, one for Addison and the other for me. I'll worry about these later. I place them on the desk and go through the papers. Half way through the file and I find it, *Last Will and Testament*.

"Found it, Addison." Skimming through the document, I read he has asked not to be resuscitated. "He has a Do Not Resuscitate order. So we need to let the hospital know."

"Okay," she says, tearing up.

"It's a lot to take in, I know. I should have been here for you more." I get up, walk around the desk, and hug her.

"Patrick, I'm going to be alone…I have nowhere to go." Shit. I didn't think about that.

"Don't you worry about it. I'll make sure you're taken care of."

"I don't even know what to think right now," she says, wiping her face on my chest.

"Let me get Dad and all of his financials sorted so we know what is going on and then we will know where we need to go from there."

"Okay."

"Oh," I say letting go of her and pick up the letter on the desk addressed to her, "this is for you." She takes it out of my hand and looks at it.

"That's Dad's writing."

"I know."

She sits on the edge of the desk and gently opens the envelope and pulls out the tri-folded piece of paper. I watch her eyes read line by line, word by word as the tears stream from her eyes. When she finishes, she holds the letter close to her chest and sobs. I pull her into my chest and comfort her. I have no idea what the letter even says.

"You need to read yours," she says in between gasps.

"I will when you're calmed down." I can feel her nod into my chest and I hold her until her breathing evens out.

"Please make sure you read yours, it's in my letter to make sure you do."

"Okay." I pick up the letter and open it.

"I'm going to get a glass of water, do you want one?"

"No, I'm fine. I'm not going to be here much longer since we found what we need."

"Alright. I'm going to go shower before I go to the hospital."

I nod, opening the letter.

Dear Patrick,

I'm sure you're confused about everything you found in my office. I wish I could have been man enough to explain it to you in person, but since you're reading this, I've probably passed on.

Let me by saying I'm proud of the man you've become. You're honorable, successful, and compassionate. I'm sorry I wasn't the best father to you. I didn't want you to turn out like me and the only way I knew to do that was to push you away. I saw so much of myself in you and it scared me.

Before I met your mother, I was rough and wild. I danced with the law several times and stayed the night at jail few times for public intoxication, but back then, it wasn't a big deal like it is now. I was heading down a road of destruction until I met her. She made everything change…until the first time I raised my hand to you, and I couldn't stop until I made sure you turned out nothing like me.

I pray to God everyday that you'll turn out nothing like me, especially when it comes to being a coward like me. From what I can see, you haven't. You're the son I've always been proud to have, but too stupid to honor.

I know this is a shit attempt to apologize, and there aren't enough apologies in the world to tell you how sorry I am.

I hope I haven't left you and your sister with a lot of debt. There is money is the false bottom of the drawer you got this letter from and a few insurance policies. I hope it helps.

Please take care of Addison. She loves you and you mean the world to her.

Love,

Your father

Harrold F. Matheson

I crumble up the letter and throw it. How in the fuck can he tell me everything in a damn letter?

"Argh!" I knock several boxes to the floor, their contents flying everywhere. Shit.

"Are you okay," Addison breathlessly asks as she runs back into the room.

"Yes, I read my letter."

"Did yours tell you about the money?"

"Yes."

"Good. Everything should be taken care of."

"I think so."

"I need to get out of here. I'm feeling closed in here, I'm suffocating."

"Alright. Do you want me to tell the hospital about the will?"

"No, I'll do it. It lists me as the executor of the estate. I'll call them tomorrow. Enjoy your night with him."

"I will," she says as she gives me a hug.

I pick up the wadded up letter and files and carry them out to the car, and throwing everything in the passenger seat when I get in. I need to talk to someone…

Emily

M̶y phone rings as I put my SUV in reverse and I answer, not waiting for Siri's voice to play through the speakers.

"Hey, Mom."

"Um. That's a first. Daddy a few times, but definitely not mom."

"Oh shit. Sorry. I assumed you were my mom. She calls me about this time most days." I giggle. "And I wasn't expecting to hear from you so soon."

"I can let you go."

"Nooo! That's not what I meant. I mean, how are you? I swear some days my mouth opens before I think about what I'm saying."

He laughs. "Well, can I take you up on that friend thing? I really could use your opinion."

"Of course."

He begins by telling he was at his parents' house and everything he found and the letter. I can hear the pain and emotion in his words, and I bet his heart is thumping and his palms are sweating because he is talking so fast. I actually can't believe he called me for my opinion.

"I don't know what to think. I…I'm somewhat lost here. What do you think?"

What do I think? I don't even know what to think. I really want to see the letter, but I really don't think this something that should be discussed over a phone call.

"I think we should have this conversation face to face. We're both driving and these are your emotions we are talking about."

"Come to my house for dinner?"

His house? Dinner? Can I trust him? I mean I know of him, but do I know him? Yes, I can trust him, and he did say the friend thing earlier.

"Sure. Time and address?"

"Six and I'll text you so you can put it in your GPS."

"Okay."

"Any food you don't like?"

"No, and no allergies either."

"Perfect. I'll see you in a few hours." He hangs up.

I'm in a daze and I have to slam on my brakes, trying not to get hit by the idiot driving a Mustang that decided he needed to pass me and cut me off. After twenty minutes of dealing with rude drivers, I make it to my apartment, and run inside. I want to shower and change before I go to Patrick's and I know I'm going to have to rush as I saw his address is southwest of the city on

Rancho Verde

Ahhh! I don't even know what I'm going to wear.

After my shower, I pick out a maxi skirt and T-shirt with a pair of sandals. I look nice and it's comfortable. I pull my hair in a loose bun at my neck, and I apply a little makeup. I hope I met Patrick's expectations. I grab my sunglasses, purse and keys, and head out the door.

CHAPTER EIGHT
Emily

I MISS RUSH HOUR TRAFFIC AND I'M PULLING INTO HIS DRIVEWAY thirty minutes after leaving my house. I know the houses in this area aren't cheap, but I don't see them as his style, or what I thought was his style. I keep learning new things about him every time we talk or I see him.

Evergreens and tall grass landscaping line both sides and the exterior of the two-story house is gray clapboard with white trim. Finishing off it all off is a gray aluminum roof, several windows in the front of the house, and I'm sure there are more in the rear since they look out to the mountains.

I park my SUV in the U of the drive, not blocking the garage door in case Patrick needs to leave immediately. As I get out, I take a deep breath and wipe my sweating palms on my skirt. I don't know why I'm nervous. This is two friends getting together for dinner and conversation. What if he wants more? Maybe I want more too.

Before I can think about it further, Patrick opens the front door and he's waiting for me to enter. I'm glad I still have my sunglasses on because Patrick looks ruggedly good-looking in a pair of tight fitting faded jeans and a muscle hugging T-shirt. He looks fine in suits, but he looks even better in jeans and a T-shirt, and I can't take my eyes off is his chiseled body.

"Glad to see you didn't have any trouble finding my house." His smile is bright and down right devilish with both dimples showing. Um. Down girl. Friends, remember?

"None at all. The GPS brought me right here." I remove my sunglasses so no more staring at his muscular arms.

"Good. Hungry? Dinner is waiting. I ordered Chinese. I hope you like sesame chicken," he says as he closes the door and leads me into the open kitchen. A slate bar sits in the middle of the space with two plates with silverware, napkins, and glasses sitting in the center of the slab.

"My favorite, thank you." He pulls the chair out for me to sit down in and I do after placing my purse on the back of the chair.

"I'm kind of limited with drink choices; wine, bourbon, or Coke. I need to go to the grocery."

"Coke is fine since I'm driving."

He grabs the glasses from the bar and fills them with ice, and he gets in the fridge. He comes out with two cans of Coke. He carries the glasses and the cans to the bar, and he walks over to the wall that looks like an oven with a warming drawer. He opens the drawer and pulls out a brown paper sack, the food, and brings it to the bar, setting it out for us to eat.

"Sorry I'm not too fancy here. I'm rarely home so everything is pretty basic."

"Oh, no need to apologize. Your house is beautiful."

"Thank you. When we finish eating, I'll give you the tour."

"Sounds great, thanks!"

We get out containers of food and put out what we want to eat on our plates, and cover up the leftovers so they stay warm if we want more later.

"How long have you lived here," I ask, being a little nosey.

"Almost five years. I bought it after I was hired on full-time with CUGC."

"Very nice. I live in an apartment close to UNR. I can't bring myself to buy a house. I like being able to call the landlord to fix things." I smile and he laughs.

"Good perk to renting. I wanted out of the city and this house was perfect. I haven't done anything to the house, as I'm not much of a decorator. Everything is pretty much how I bought it," he admits, almost embarrassed.

"It's a classic design. There isn't much I would change from what I've seen so far." I give him a reassuring smile—the house is gorgeous and immaculately clean for a bachelor pad.

"If you're finished, I'll show you the rest of the house." His eyes light up like a child showing off a new toy.

"I am. Dishes?"

"I'll get them in a bit," he says and gives me his sexy grin.

I smile and he offers me his hand, and I hesitate, but place mine in his, and I feel a magnetic pull that pushes my hand further into his hand. The tingles of the connection radiate up my arm and throughout my body. I look up at him and he smiles, and all I can do is lick my lips.

He hesitates for a moment, looking a little lost for words. "Well, you saw the entry and the combo kitchen and living room. Over here is the all seasons room." He pulls me through the doorway that meets up with the entryway of the house, and the view is spectacular.

"This door," he points to a door to our left, "is a guest bed and bath. He walks over and opens the door so I can peek in. I'm sure the view is amazing from that room too, but the curtains are drawn. "There's a den at the front of the house, but I use it as a small library."

"Nice, you like to read?"

"I did when I was younger. I don't get the time to do much reading now."

"That's a tragedy." I smile and wink at him.

"You read?" he asks.

"As much as I can."

"I might be a little jealous," he says as he gently squeezes my hand.

"I'll share my books with you, but I don't know if they are your genre…"

"You never know." He winks. "Upstairs is my bedroom, office, and a loft." He pulls me up the stairs that are by the entryway. We make our way up the stairs and they open into the loft. The loft in in front of the house and has a big window that overlooks his front yard and beyond. There's nothing in this area except for a few pieces of art, and I think to myself this would be an amazing place for a reading area.

"Prepared to see the rest?"

"Yes." He pulls me to the door a few feet from the staircase and I have no idea which room it is.

"My office. This is the only room I've done anything with." He lets go of my hand so I can look around, and I see that he's framed his degree and accreditations. I see a picture of him with a woman and a younger girl. His mom and sister maybe? There are also a few pictures of him and the girl alone, but no pictures of him and his dad.

"The space and view is magnificent. I don't know which I like better, here or the all seasons room."

"This one. Because you can see farther out and at night, it's breathtaking. This office is what sold me on buying the house."

"Really?"

"Yes, because it faces the east, so the moon comes up and the stars are close at night. You almost feel like you can reach out and touch them."

"I think I should be the one that's jealous." I giggle. "Too much light pollution to see much at my place."

"Well, stay a little longer and you'll get a show before you go."

"I might take you up on that."

He smiles and grasps my hand and pulls me out of the room. "The only room left is my bedroom…and it's just a room."

"That's your private space; you don't have to show me."

"Truth is, I didn't make the bed, and I might have dirty clothes on the floor."

"Gasp. You live in filth." I dramatically place my hand on my chest and laugh. "Mr. Matheson is human, folks." At first, I think he thought I was serious until I laughed. "See, I told you I had bad jokes."

"That was pretty good I have to say. You had me for a moment."

"I'm sorry. I was totally kidding."

"That's good to know. I would hate for you to think I was a dirtball or something."

"Definitely not." I smile, trying to make him see that I don't think anything bad about him.

"Let's go in the all seasons room, and we can talk about the reason behind your visit.

"Okay."

He walks down the stairs, still holding my hand, and I don't mind following behind him. I feel…safe with him.

"Want another Coke?"

"No, I'm good. Thanks."

He grabs himself a Coke, sans glass and ice, and we head to his all season room. Since the sun is setting on the other side of the house, the room isn't hot. The room has large oversized blue canvas couches and chairs to relax in. Patrick unceremoniously falls down into the couch, pulling me in with him.

"Oof."

"Sorry. I guess I didn't realize I still had a hold of your hand."

He slowly removes his hand from mine, and my hand wants to follow his. I look up at him, gazing into his eyes. Lost within my thoughts, I want to smile every time I think of him, look at him. I'm infatuated with him. There I said it. I'm totally crushing on Patrick.

"It's okay. So…do you have the letter?"

"Shit. I do. I left it in my car. I'll be right back." He gets up and goes into the house. I few moments later I hear a door open and not much after that. A few minutes pass and I hear a door close, then he's walking into the room. This time he sits like I thought he would the first time.

"Sorry it's a little crumpled up. I wadded it up after I read it. I was so angry, I don't know what to think or feel. I was confused and hurt," he says as he hands it to me. "Well, I still am."

I read the document, word for word, trying to understand what his dad was trying to say to him. There's a lot of grief in the words, so much pain and regret, and since his dad can't verbalize his apology, there are so many things that are probably being left out that he implied but couldn't bring himself to actually say the words. I want to give Patrick my honest opinion, but I don't want to be too far fetched.

"Well?" he says after I've stared out into the hills too long.

"This is what I think. You can take it with a grain of salt or whatever."

"Okay," he says, gently squeezing my hand to urge me to continue.

"I believe he's genuinely sorry for failing you as a father figure. He's proud of you, and I think he regrets not telling you that." I pause, thinking how to word the rest of what I want to tell him. "He means every word that he wrote. It's hard to say sorry, especially when you've been wrong for so long and caused a lot of pain. He's sorry for that pain, but he's not sorry that you turned out to be so much more than him."

I place my hand on his, and he turns his palm up so our fingers intertwine. I watch him lazily trace circles in palm with his thumb, as he lets my words soak in. The room is silent except for our breathing, and I don't know what else to say to calm his troubled mind.

Patrick

*H*ER VOICE, HER TOUCH, JUST HER BEING HERE RELAXES ME. I so want to believe every word she said about my dad, but what if she's wrong... I guess I won't know either way, unless he makes an extraordinary recovery. Anything is possible these days.

"Want to tell me a more about your father, like anything

positive you remember about him growing up?"

She looks up at me with her big, brown eyes, waiting to know more about my fucked up family and me. What do I say? I don't remember anything good about my childhood, and I close my eyes, willing my memory to recollect something, anything.

"I don't remember much. I remember when Addison was born. Everyone was happy, and we were a family then. My dad worked a lot, but he was still a good guy. Then I saw less and less of him and when I did, he said mean stuff to me. I'll never forget the first time he hit me. I messed up on a math problem. He told me I was worthless and backhanded me. He didn't apologize, but he didn't do again for a while. The next time it happened, it was like the dam broke and I was getting smacked around for everything and continued to do so until my mom died..."

"Oh, Patrick." She squeezes my hand.

"I sometimes wonder if the age difference between my parents caused issues too. My dad's fifteen years older than my mom, and so much changed in the way people were raised in those decades. I don't want to make excuses for him, though."

"Maybe it's time to let the pain go?" she says quietly.

"I don't know how." I wish I did.

"I think talking about it will help you a lot, and I'm honored that you trust me with this private part of your life."

"You're easy to talk to—I enjoy talking to you. You're not interested in my bank account," I say with a chuckle and she stills, looking at me wide-eyed. "Oh yeah. There's been a few of those."

"Wow. Some women have no class. What happened to being interested in someone's mind instead of their looks and money?"

"So you're here just for my mind?" I deadpan.

"Umm. Yes? I mean, I like talking to you too and it's refreshing to have someone who's horrible at being sarcastic too."

"I'm not that bad am I?" I mock the look of being hurt.

"It's a close tie for who's the worst." She giggles, and I want her close to me.

She feels amazing in my arms as I pull her into my chest for a hug. I thought she might tense up, but instead, she melts into me as I feel her taking in a deep breath, inhaling my cologne, and relaxing into me even more. The closeness of our bodies sends a jolt through mine, warming every surface of my skin where she's touching. My chest feels like it is on fire from the touch of her hands and face.

I'm getting too hot from our body heat and I slowly push her up. A flicker of disappointment shows in her face, but it quickly disappears as I pull her onto my lap and kiss her. As soon as our lips touch, I'm lost. I consume her, not wanting to ever let go, I've wanted a taste of her since the first day I met her. Kissing her is better than I ever imagined, but I slowly end the kiss, leaving us both breathless and wanting more.

"Sorry, I didn't know how else to thank you for listening to me."

"I enjoyed the hug too." She smiles.

She's gorgeous when she smiles, and she makes me feel like

I'm normal and not some tortured boy. I look outside to keep myself from taking her on the couch and notice the stars have begun to come out.

"And now for the feature presentation, the stars over the mountains," I say as pull her into my chest. She's exactly what I need to help let the pain go.

"Wow, I didn't even notice until you said something…" She inhales. "You're right. You feel like you can touch them." She looks at the stars in amazement, and I'm not in a hurry to do anything but sit here, so I can enjoy looking at her while she looks at the stars.

A little time goes by and she squirms. "Um, where's the restroom again?" she asks embarrassed.

"You can use the one in the guest bathroom, through that door and to the left. I'll turn the light on for you so you can see." I help her up, and I get up, grabbing her hand, and lead her into the bathroom. I return to the couch, giving her privacy.

"Thank you," she says when she comes out, shutting the door behind her. "I hate to rush, but it's getting late and it's almost my bed time."

"Thank you for coming over and listening to me. Please come over whenever you want." She blushes a little and smiles.

"I'll just have to do that," she says as I walk her to the front door. "Have a good rest of your evening. And if you ever need anything I'm just a phone call away."

"I'll remember that." I pull her in for another hug, and this time I don't want to let go.

"Night," she says, slowly pulling out of my hug.

"Good night, Emily."

I stand outside without shoes on as she pulls out of the drive and honks as she drives down the road, and I watch her taillights until I can't see them anymore. A bug crawling over my foot gets my attention and I realize I'm still standing outside watching non-existent taillights in the dark.

Turning around, I walk in the front door, and I can faintly smell Emily's lotion or perfume. The smell is citrus with a hint of something soothing, just like she is. I go into the kitchen and clean the dishes from dinner. There's not much else to do downstairs, so I head upstairs to my office to check my email and to work on reports that need completed by the end of the month.

I glance at the clock every few minutes, wondering if Emily has made it home yet. Instead of sitting here worrying, I pick up my cell phone and send her a text.

ME: *Please let me when you make it home.*

I get an instant reply:

EMILY: *I'm driving. I'll message you when I can.*

Good girl.

I dive into my reports and get most of them finished when I hear my phone chime with a text message.

EMILY: *Made it home. Thank you again for dinner. I had a good evening. Goodnight.*

ME: *Good. Me too. Good night to you.*

I set my phone down on my desk and work on finishing the last report that I need to complete. Once it's finished, I hit save, and close my laptop. I put my files in my briefcase and close it, and I grab my cell phone and walk to my bedroom.

I hope the next time Emily comes over, I can give her the full tour of my room, and I take off my clothes and get into bed. Thoughts of Emily take over my mind when my head hits the pillow, and I can feel myself falling to sleep.

CHAPTER NINE

Emily

*A*FTER PATRICK'S TEXT WEDNESDAY NIGHT, I HAVEN'T HEARD from him since. Thirty-six hours without anything from him has me second guessing his feelings for me. Is it possible I misread his body language and he only wants to be friends? I'm not sure though. The hug before I left was nice and I didn't want to go, but I was getting sleepy. Since I like to be at work early in the morning, it doesn't allow for any kind of night life.

I pull into the parking lot at work and hesitate getting out because I notice Victor hanging out by the entrance. He needs to go on in and not wait for me. I decide to call my mom so it looks like I'm going to be a while.

"Good morning, Emily." She sounds perky this morning.

"Hey, Mom. How are you today?" I ask as I play with the zipper on my briefcase.

"I'm doing okay. I'm sitting outside drinking a cup of tea and watching the birds before it gets too hot. How's your morning."

"Good so far. I just got to work so it's hard to say how the rest of the day will go." I hear my mom put her hand over the receiver to mute her side of the call. "Mom... Mom?"

"I'm here. Sorry."

"Everything okay?"

"Yes, I dropped the phone. Well, I better let you go so you can get to work. I love you."

"I love you too, Mom." I hit end on the phone, and I look up at the entrance to see if Victor is still there and lucky for me he's not.

I get out of my SUV and head inside, and I make it to my office without seeing Victor. Thank goodness. I do my normal routine and get everything turned on and my personal belongings locked away.

As I sit down, I wish I would have stopped and got a coffee. I'll wait until someone in the office is here to make coffee. If I don't I'll end up drinking a whole pot because I don't want to waste it since no one will be in for another hour or so.

While I look through my emails, I wonder when I'm going to hear about the grant from CUGC and Patrick? Mmm Patrick. I think I have more than just a little infatuation with the man. Oh, how I wish I could see him tonight. Maybe I should ask him...out.

That is a brilliant idea. He'd never expect it, but what if he has plans for tonight? Who says it has to be tonight. Me, I want it to be tonight. Calm down, girl. I'll call him and ask him out and he can pick out the when, and the where we can decide later.

I wonder when should I call him? I look up at the clock on

the wall and see it's only seven thirty. I wonder if now would be good? I better not. I'll wait until later so I know he's awake and hopefully not busy.

Checking my email, I click on the monthly newsletter, and read about the center's celebration. At the top of the letter is our picture and while looking at the picture of Patrick and me at the top of the letter, my email dings with a new message. I click over and see it's from KCaton from CUGC. Um, who? I open the email and it's from Patrick's assistant.

> *Ms. Janes,*
>
> *I'm contacting you for a good time to speak with you. I'm working on your grant file for the board and I need some additional information.*
>
> *You may reply to the message or call me between 8am and 6pm today at the number listed below.*
>
> *Sincerely,*
>
> *Kristin Caton*
>
> *Assistant to Patrick H. Matheson*

Oh no. I wonder what else she could need. I look up and still it's twenty to eight. Screw waiting for coffee. I need to do something to kill time instead of just staring at the clock. I walk to our breakroom and get the coffee out, fill the filter full of grounds, and put it in the pot. I press the button on and the machine comes to life. I look around for my coffee cup and realize that I left it on my desk.

I walk into my office and grab my cup and turn to walk out

and run right into Victor. Where in the hell did he come from?

"Um, sorry. I didn't hear you come in," I say as I push myself away from him.

"It's okay. How are you this morning?" His hands are still on my arms and I take another step backwards, my desk stopping my movement. I feel trapped.

"I'm well. Getting some coffee, it's brewing now if you want some." I push myself off the desk and out of his grasp.

"Umm, okay." He looks disappointed that he's not touching me anymore, but I'm not sure and I don't care. I don't want to be a bitch, but I might have to be.

"After you," I say as I wave my hand toward the door, hinting to him that I want him out of my office.

He sighs and walks out my office and in the direction of the breakroom. As I walk out of my office, Kelly comes in and I've never been so glad to see her because I know she will be making a straight dash to the coffee pot.

"Good morning, Kelly. Coffee should be finished brewing."

"Oh, bless you. I need a cup. I'll be right in there," she says as she rushes past me with her arms full of files and boxes.

I walk slowly into the room and walk to the sink to wash out my mug, and she arrives moments after me.

"Good morning, Victor," she cheerfully says as she pours coffee into the biggest coffee cup I've ever seen. The cup has to be two or three cups.

"Hey, Kelly. Well, I guess I should get to the gym. Have a

good one, ladies," he says as he brushes pass me.

"Bye, Victor," Kelly yells after him. "Such a nice fellow," she says while she stirs cream and sugar in her coffee.

"Yeah," is all I say and nod in agreement.

"Any word on your additional grant?"

"No, I have to call CUGC after eight actually. They needed more information for the documentation."

"Oh, well let me know how that goes."

"Will do."

"Have a good rest of your morning. I know I will," she says as she puts the massive mug up to her lips and takes a drink.

"You too," I say with a smile. I fill my cup and head to my office.

Looking at the time, I see it's time to call Kristin. I take a deep breath, let it out before picking up the phone, and call the number listed in the email. I hope I can give her the information she needs.

After pressing the last number, the phone rings and rings. I guess I've missed her and—

"Good morning, Patrick Matheson's office, Kristin speaking."

"Good morning, Kristin. This is Emily Janes. I'm calling you in regards to the email you sent."

"Hello, Ms. Janes. It's nice to put a voice with the name. I've heard a lot about you…and the center." Oh my. I wonder what Patrick as told her.

"All good, I hope?"

"Of course, dear. Patrick tells me you're doing some astonishing work with the community. What I'm calling about is Patrick left out a few things that I need."

"Alright."

"First, how many families monthly do you see on an average for assistance?"

"For monetary assistance for things like rent and electricity, thirty to forty, and for the food pantry, the average is around fifty. However, that's slowly increasing. I'm projecting sixty to sixty five families. Or two hundred people to two hundred sixty."

"That's quite a jump for an improving economy."

"I know," I say sarcastically.

"Next question, do you have volunteers at the center or a community day of service?"

"Yes, and yes. We collaborate with the University of Nevada Reno and AmeriCorps. The college students spend hours here working with the kids or helping around the center for a stipend to use for college expenses. In the past, companies have come in and spent the day organizing the food pantry and restocking it."

"Sounds like your center is busy."

"It is, but we service a lot of people, especially at risk children. I want to make sure I do my part to try to help them be successful when they grow up."

"I think you're doing an excellent job."

"Thank you very much. That means a lot to me."

"You're welcome. I think I have everything I need now. I'll

get this finished and send it to the president and the board today. You should hear from Patrick or myself in a week, two weeks at the most."

"Great. I appreciate it. Thank you so much."

"Not a problem. Have a good rest of your day."

"You too, Kristin." I hang up, wishing I had asked her if Patrick was in. Too late now.

I check my calendar and I have an appointment in fifteen minutes, so I email Kelly about my call and get organized for my appointment. Looks like I'm booked until lunch and the morning should go by quickly.

After two appointments, my third appointment is either running late or is a no show. I wish people would at least call if they can't make it on time, I could have possibly helped someone else. I don't want to leave in case they do show-up, but I really don't have much to do.

I could text Patrick to see when is free to talk? Yes!

ME: *Hey. It's Emily. Are you free to talk?*

I'm sure he knows who it is, smooth, Ems, real smooth. I wait a few minutes and no reply. I guess he's busy so I place my phone down. A few minutes later, my phone buzzes with a new message.

PATRICK: *Hey, anytime.*

ME: *Now?*

PATRICK: *Yes, now would be included in 'anytime'.*

ME: *Sarcasm doesn't suit you.*

PATRICK: *Are you going to call me?*

ME: *Maybe.*

I press the call button that's next to Patrick's name and the phone rings once.

"I thought you were kidding or pulling out one of your jokes."

I chuckle. "No, but if you need one I'm sure I can come up with something."

"I'm good right now, thanks though. So…you wanted to talk?"

"Yep. Actually, I want to ask you something."

"Alright."

"I was wondering if you would like to go out to dinner." Silence greets my ears; I can't hear anything from Patrick. "Um, are you there?" There's more silence and my stomach flip-flops. Did I misread his cues?

Patrick

"You want to go out with me?" So I didn't imagine the effect I had on her.

"Yes, or I wouldn't have asked." Sassy. I really like this.

"When?" I ask, pulling up my calendar on my computer.

"Whenever works for you, as my schedule is open." I think I can change that.

"How about tomorrow night?" I wish it could be tonight, but I told Addison I would be with her when they transfer Dad to hospice. He's holding his own after they removed him from life support.

"That works." There's a hint of excitement in her voice.

"Text me your address and I'll pick you up. Even though you asked me, I'll pick up the tab."

"Fine. You pick the place too." I laugh at her exasperation.

"If anything would happen to change on my end, I'll let you know."

"Likewise. Have a good rest of your day, Patrick."

"You too, Emily."

I get to work on the month end numbers. Kristin told me she talked to Emily this morning and really thought she sounded like a very sweet woman, and I couldn't agree more. I think about what sounds good for dinner, and get lost in planning my date with Emily.

Four thirty rolls around and I'm dreading leaving the office. I know I need to be strong for Addison and get Dad's estate in order. The finalization of paperwork won't happen until he passes away, but we know it's inevitable. Not if but when he does at this point.

As I walk into the hospital, and I don't stop until I get to the waiting room on the floor our father's on. I send Addison a text letting her know I'm here, and I sit in an uncomfortable plastic chair until she gets here.

"Hey," she says as she walks in the room and plops down in the chair beside me.

"Any change?"

"Yes, they are getting some brain activity now. He's still breathing on his own. They don't know if taking him off the vent kick started something in his brain or not. The outlook is still grim and they said it would be best for him in hospice."

"Okay. Then that's what we will do."

"I have all of his things that are in his room bagged up and ready to go. They are taking him there by ambulance. They just need your signature on the paperwork."

"Lead the way."

She slowly stands and I stand with her, pulling her into me to lean on me for strength. We walk to the nurse's station and talk to the charge nurse to get everything signed and prepared for his transfer. Hospice care is ten minutes away from the hospital and closer for Addison to drive to. She can't stay the night with him there like she was here, but at least she will be close if something happens.

"I'm going to head to the facility to make sure Dad's room is all ready for him and put some things out to make it all more cheerful."

"Do you want me to come?"

"You might want to in case they need information from you."

"Okay, I'll meet you there. Love you." I kiss her temple and hug her again.

"Love you too." She grabs the bags that are outside of Dad's room and take them with her.

"I'll help you carry those.

"I got them, they aren't that heavy. Thanks though." She walks to the elevators and gets in when they open.

I find the stairs and walk down them and out to my car. Once I'm outside, the sky opens up and rain comes pouring down on me. I think about running, but the result still would be the same. Walking in the rain to my car, I remember what Emily said about letting go of the pain my father caused, and I know she's right. I let the rain fall down over me, soaking me to my undershirt, and take away the years of hurt and anger that's made me a cold person.

When I get to my car, my suit is rain soaked and ruined, and even though the suit weighs a ton, I feel lighter. A small weight lifts from me, and I would have never tried to let go of my pain if it wasn't for Emily's suggestion. I know it's not all gone, but I'm trying—I need to keep trying. Not for Emily or Addison but for myself—I have to want this.

I pull off my suit coat that sticks to my body and hang it on the coat hanger in the back seat. Water drips off the cuff and onto the seat of the car. There's nothing I can do about it, and the driver's seat isn't going to be much better. As I pull out of the parking garage, the rain stops, and the sun peeks through the rain clouds—I have to laugh at the irony of the situation.

The drive to the hospice facility is short and I pull into a parking spot next to Addison's Honda. I think she needs to get a newer more reliable car. I should buy her a car so I know that she won't get taken advantage of and she's safe driving wherever she needs to go.

I get out of my car, not even worrying about putting my coat on, and head toward the front of the facility. Addison is waiting for me under the canopy.

"You look like a drowned cat."

"I feel like one."

"I guess the downpour got you?"

"Yes, I was too far to run to my car and too far to run back inside the hospital."

"I'm sorry, but at least you smell better," she says as she scrunches up her nose.

"Har, har."

"I talked to the nurse that will be in charge of Dad's care and she needs a few things from you. I didn't want to tell her the wrong thing. I told her you would be here shortly."

"Okay, let's get everything taken care of so you can stop worrying."

"I'm not worrying."

I shoot her a *you can't bullshit a bullshitter* look.

"Alright, maybe a little bit…okay, a lot."

"I figured."

"Thank you, Patrick. I don't think I could have done all of

this on my own."

"You're my family; I would do anything for you." I pull her in for a one arm hug and walk inside the building.

By the time the nurse is finished talking with us, they have Dad in his room and everything in place for his stay, however long that may be.

"I'm going to say good night to Dad."

"I'll wait for you so you have someone to walk out with."

"Okay."

I walk down the hall, into a small waiting room and sit down in the hard plastic chair. I pull out my phone from my pants pocket and realize it's water logged. Shit. I'll need to get a new phone tomorrow. I don't even know what time it is.

The wait seems like it's taking forever, I'm sure it's because I'm just sitting here watching the hallway, willing Addison to hurry up. A few minutes later, I see her walking toward me, I get up and meet her, and we walk out the entrance.

"Hungry or anything?"

"Yes. You want to get something to eat with me?"

"Yes, if you don't mind people seeing me looking like this."

"I'm sure no one will notice your soggy clothing."

"Perhaps if we go to McDonald's," I say blank faced.

"Sounds good. You can drive," she says as she bumps me with her hip and walks to the passenger side of my car.

"Teenagers." I shake my head and get in the car, taking Addison to McDonalds. She looks carefree at the moment and

I'm glad to see a smile on her face.

CHAPTER TEN

Emily

𝒯ICK. TICK. TICK. I PUT MY PILLOW OVER MY HEAD, TRYING TO persuade my head that I need to sleep longer, but my heart and mind is racing with excitement. When I texted Patrick my address yesterday, he replied he would be here at five thirty, in exactly twelve hours and eight minutes. I take a deep breath, trying to calm my rapidly beating heart and I give up. I'm wide awake; I might as well get up and kick off my day.

I open the windows in the living room and let the outside filter into the room. The sky looks stunning at this time of morning. I go to the kitchen and brew a pot of coffee. While I wait for it to brew, I pour a bowl of Special K cereal with milk, and go into the living room and turn on the TV.

The news drones on about the same dull stuff over and over so I flip through the channels. There is nothing on at this time of the morning. I come across a cooking show and leave it on the channel. I can't cook to save my life. I burn water. Yes, it's possible. Whatever the woman is making looks amazing and it makes me wish I knew how to cook, and the lady's techniques pull me into the show and I end up sitting there watching four episodes without moving. Oops.

I pour myself a cup of cold coffee and heat it up in the microwave, and I wonder what my mom is up to this morning. I only talked to her a few moments yesterday. Actually, I've only talked to her a few minutes the past few times I've called her, and I grab my phone out of my bedroom, taking it and my coffee into the living room. I dial her number and hit send.

After a few rings, she answers.

"Hello, Emily," she says with a shaky voice.

"Hey, Mom. Are you okay?" I asked concerned.

"Yes, it's just a rough morning," she says more even toned.

"Do I need to come over?" I'm still worried.

"No, no. I'll be okay." She's trying to shake off my concern.

"Are you sure?" I don't believe her.

"Yes, darling. You have plans today. I'm not going to make you cancel them." Her tone changes and she's in mothering mode.

"Patrick would understand, Mom," I plea to her.

"I'm fine, so no worrying," she huffs.

"As long as you're okay." I sigh because I know she's not telling me something.

"I am. So, tell me more about Patrick." Wow. She's not rushing me off the phone.

"Well, I think I told you he works for CUGC, and he's very good looking and very kind." I smile as remember the feeling his body close to mine. "And many other things that I haven't discovered about him yet. There's just something about him that every time I talk to him or see him that I want to be around him more. I'm kind of infatuated with him."

"Just be careful. Sometimes those guys in power tend to try to use their power in relationships too."

"I don't think he's like that. He's told me a little bit of his past… I don't think he'd ever raise his hand to a woman, or child. Just that feeling I have about him."

"Okay, I trust your feelings."

"He's someone I think Nate would—" The words are out of my mouth before I can stop them. "I miss him, Mom. I can't not think about him."

"I know, I miss him too, and if Patrick treats you well and you like him, I'm sure Nate would have liked him."

"I love you, Mom."

"I love you too, Emily."

"I'm going to get going so I can spend some time outside before it gets too hot. I'll talk to you later."

"Okay, Mom. Enjoy your time outside."

"Thank you, bye, darling."

"Bye." Her lack of telling me what's happening with her nags at me, but she'll tell me when she's ready to.

I look at the time on my phone and it's only eight. What can I do with my free time? I need to go to the grocery store and pay bills, and I guess now would be good as any time to go. In my bedroom, I throw on underclothes, a tank, and shorts. I dig around in my closet for a pair of flip flops and put them on as I head to the bathroom to brush my hair and put it in a messy bun, and I quickly brush my teeth and apply deodorant. I'm worthy of Walmart.

My purse and keys are by the door, so I grab them along with my sunglasses and head out to my SUV, locking the door behind me. I press the remote starter as I walk to the SUV so the AC has a head start cooling down the interior, and as I open the door, the enclosed hot air blasts me in the face.

I roll down the window and get in, shutting it behind me. My bare legs instantly stick to the leather of the seat and I silently curse myself for not getting cloth interior. The air quickly becomes cooler and I roll the window up, allowing the cool air to lower the temperature.

The first stop will be at the leasing office to pay next month's rent, then off to the grocery store where I'll spend too much money on nothing. Isn't that always how it goes? You think you need this and this and this, and when you get home, you didn't even buy what you originally went to the store for.

For nine in the morning, the store was crazy busy. Kids were running around yelling and crying. I felt like acting the same way, but since it's so busy, I don't do much looking. The frozen section is where I need to go, and I get my supply of pizza, Chinese, and Weight Watchers frozen dinners, and hurry to a checkout lane to get out of the zoo.

Arriving back at my apartment a short time later, I get the food put away and look around at what needs to be done. Nothing. I haven't been home enough to really mess up the apartment. Perhaps since it's not too hot out yet, I should go for a walk? I change my shoes, grab my earbuds, phone, and keys, and head out for a walk.

I make it halfway down the drive in my complex and I remember sunscreen. I know better than staying out too long without it. When I get back to my apartment, I decide to say in. I'll pamper myself before I go out tonight. My nails could use a new coat of polish.

After a two hour bath, a shower, painted toe and finger nails, straighten hair, and make up, I'm sitting nude on my bed in front of my closet trying to decide what to wear. I have an hour to decide. Why am I worrying about how I look? He's seen me in a T-shirt and shorts and business suits. I get off the bed and look at every piece of clothing hanging up, and think that I might need to update my wardrobe.

Grabbing a teal midi dress that's hanging in the closet, I hold it up to my body and throw it down to the floor, only to pick it up again. I throw it on a bed as a possible and look at what else I have—I have a royal blue short maxi dress and I hold it up. This one I like, a lot, and decide this is what I'm wearing. I finish my hair and makeup and put the dress on after I brush my teeth, and I add black wedge sandals to the outfit and change my purse to a small clutch to polish the look.

I look at myself in my floor length mirror and I think I look good, I hope I don't look like I'm trying too hard or I'm desperate. I double check my hair and makeup and reapply a thin coat of lip gloss.

Time seems to be flying by, and I check the time, seeing as I still have twenty minutes before he's supposed to get here. I go through my apartment and make sure that everything is neatly organized and clean, and I shut the blinds and curtains and turn on the table lamp since I probably won't return until after dark. Impatiently, I sit down on the couch and wait for Patrick to arrive.

Patrick

J PUT EMILY'S ADDRESS IN MY GPS AND WHEN I SEE WHERE she lives, I realize I know the area well. When I was at UNR, I lived in a rundown apartment with five guys down the road from her complex.

My excitement has me arriving at her place thirty minute early and I know I need to kill some time. If I remember correctly, there is florist a right off campus. Emily seems like she would enjoy getting a bouquet of flowers. I ask Siri for directions to a florist and several pull up, and I choose the one closest to Emily's apartment.

When I get inside the shop, all different types and colors of flowers welcome me inside. I know most women love roses or at least love getting them, but I don't want to be cliquish. An older gentleman welcomes me as I get farther into the shop.

"How can I help you?"

"Well, I'm looking for flowers for a girl…friend."

"I have any color of roses you could want."

"Would they work for a first date?"

"Oh, first date, eh? Skip the flowers. Come and see me when she's having a bad day or a few dates down the road."

"Hmm. Okay."

"I know from experience. Women think you're up to something when you present flowers in the beginning. It's like you're saying *I'm sorry* before anything has happened."

"I guess I didn't think about that." He winks.

"I've been down this road a few times; buy her something reminiscent of the date, not flowers."

"Okay, I'll take your word. I hope to see you in a few dates."

"I'm sure I will, son. Have a good time."

"Thank you." I chuckle as I walk out to my car and hope something catches her eye tonight.

I pull out my new phone and text Emily that I'll be there in a few minutes, and she quickly replies she's ready. The drive to her apartment from the florist takes eight minutes, and I pull into a vacant spot next to her SUV. I check my breath in my hand and pop a breath mint to make sure my breath smells good, and get out of my car, heading to her door.

A small porch covers the old, metal faded door to her

apartment, and I knock on the metal door and wait for her to answer. I can hear her unlocking the chain lock and deadbolt, and she opens the door. I have to bite my lip to prevent myself from gasping at her radiating beauty. The blue dress she has on fits her in all the right places, showing off her curves and long legs. I'm sure I look like an idiot standing here, staring at her.

"Hey," is all I can get out.

"Hi. Want to come in or go?"

"If you're ready, we can go ahead and go."

"I am; let me grab my purse off the couch."

She walks in and I stick my head in, looking around her apartment. I watch her as she bends over, showing a lot of her toned, tanned legs as she grabs her purse. She turns around and catches me watching her and she blushes. She makes her way to the door and I step out of her way so she can shut and lock the door.

"I hope you like Mexican."

"It's my second love behind Chinese."

"Good. I think it's my favorite. I could eat it anytime."

"Me too."

We make it to my car and I open the door for her, waiting to make sure she's inside before I shut the door. I walk around the car, feeling nervous. I can stand in front of people worth billions of dollars and not break a sweat, but when it comes to Emily, I can't even think about her without my palms sweating. My stomach is doing that jittery thing. I hope she likes what I have planned.

On the drive to the restaurant, we make small talk and the jitters slowly fade, but my hands haven't caught up with my stomach. I pull into the parking lot and find a spot close to the door. I turn off the car and get out, hoping to help her with her door.

By the time I've made it around to the passenger side, she has the door open but hasn't got out. I offer her my hand and she looks up and smiles. She places her hand into mine and gets out of the car. I don't let go of her hand and instead, intertwine my fingers in hers, and walk into the restaurant.

We don't have to wait long for a table and as soon as we sit down, chips and salsa arrive at the table. Not in a rush, we make small talk over the menu, and decide we both want shrimp fajitas. I guess I won't have to worry about my breath later, I think to myself.

Ten minutes after ordering, our very hot and sizzling food arrives to our table. With all the excitement and noise, it's hard to hold a conversation. After the food cools and half of it's gone from the skillet, we can talk again.

"Those were amazing," she says as she pushes her plate away from her.

"I have to agree. Are you saving room for dessert?"

She looks at me horrified. "There's no way I could eat dessert after eating that." I chuckle at her expression.

"Okay, doggy bag?"

"Please, if you don't mind your car smelling like Mexican food." She laughs.

"Not at all."

We finish our drinks and I pay the check while she is freshening up in the restroom. Now to move onto the second part of the date, the bookstore and coffee shop. She makes her way to our table.

"I'm all set if you are," I say before she sits down.

"I am." She smiles and picks up her to go box.

I put my hand on the small of her back as we walk through the restaurant and out the door, and I take her to go container and replace it with my hand. When we get to the car, I pop the trunk and put the container in a box I have in the trunk, and walk her around to the passenger door to let her in the car.

The drive to the bookstore is quiet but the silence in comfortable. I reach over and gently grab hold of Emily's hand and put her hand in mine and pull it over to my leg, and smile at her when she looks over at me. A red light stops us, so I pull her hand up to my lips and kiss the back of her hand. Her skin is so soft to the touch and smells so good.

"A bookstore," she asks as we pull in front of the large building and a coffee shop.

"Yes, I was hoping you'd introduce me to some of the books you read."

"Seriously?"

"Yes," I wink at her, "maybe I'll learn a thing or two."

"Uh huh…" She smiles as the blush creeps up on her face and her reaction makes me curious to how sexually experienced she is. "It's fun to try things you've read about," she says as she curls her tongue on her lip, moistening them. Oh, she's a little vixen.

"With the right partner too, I bet." I think I should get out of the car or I'll be practicing with her, sans a book.

"Mmm. We might want to head inside."

"I'm fighting the urge to make you the happiest woman—"

"On earth tonight," she says, giggling. "Nice. Excuse me, but I think I dropped something."

"My jaw."

"Who knew Patrick Matheson knows cheesy pick-up lines," she says through her giggles.

"Who said they were cheesy. Some of them work." I deadpan. "Kidding." I wink at her.

"Just when I think I have you figured out, you reveal a little more about yourself then I have to try to figure you out all over again."

"Is that good?"

"Yes." She smiles and her eyes twinkle with delight.

"Good." I place my hand at the nape of her neck and pull her in for a kiss. Her lips are soft and I tease them with my tongue, begging for access of her full mouth. She willingly opens for me, and I consume her, making her breathless. I slowly pull out of the kiss and rest my forehead on hers.

"Ready to go in?" I ask as I try to catch my breath.

"If you are," she says, softly.

"I'll be around to help you out."

I turn off the car and get out, making my way to help her out. I grab her hand and don't let go as it fits perfectly in mine and they feel like they belong together. This woman is undoing me...I don't know what it is, but I like it. I like that I want to touch her, breathe her in, and make her mine.

CHAPTER ELEVEN

Emily

$\mathcal{I}$M LYING IN BED HALF AWAKE AND MY CELL PHONE BUZZES with several text message notifications. Who would be texting me at this time of the morning. Rolling over to the edge of the bed, I pick up my phone from the nightstand, looking at the notifications when my eyes can focus on the letters. I guess it's not that early as my phone reads a little after eight.

Patrick messaged me a few times after he dropped me off at twelve thirty, I hadn't been out that late for a while, telling me he had a good time and letting me know he made it home okay. Both made me happy. I wonder when our next date would be?

I read the messages and they are from department stores letting me know about their holiday sales, I was hoping they were messages from Patrick. I put the phone down and get out of bed. I need to shower and breakfast out sounds good. I stumble as I walk into the bathroom, and I wake up when I hit my elbow on the door jam. Ouch. After cursing like a sailor, I get underway with my morning routine.

Before I leave, I call Mom to see if she wants to meet up for breakfast. I haven't seen her since last weekend and I'm kind of worried about her since she was upset yesterday. I try calling her and it goes to voicemail. I don't leave a message. I wait a few more minutes and call her again. Voicemail again. Maybe she's getting a shower? Perhaps. I call again and voicemail. I leave a message this time. I guess I'll be going to breakfast alone.

I head into a little hole in the wall place not far from campus. They have amazing coffee and huge omelets. I don't mind going in there because alone because normally there are lonely college students in there studying or eating.

The diner looks to be slow with I arrive and I sit at my normal table facing the outside. I order my usual two egg omelet and two pancakes with coffee and orange juice. I pull my phone out of my purse to see if my mom has called back and she hasn't, and I go to turn off my phone but it vibrates with a new text message.

Patrick: *How to do you feel about golf?*

I can play, decently. You have to when you work for a non-profit.

Me: *I like golf. Do you have a long putter? ;)*

The waitress brings me my drinks and I sip on my coffee waiting for his reply to my attempt to be naughty.

Patrick: *Saturday. Tee time is 9:10. I'll pick you up at 7:30 for breakfast and golf.*

He totally ignored my putter question.

Me: *It's a date.*

I'm kind of bummed he didn't reply to my naughtiness.

PATRICK: *Bring your A game.*

I'll show him A game. More like C game.

ME: *Smack talk, huh? Remember basketball a few weeks ago?*

PATRICK: *I let you win so you'd like me.*

Really? That's what they call that.

ME: *Oh, Mr. Matheson. I'd have liked you even if I'd have lost.*

PATRICK: *Good. I won't feel bad about beating you at golf then.*

ME: *Make sure your balls are clean.*

Wonder what his comeback will be for that?

PATRICK: *You are talking about golf balls, right?*

The waitress brings my food to the table, and it looks amazing.

ME: *Talk to you later. I need to eat.*

PATRICK: *Okay. Talk later. And yes, I have a long putter. ;)*

Oh. My. I can feel my cheeks slightly blush as I squirm in my seat because our little tease session turned me on. I fan myself with my hand, trying to quell my raging hormones, as it's been a while since I've had sex. This time of year is insane with writing grants and clothing kids for school, and they consume my life.

I take a bite of pancake and syrup runs down my chin, and I use my fingers to wipe it off and lick the syrup off my fingers.

I feel someone watching me and I look up and see this guy sitting at a table across the diner from me, entranced with my movements, and he becomes embarrassed when he sees that I'm looking at him.

I think I might have moaned out loud instead of in my head. Oops. As quietly as I can, I finish eating so I can get out of here without further embarrassing myself.

*A*s soon as I leave the diner, I try calling my mom and I still don't get an answer. I begin to worry, but I don't want to suffocate her. Since there's nothing to do at my apartment, I don't want to go home and sit. I think about what I haven't done for a while and a visit the museum pops in my mind. The Nevada Museum of Art should be quiet at this time of the day since people are still at church, and it's about fifteen minutes from where I am.

A few blocks from the museum, my phone rings through my speakers. Patrick.

"Hey, how are you?"

"Good. I just finished up a round of golf."

"Sounds fun and hot."

"It was and worth it because I shot under my normal handicap."

"Forty-five?" I say sarcastically.

"Funny. Try twenty."

"Oh, very nice. I might have my work cut out for me then." Please don't ask me my handicap.

"Maybe. What are you up to? Would you like to grab brunch?"

"I'm still full from earlier, thank you, though. I'm pulling in at the art museum now."

"Ah, okay. Well, I'll let you go."

"Okay, I'll talk to you later."

"Bye." My speakers go quiet. Why didn't I invite him to come with me? Ugh.

As I walk to the entrance of the museum, I keep thinking about texting him to come join me but I don't want to sound desperate. I turn the ringer off on my phone and put in my back pocket so I can feel it if my mom would happen to call.

I walk around the newer exhibitions that I haven't seen yet and stroll to the contemporary collections. Something about these pieces of art pulls me in and my mind goes wild. I stop in front of Petah Coyne's *Untitled #1205, (Virgil)*, and I become oblivious to all around me.

"You're a hard person to find." His warm breath tickles my ear, causing me to smile. I turn my face toward Patrick, delighted to see him.

"I didn't know you were looking for me."

"I didn't either until I found you." Did I hear him right?

"Oh?" I turn my body to him and he pulls me into him, slamming his lips into me, kissing like there's no tomorrow. I sway because he makes me lose all my senses. He pulls away, looking me in the eyes, and I know he meant every word of what he said.

"Tell me I'm not imagining this," he breathlessly asks.

"No, I feel it too." My heart hammers in my chest at his confession.

"I thought I was going crazy. From the first day I met you, you've been on my mind, in my dreams. I don't even know how to put what I'm feeling into coherent words."

"This is so…new…and so exhilarating. I enjoy spending time with you…being around you…being with you."

"Are you finished here?" His eyes burn with passion.

"Yes…"

"Let's go. I have somewhere else in mind," he says as he grasps my hands and takes the lead.

How could I say no to this handsomely determined man?

Patrick

I'VE BEEN HARD SINCE SHE SENT ME THE MESSAGE TO MAKE sure to clean my balls. Her comment went straight to my cock, and it made it difficult to play the last three holes. Although, I think she was my motivation to hit two birdies and an eagle so I could get showered and downtown.

"Umm. Do you think my SUV will be okay here?"

"Let's take it back to your apartment."

"Okay. Do I need to change or grab anything?"

"That's up to you."

"Okay." She smiles and the apple of her cheeks blush.

We walk to the parking lot in silence, and luck is on my side today and I'm parked a few spots down from her. She walks to her SUV and I open the door for her and make sure she's safe and sound before I head to my car. She pulls out of the lot, and I follow behind her, making it to her apartment in twenty minutes.

I get out, opening the passenger door, but she says, "I'm going to run in and get a few things. I won't be long." I don't think so. I shut the car door, locking it behind me, and meet her at her door before she can get it unlocked.

As she opens the door, I pick her up by her waist and carry her into the room, shutting the door with my foot. She giggles in delight and I place her down, turning her around to face me.

"Sorry, but I don't want to wait…"

I quickly close the gap between us, placing both of my hands gently on either side of her head, running my fingers into her hair, and tug her into a kiss, shattering her as I push her up against a wall. She drops her purse and keys and runs her hands up my shirt, grabbing hold of my sides, pulling me into her. I can feel her heart wildly beating as our kiss deepens, and I become crazed with her intoxicating taste, pulling away from her slowly I know I need more than just a kiss.

Gently pulling her hair, tilting her jaw to expose her long

neck to me, and I place kisses from her jaw all the way down to the neck of her shirt.

"This needs to come off…" She looks up at me, overcome with desire, and smiles seductively.

"Oh?"

She lets go of me as I remove my hands out of her hair and place them on the wall, trapping her in. Emily reaches for the bottom hem of her teal Dave Mathews Band tank and pulls it over her head slowly, teasing me inch by inch. In one quick move, she ducks under my arm as she pulls the shirt the rest of the way off. I just look at her, stunned that I didn't see that coming and at her beauty.

Licking my lips, I think she wants to play a little cat and mouse, and this cat is ready to pounce on his mouse. I take a step toward her, and she takes a step backwards.

"Going somewhere?"

"Uh huh." She winks and takes another step.

"Your bedroom?"

"Yes…"

She crooks her finger, begging me to come to her, and I go to her. Before I get to her, she turns and runs down the hallway, ending in her bedroom, and she spins around to face me before she gets to the bed, sliding her shorts down her tan legs as I come to a stop a few inches from her. My cock twitches, as she stands before me in a blue lacy bra and matching panties. Holy fuck. She is gorgeous.

"I think you need to catch up," she breathes out, running her fingers down the side of my face, "you have too much on."

I kick off my shoes, unfasten the buttons on my polo, and pull it over my head, tossing it on the floor next to the bed. She looks at me as I unfasten my belt, biting her lip as I take my time. I stop, leaning in to taste her pouty lips. They were begging me to kiss them.

She moves my hands out of the way and finishes unfastening my belt and pops the button on my shorts open, and languidly pulls the zipper down. Placing her hands on either side of my hips, she pulls the restrictive material down my legs. As she uncovers me, she gasps as the sight of my cock strains against the taunt cotton of my boxer briefs, and lets my shorts fall to the floor.

I hesitate for a moment, and she becomes the aggressor, pulling me into her, kissing me. She wraps her arms around my neck and leads us onto the bed, and I put my arm around her waist and lay us down on the bed, not stopping our kiss, leaning on my forearm. I move my arm from underneath her and caress her silky soft skin on her abdomen to her breasts, stopping at her breasts to tease her nipples through the lacy material as I move to my side.

Emily squirms under my touch and I tug on her nipple, causing her to gasp, breaking our kiss. She moves her arms from my neck and runs her fingers across my shoulders, down the backside of my arms and back up the front side, stopping at my pects for a few seconds. She gets a glint in her eyes, like she's thinking about teasing my nipples, but decides not to and rubs down my abs to the elastic of my boxers.

She dips her fingers in between my skin and the fabric, teasing me, making me needy for her touch. I look at her with a look of "are you sure you want to go there?" and she doesn't hesitate as she puts her hand all the way in, grabbing my throbbing cock in her soft hand. My hips thrust into her, pushing my cock all the way into her hand. Her eyes widen as she feels the size of my manhood in her hand.

Two can play at this teasing game. I tease her nipples again and move my hand down her body to her clit, massaging it until she's withering under my body. Her hold on my cock is tight and can't wait to feel other parts of her around it.

"Please, Patrick," she says breathlessly.

"Please what?" I play dumb as I continue to massage her.

"I'm almost there, please keep going…"

"I hadn't planned on stopping, baby." I lean down and kiss her, consuming her thoughts so she doesn't know if she's coming until she's coming. She moves her hand from me and places it on my arm, squeezing it as she gets closer to her release.

She tenses under my hand and moisture coats my fingers as she starts to moan into my mouth, and I feel her body trembling next to mine. That will be the first of many orgasms. She pulls away from me, trying to catch her breath and she looks at me with a look of bliss on her face.

"Ready for another?"

"Um. I can't come more than once," she shyly states.

"I bet you I can make you come again." I wink

"I would enjoy you trying."

"Challenge accepted." I rip her panties from her body and she gasps. "I guess I should have asked if you liked them."

"Let me take my bra off, because I do like this one." She laughs and she raises up, but I help her take it off, and her breasts escape from the lacy material and I can't stop staring the pertness of them, licking my lips wanting a taste.

"Do you need help with your boxers?" she asks after she cleared her throat.

"Maybe."

She leans over, hooking her thumbs under the material and pulls down as I lift my hips up to help her get the boxers off my body. Her eyes widen as my cock springs to life after the fabric trapping it is gone, and she gets the material to my knees and I finish kicking it from my body. She timidly takes my cock in her hands and strokes it from base to the tip, making me groan in pleasure.

I move myself between her legs, pushing her back onto the bed, and kissing her as I fall on top of her, my hands stopping my body inches from hers. She raises her hips, wanting me to fill her. I line myself up to her and as I'm about to enter her, it dawns on me, I'm not wearing a condom and freeze. This has never happened.

"Um?" she says, confused.

"I forgot the condom. I have one in my shorts." *Idiot.*

"Oh. Yeah, good call." She smiles as I move off her and pick up my shorts off the floor, digging in the pockets for a condom, one of five I'd placed in there.

"Got it."

I rip the package open with my teeth and roll the condom on before resuming my position. She is waiting for me, and I enter her in one fluid motion, filling her, stretching her, overwhelming her.

Thinking to myself, I don't want this to be quick, but I don't want it to last all night. I have plans that include her, and I pull out of her, languorously, and slam into her, causing a soft moan to pass over her lips. Making her come again will be fun as I fuck her into bliss.

A thin sheen of sweat covers our bodies, and I can feel her pleasure building, as mine is about to explode. I move my hand in between our bodies, finding the center of her desire, and massage it until she's panting underneath me, about to come undone.

I remove my hand and she pouts a little, and I bite her lip, turning the bite into a deep kiss. Shorting my strokes into her, I pick up the pace as I put my hands under her ass, and she tenses—she's on the edge of releasing. I can't hold on much long, she's milking me, making me want to come.

"Come, Emily. You know you want to," I say, strained.

"I…I'm…" is all she can get out as I slam into her, coming

as she comes on my cock. Her body's trembling under me with a look of utter satisfaction on her face. She's gasping for air, trying to catch her breath.

I pull out of her slowly, looking around for a trash can or something. I spot Kleenex on her nightstand and notice a trash can next to it, and I carefully get off the bed and make quick work of disposing of the condom. I return to the bed to lie next to her, caressing her body as she catches her breath from our passionate experience.

"I've never…" I kiss her, not wanting to hear about the others before me.

"Me too." I've never had a connection like that to a woman, ever.

"Wow. I think I need a nap." She says as she rolls over, grabbing a blanket on her bed and covers up. "You?"

"I think that sounds like a great idea." I pull her into me, my sensitive cock stirs, but I will it down as I rest my head on a pillow that smells like Emily and I feel myself drifting to sleep.

CHAPTER TWELVE

Emily

Three long days since Patrick made love to me. Three days that I've wanted him to pound me like there's no tomorrow. Monday and Tuesday, neither of us was off work in time to see each other before it got too late. Monday, I had a work emergency and had to go in after someone broke in, and yesterday, Patrick had a day trip to Vegas and I hadn't talked to him since the plane landed there, but we had texted on and off until I fell asleep waiting for his call.

He was supposed to return to Reno last night, but I haven't heard from him since eleven thirty last night. Since I have some comp hours from Monday, I'm taking off before lunch. I'm planning to surprise him at his office, but I had better call Kristin to see if he's in today. I pick up my cell phone and dial the number that I saved as Patrick's office.

"Patrick Matheson's office, this is Kristin. How may I help you?"

"Hi, Kristin, it's Emily. Is Patrick in today?"

"Hello, Ms. Janes. Yes, he is. I'd transfer you to him, but he's in meetings at the moment and it would be voicemail."

"Oh, good, I was worried. Will he be finished by noon?"

"I would think so."

"Fantastic. I'll come see him at lunch, don't tell him though."

"Your secret is safe with me. When you get downstairs, have security call me and we will get you up here."

"Thank you so much, Kristin."

"No worries, dear. See you in a bit."

"Bye."

I hang up the phone and smile, thinking that I can't wait to kiss him and feel him close to me. My next client should be arriving in a few moments, so I try to focus on work instead of replaying Sunday afternoon in my mind.

"Come, Emily..."

I've never had anyone talk to me like that and made me hotter, turning me on hotter than I've ever been, and desire builds in my body. I find a piece of paper on my desk and fan myself with it, trying to cool myself down.

A knock at the door pulls me out of my lust for Patrick as I see my client waiting at the door for me. I stand up and show her in as I close the door behind her, and I hope work can refocus my attention.

"Hello, Ms. Orhe. How are you?"

"I've been better," states the elderly woman. "I have my grandchildren living with me now. I need some assistance until the state gets their paperwork straightened out."

"Okay, let me see what I can do. Do you have everyone's birth certificate or documentation that they are living with you, income verification, and utility bills?"

"Yes, ma'am. I included all the paperwork I've received from the state too. That way you would know where they were in their process."

"Thank you. That will be a big help."

"Let me get this info entered into the computer and then I'll have some questions for you, okay?"

"Yes, thank you."

I look through the paperwork and the sixty-eight year old grandmother has custody of her eight grandchildren. Their parents are in various stages of the Nevada corrections system. She decided to adopt them instead of them having to deal with an unstable life with their parents if she just fostered them. She works full time as a pharmacy tech at a small drug store not too far away.

After inputting all her information and all the children's, it's evident that I would be able to offer her most of the services that we have here. She'll receive food, clothing, assistance with her utilities, and afterschool care.

"I can offer you help with everything you need help with. Also, we have before and after school programs and a summer program too at no cost to you."

Tears well in her eyes, she wipes them away, but more come

and fall down her cheeks.

"Oh, bless you. I was so afraid I wouldn't be able to get help. Oh, God bless you," she says over and over.

"You're welcome, Ms. Ohre. Let's go get you some food to take home. You can come twice a week for food, and if you see you're running out, please call me."

"Thank you. You're very kind."

We walk to the pantry and I help her get enough food to last a few days. I make a mental note to call my friend at another pantry to get her on the list as well. This food won't last too long with eight growing children.

I help her take the groceries to her older van and load them in for her.

"Thank you again, Ms. Janes. Bless you."

"You're welcome. See you in a few days, Ms. Ohre."

She drives away, and I feel amazing that we were able to help someone make sure that children didn't go hungry. I walk into my office and finish my notes with her case, but my throat dries out and I need a drink.

I head to the Coke machine and purchase a Coke, and as I return to my office, a florist walks in with a beautiful bouquet of creamy yellow and red lilies.

"Delivery for Emily Janes," says the rushed driver.

"That's me."

"Sign here, please." He hands me a clipboard and I sign. "Thank you, enjoy the flowers."

"Thank you," I say as I look for the card to figure out whom they are from.

I take them to my office, sitting down at my desk opening the tissue paper around them so I can see the entire bouquet. Even the vase is gorgeous. In the center of over two dozen blossoms is a white envelope that simple states *Emily*. I open the small flap, pulling out the heavy cream colored cardstock, and read the message.

> *Dearest Emily,*
> *I'm sorry I haven't called—phone mishap.*
> *Please accept this as my attempt at an apology.*
> *I'll call as soon as I can.*
> *P.H.M.*

Dearest? Did he write this himself? Him referring to me as dearest is romantic and his handwriting, I am stunned as it puts mine to shame. I wonder when he did this? He would have had to do it early this morning to have them delivered before noon.

Noon! I was going to leave by noon. I hurry up and get my paperwork done, and turn off my computer. I leave the flowers on my desk so I can enjoy them, if I take them with me, they will wilt in the SUV when I go see Patrick. I grab my purse and briefcase from the drawer and head out the door, locking my office behind me, deciding that Mr. Matheson deserves a kiss, a long sensual kiss that leads to sex!

The drive to CUGC is a short one as it's on the other side of the interstate a few blocks over. Traffic is moving at a good speed and I make up time. I pull into a garage next to the building and park as soon as I see an unreserved spot. I take my time walking to the front of the building, trying not to make myself a sweaty mess since it's so hot outside.

When I get inside to the security desk, I tell them what Kristin told me, and security gave me a visitor's badge and told me which elevator to use. I walk to the elevator, my heels clicking as I walk across the vast lobby. The lobby decor is old fashion mining equipment and mining pictures, showing the history of the company. I would love to know the history behind everything down here.

The elevator quickly arrives, once I'm in, I press the button for the eighteenth floor, and it slowly takes me up the eighteen flights. The doors open slowly and I get out, unsure in which direction to go. An older woman is walking toward me and I'll ask her which direction I need to go.

"Hi—"

"Ms. Janes?"

"Yes?"

"Hello, it's nice to finally meet you. I'm Kristin, Patrick's assistant."

"Oh, hi! Likewise. I was about to ask how to find you and here you are. Thank you so much."

"No problem."

"Is he out of his meeting?"

"He is. I'm sure he will be glad to see you," she says as we walk down the hallway.

In the hallway hangs a picture similar to the ones downstairs showing the timeline of the company's accomplishments. The hallway opens up into an open area, beautifully decorated in gold and dark brown. There are pictures of several older gentlemen and then I see Patrick's photo. They must be all of the CFOs of the company.

"Let me make sure he's not on the phone or anything."

"Okay, thank you."

She walks over to her desk, picking up the phone and talks to him.

"He's available; let me open the door for you."

She walks over to the large wooden door, knocking, she opens the door, revealing Patrick holding a woman in his arms, hugging her.

"I…um… Sorry to interrupt," I say as I back out of the office.

"Emily! Wait."

I stop.

"Emily, I'd like you to meet my sister, Addison."

Sister? Shit. I look at her again, and she favors Patrick. I feel like an idiot.

"I didn't want to bother you two," I say, trying to cover myself.

"You're not. We were just talking about you before Kristin called. Addison was getting ready to leave."

"Oh. Sorry." He grabs my hand and walks me into his office.

"Addison, this is Emily. Emily, this is my sister Addison."

"Nice to meet you, Emily. Patrick told me a lot about you today. Glad he found someone who keeps him on his toes."

"Thank you."

"Well, I need to go and check on Dad. I'll call later. Love you, Patrick. Bye, Emily," she says as she walks out the door, closing it behind her.

"Who knew, Ms. Janes had a jealous streak." He reaches for me, clutching onto my hands and holds them in his.

"I do not," I lie.

"You don't fib very well, gorgeous," he says with a wink.

"Ugh. You caught me. Sorry. You're you and all hot and sexy…and I can't contain my…overwhelming need to claim you as mine."

"Like pee on me like a dog?" Looking at me like he's appalled.

"No!" I say, pulling my foot from my mouth.

"Well, I *am* yours. I didn't pour out my feelings in an art museum just for a one time fuck," he says seriously. "Actually, I haven't been in that museum just to be there until you. So I think it's safe to say I'm yours."

I feel like an idiot.

"Come here, you," he says as he pulls my body into his, lifting my chin and kisses me, making me needy with desire and wanting.

Patrick

$\mathcal{S}$HE TASTES LIKE CITRUS AND VANILLA CREAM, AND I CAN'T GET enough of it. I've been craving her taste since I left her house early Monday morning. I reluctantly pull out of the kiss as I hear her stomach growl.

"Hungry?"

"Yes. I was actually going to ask you if you wanted to go to lunch. I'm off the rest of the day."

"Nice, how about Lulou's?"

"I've never been there."

"Then that's where we'll go."

"Alright." She smiles at me, teasingly biting her bottom lip.

I know I have to get out of this office or I'll be having her for lunch on my desk. I take her hand and head out of my office, stopping to let Kristin know I'll be gone for a few hours. She tells us to enjoy and we head to eat.

As we are walking to my car, her cell phone rings.

"Excuse me, I need to take this."

I nod as she answers the phone. A few moments go by and she cries out, tears running down her face. What the hell just happened. She hangs up the phone, putting it in her purse, and digging around for something.

"I-I-I can't go to lunch. I-I need to go. M-m-my mom is in the hospital," she stutters out in between breaths.

"I'll drive you; you're in no condition to drive. Where is she?"

"She's in Carson City at Carson Tahoe Regional."

"Okay, let's go."

I hold her by the waist and direct her to my car; thinking I'm glad that my car is parked on the first level of the parking garage, and I get her in the car. I make sure my new phone syncs to Bluetooth and call Kristin to leave her a message that I'll be in the office later today or tomorrow, and we are quickly in route to the hospital.

Emily looks out the window withdrawn as I drive to the hospital, and I wish I knew what to say or how to console her, how to make her relax. Placing my hand on her thigh, right above the hem of her skirt, my thumb caresses the exposed flesh below the hem. Goose bumps appear on her skin from my touch, and she looks over at me with a small smile.

"Thank you for driving me. I don't know how I would have made it if I had to drive myself."

"Not a problem, gorgeous. I don't mind at all."

"I'm just worried. I hadn't talked to her in a few days, and this guy called me using her cell phone. I should have gone to see her Sunday."

"Maybe she didn't know she had something going on?"

"Perhaps…but I don't know. I have a feeling she wasn't taking care of herself. She told me she was doing better with handling Nate's death, but I think she told me that so I wouldn't worry about her."

"I think that is something you need to talk to her about."

"I will once I know she's okay. I just feel so helpless right now."

"I'm sorry. I'll get you there as soon as I can so you can figure out what's happening."

"Thank you, thank you so much," she says as she wipes the tears from her face.

I look away from her and look down at my speed, and I press the accelerator down more, increasing my speed. She needs to be there quickly to be with her mom, but I need to make sure I'm driving safely.

CHAPTER THIRTEEN

Emily

𝒯HE DRIVE TO THE HOSPITAL SEEMS TO TAKE HOURS, AND I FEEL the bile rising in my throat. As soon as we arrive at Carson Tahoe Hospital, I have the urge to run from the car to Mom's room, but I've never been here and I don't know where I'm going. Patrick takes my hand and guides me in the direction the information desk, and they tell us where we need to go.

My stomach continues to churn with nerves and worry. Why did this have to happen to my mom? I hope the doctor is able to explain why she's here, how to make her better. We walk by the nurse's station and I overheard them talking, "Did you see who's in there with her? That actor guy from that one movie, you know that Sci-Fi film with Lawrence Fishburne…" I don't hear the reply as Patrick continues walking with me in tow.

Patrick stops us outside of room 210. The door has a small rectangular window, I look through it, and I see my mom in bed, resting. I place my hand on the door handle, pushing it open, and walk in the room, Patrick follows closely behind, still holding my hand. My eyes land on a man sitting in a recliner in the corner of the room, the man under the willow trees, and I stop midway through the door.

I gasp, startling my mom awake; he's whom the nurses were talking about when we walked by.

"Emily." Her voice is hoarse, and she looks a lot older than her fifty-six.

"Mom," I walk over to her bed, and pull up a chair, "what happened?"

"I'm fine, I just passed out, and Kenneth thought I needed to be seen."

"Who? And Mom, this is Patrick Matheson, Patrick, this is my mom Cassandra."

"Nice to meet you, Patrick, finally."

"Likewise, I wish under different circumstances, though."

"I agree. Emily—" she licks her lips, thinking about how to word what she wants to say "—this is Kenneth," she states gracefully waving her arm in his direction. "Kenneth, this is Emily…" She lets her words trail off like there's more she wants to say.

"Nice to meet you, thank you for getting my mom here. You look familiar. Were you at Nate's funeral?" I ask, trying to piece together everything that's happening.

"It's the least I could do as I blame myself for her condition," he says concerned. "Yes, I was, although I didn't think anyone saw me since I wasn't near the burial plot."

"Oh?" What the hell? Hopefully he will explain further—I'm about to lose it, because I'm obviously in the dark about something. *Who the fuck is this Kenneth guy?*

"Emily, there are some things I need to tell you." My mom sighs as she tries to push herself up in the hospital bed.

"I'll step out to give you privacy," Patrick says, squeezing my hand. I don't know if I can handle anything right now.

"No, please stay. I'll be telling you anyways, might as well hear it from my mother." I silently beg him not to leave me.

He nods in okay as if he understood me, and I look at Mom to make sure it's okay, and she doesn't say no.

"I don't know how to say this without upsetting you, so I'm just going to say it." She takes a deep breath, tears running down her face. Oh, hell. Is she dying? "Emily…Kenneth is your father, and he probably looks familiar to you. But you don't know him as Kenneth Reed, as it's his real name, not the stage name you know."

She takes another shaky, deep breath, continuing, "I'll give you the short version. I was an extra on a movie set and became romantically involved, and you and Nate were a product of that love. Kenneth's career took off and I let him go, without telling him I was pregnant. He didn't know about you and Nate until he was on a USO tour and met Nate. Kenneth reached out to me when he returned stateside and I refused to let him in." She sobs, and Kenneth gets up and tries to comfort her. He loves her, even after all these years that much is evident in his eyes.

"I didn't try hard enough to see you and Nate. I should have stood firm and demanded, but you were adults and I couldn't just pop into your lives after all these years. Once I heard about Nate's death, I knew I had to at least meet you, but I wanted to see your mom first and tell her that either I could do it with her support or I was doing it on my own." He kisses her temple. "I didn't realize that showing up would cause her to react like this. I'm sorry I wasn't part of your life…"

"I…I…don't even know what to say. I have a father? But my mom wouldn't let him be a part of my life? I don't even know how to feel. Mom, how could you keep this from us, from me?" My voice threatens to raise, but Patrick rubs my knuckles, soothing my overheating temper.

"I thought I was protecting you. Keeping you from getting caught up in the fast life of Hollywood. I was trying to be a mother." His voice is quiet, she looks so broken.

"Emily, I know we don't know each other, but please try not to be too hard on her. There's a lot that needs to be told about our relationship, but I'm not mad at her," Kenneth says as he rubs Mom's hand.

"I'm completely overwhelmed right now. Let's work on one issue at a time and go from there." Patrick squeezes my hand, letting me know he agrees, but isn't saying anything because he knows it isn't his place to.

"I can go with that," Mom says, regaining her composure.

"How long are they keeping you?" I ask, trying to figure out what I'm doing.

"Tomorrow, if I have someone staying with me—"

"I can do that," Kenneth says before I have a chance to think about how to handle the situation.

"Oh. Okay, thank you. Are you taking her to her house or somewhere else?" I raise my brow at him, making sure to know exactly where my mom is going to be.

"I'll take her to my ranch outside of Sparks. She needs to get out of her house and recover, heal from the events of the past month."

The awkwardness of the situation evaporates and everything seems to be under control for the time being, and I sit back in my chair, trying to gather my racing thoughts. My upset stomach has calmed down along with my nerves, and even though I don't have everything organized, I'm not going to freak out about it now.

"I agree with you there. Before I leave, I'll exchange numbers and addresses with you so I can visit with her when she gets settled in." I take a cleansing breath, hoping I can make sense of everything later.

"You're being awful calm," Patrick whispers in my ear.

"Because you are here," I murmur.

"Kenneth, are you staying with my mom here at the hospital as well or do I need to stay with her?"

"I hadn't planned on leaving her, but if you don't mind, I'm going to step out and make some phone calls."

"That's fine, take your time."

"Thank you." He kisses my mom on the head and walks by me, patting my arm gently and walks out of the room.

"I'm going to go out and get a coffee; do you want me to bring you something back?" Patrick asks after looking at his phone.

"A bottle of water, please." I give him a small smile.

"You got it." He squeezes my shoulder. "I'll return shortly." He turns and leaves the room after smiling and nodding at my mom.

As soon as the door latches, I look at my mother, time for some answers. "So. I just got the bullshit story of why you're here. Mind telling what's really going on?"

She sighs, trying to avoid telling me the full truth. "Fine. I should have known I wouldn't be able to keep it from you. I haven't been taking care of myself. I can't eat or sleep. All I can keep down is tea. I don't know what's wrong with me."

"It's called grief, Mom. I understand. I so understand. I find myself calling his cell phone, hoping he answers, but he doesn't. As much I hate it, he's not coming back. I know it's hard, but you have to try to pick up the pieces and place them together again. I'm here and I'll help you through this, we can work through it together, just don't shut me out anymore. I can't help you if you don't talk to me."

"I thought I was okay, I thought…I thought wrong. I'm so sorry, darling. I'm sorry for making you come here and having to check on me, having to worry." Tears run down her face. I crawl into bed with her, holding her.

"I love you, Mom. Please don't ever forget and it's okay to lean on me if you need to."

"I love you too." She squeezes me tight, holding onto me like she did when I was a child.

Her breathing evens out and her hold relaxes, she's fallen asleep. I gently pull myself from her arms and get out of the bed, making sure the covers are around her snugly. I need to get out of the room; I need some air, something that I can't get from this room.

I back out of the room, making sure she doesn't wake from the clicking of my heels on the concrete floor in the room, and I open the door as quietly as I can and latch it shut after I'm in the hallway. I take a few steps down the hallway and lean on the wall for support. My life, the simple life I knew growing up was a lie, and I slide down the wall, crumpling down the floor.

"Emily!" Patrick says, dropping everything in his hands and runs to me.

"I had to get out of there, I couldn't breathe," I breathlessly respond.

"Let me help you up, are you hurt?" he asks with worry lacing his voice.

"No. I'm fine, I couldn't stand anymore." He pulls me up in his arms, holding me close. I can feel his heart beating frantically in his chest.

"I shouldn't have left you," he says, beating himself up.

"I'm fine—"

"You're not. I just found you on the floor," he cuts me off.

"I had a little anxiety attack. I'm okay."

"If you say, but I'm not letting you out of my sight for the rest of the evening."

"Okay." I don't want him to worry about me. He has enough going on.

"I need to get that cleaned up. I hope your sandwich is okay."

"I'm sure it is. I'll help you."

"I got it, I got you."

He helps me into Mom's room, making sure I'm okay and returns to the hallway to clean up the mess. He's returns to the room within a few minutes with a brown paper sack containing a ham and cheddar on wheat, my favorite.

Kenneth walks in the room as I'm finishing my sandwich and has a conversation with Patrick, I can't hear. They keep looking at me and I know they are talking about me. I'm sure Patrick will tell me what it was all about later, and I see him fishing in his inside coat pocket, producing a business card and hands it to Kenneth. They shake hands and walk further into the room, next to Mom's bed and me.

"Emily, I talked to Cassie's doctor while I was out, and he will see you in a bit. From what I gathered from him, your mom is scheduled to be released in the morning. Everything came back within the normal ranges. The preparations for your mom in my country home are underway, and I have a psychologist friend that's coming over to talk with your mom in the next few days. You're more than welcome to meet with him too."

"Thank you. I think that will be a tremendous help to her, and I might take you up on that offer, especially to learn how to help Mom out."

"Good thinking. While I was making calls, I wrote down all the info you wanted. The top number is my cell phone, the second number is the home phone, and the next few numbers are my manager and my driver. If you can't reach me, they will know where I am. They are aware who you are and they know they are to assist you if you should call. The first address is the address to my country home and the second is my ranch in Montana. I'm trying to be as transparent as I can with you."

"I appreciate this." I hold up the paper. I dig around in my purse and find a business card. Pulling out a pen from the side pocket of the purse, I write down my address on the back of the business card. "My cell phone is the first number listed and my office number is second. My apartment address is on there as well."

"Thank you. I'm going to give you a heads up, once it gets out that you're my daughter, people will be contacting you, trying to get interviews or pictures. Just be polite and say no comment. Hopefully we can stay under the paparazzi's radar until we can get a plan into place."

"Yes, because I don't want to be used by anyone—"

"I won't let that happen," Patrick interrupts.

"I'm glad you're watching out for her, Patrick," Kenneth says in a fatherly tone.

"You have my number as well. If you see anything that might come her way, let me know. I'll make sure it's handled."

"Will do. Emily, I'll have Cassie make sure she contacts you as soon as she's settled in tomorrow."

"Perfect. I might come over if you don't mind."

"Not at all. Both of you come over for dinner; I'll cook."

I look up at Patrick and he nods in agreement.

"Okay. I guess there's nothing else to discuss right now. I would like to see the doctor before I leave—" Knocking on the door stops me mid-thought and we all turn to the door. An older gentleman walks in, with a clipboard in hand.

"Ms. Janes? I'm Dr. Sabean. I've spoken to Mr. Reed about your mother's condition, and I'm glad I'm able to speak to you as well." He walks over to me and shakes my hand.

"Thank you, Dr. Sabean." I give him a polite smile.

He goes over everything they've done and her prognosis with me. After speaking to me, he checks her over again and tells us that she's doing better and will be able to leave tomorrow. This could have been a lot worse than just minor dehydration and depression. Even though I don't know Kenneth, I have a feeling I'm not going to have to worry about the quality of care my mom receives in his home.

For once, someone is looking after my mom.

Patrick

$\mathcal{I}$M STILL TRYING TO WRAP MY HEAD AROUND EVERYTHING that's happened in the past four hours. Poor Emily, I can't even imagine what's going through her head, and I hope she talks to me and doesn't shut me out. I know what that can do to a person, and I'm glad that I am the one that is here for her. I don't mind her leaning on me or looking after her. She's always worried about everyone else; it's time for someone to take care of her.

"Are you staying the night with your mom or do you want me to take you home?" I whisper in her ear.

She looks up at me, with her beautiful whiskey colored eyes, and says, "I'm going home. I think Kenneth has everything under control. I don't want to add to her stress of worry about me missing work and all the other stuff that goes through her head."

"Okay, let me know when you're comfortable with leaving here and I'll take you wherever you need to go."

"Thank you, Patrick." She smiles, warming me in places that I never knew that could feel.

I pull out my cell phone, sending a text to Kristin to let her know I would be in the office tonight to address anything I missed while I was out of the office, and have her look into security companies for a personal bodyguard. I have a feeling once it's out that Emily is Kenneth's illegitimate child, life is going to get crazy for her. I want to be prepared for the worst and hope

I've overreacted.

Looking up from my phone, I notice that Emily is talking to her mom, and she gives her a hug. Looks like it might be time to leave. She tells Kenneth bye and hugs him. I think once the shock of everything wears off, they will have a good relationship, or at least I hope so.

"Ready?" I ask as she walks toward me.

"I am." Exhaustion is evident in her voice.

"Bye, Ms. Janes, Mr. Reed. See you tomorrow."

"Bye, Patrick," Cassandra replies as Kenneth waves.

I grab Emily's hand and walk out of the room with our fingers intertwined. She's quiet on the walk to the car and I know she's trying to process everything that's happened.

"Stay the night with me," she blurts out.

"You don't have to ask me twice."

"I need to get my SUV from your office, though."

"We'll get it all worked later, okay?"

"Alright," is all she says, not offering to question me further.

The drive to her apartment is quiet and I glance at Emily looking out the window, watching the scenery as we drive by. As I pull into her complex's parking lot, a sense of relief falls over her face. I think it's because she knows everything here is what it seems to be.

She waits for me to open the door for her and we walk to her apartment. She unlocks the door and the smell of citrus and vanilla greets my nose, the scent I crave.

"I'm glad your mom will be okay and taken care of," I say, sitting down on the couch next to her as I loosen my tie.

"Me too. I'm still…confused. I mean I understand why she did it, but I feel sorry for Kenneth because he missed so much. I'm glad that he got to meet Nate, but he didn't get to know him, have that fatherly relationship. I think I'm more sad than angry. Although, I might be angry once everything soaks in, but I doubt it. I realized after Nate's death, life is way too short to waste it on ill feelings." She places her hand my thigh and rubs circles with her thumb.

"I wish I could agree with you," I say, looking over at her.

"One of these days you will. Once you've let go of what's up here," she touches my forehead, "you'll feel different, and you won't let anything else bother you like that again."

"I hope you're right," I say, *Only if I can let go the remaining pain caused from my father.*

"I am." She smirks.

"I'll let that one slide since today's been crazy. Just remember I give one freebie and you've collected it," I deadpan.

"A day, right?"

"No, ever."

"Uh huh." She giggles.

She grabs the remote to the TV, turning it on, and flips through channels. I can't remember the last time I sat to watch TV just for the fun of it. I don't have time to watch sports or weekly programs. I try to pay attention to the Dow Jones, NYSE, and

NASDAQ, but normally Kristin keeps tabs for me. Emily stops on some sort of a reality program about people who want to be singers. As the people come on to sing, she becomes enthralled with their stories, and I see the tears in her eyes as she feels for these people, people she doesn't even know. Her heart is huge, and I'm lucky she's given me a chance to be in her life.

After watching new performer after new performer, it's hard not to feel for them. I know I had a rough childhood, but my life was nothing compared to theirs. I'm glad the work that Emily does in the community is able to reach some of these people, and I really could take a lesson or two from her. She gives and gives and wants nothing in return, and I'm always giving and looking for something in return.

If I'm ever going to be able to completely let go of the resentment I feel toward my father, I'm going to have to stop thinking as I do. I need to give to people because I'm financially able to. Not to prove myself to my father or to others. I have to do it because I want to make a difference, make a change.

I glance at Emily and I notice she's dozed off, and I get the TV remote and turn off the show. Gently pulling her into my arms, I carry her into her bedroom and carefully undress her all the way down to her panties. I take her bra off and replace it with the tank top that is on her bed. I turn down the covers and put her in bed, covering her up. I quickly undress and slide into bed behind her, pulling her into my body, and I close my eyes as I inhale citrus and vanilla, drifting to sleep.

CHAPTER FOURTEEN

Emily

I ROLL OVER IN BED, NOT REMEMBERING HOW I GOT HERE, AND notice that Patrick isn't here and where he would sleep isn't warm either. My heart jumps up in my throat Did he stay with me? Did he leave? I sit up in bed and see his keys sitting on my night stand, then notice a piece of paper under them, and I move his keys and pick up the paper to read.

> *Dearest Emily,*
>
> *Sorry I won't be here when you wake, I tried waking you when I left, but you didn't stir when I kissed you good-bye. I needed to get to work to tie up some loose ends for meetings today. I left you my car to use because I'm assuming you'll go to work. When you get off, please come by the office to pick me up, and we'll go to Kenneth's for dinner.*
>
> *Have a great day, gorgeous.*
>
> *P.H.M.*

I look at the clock and see it's six in the morning, and

I wonder what time he left. I know there's no sense in me staying at home because I'll be bored out of my mind and I'll be unnecessarily worrying about my mother. I finish my normal morning routine and thinking if I should take an extra change of clothes for dinner tonight.

Deciding against changing, I put on a teal sleeveless dress that I'll feel comfortable in at work and at dinner. I'll include a cropped black jacket so I'm not showing too much skin at the office. I apply my makeup a shade darker than normal, lining my eyes with a black eyeliner, and I leave my hair down. I'm sure by the end of the day I'll have it pulled up in a bun.

I pick the keys off the nightstand and head to the living room where I remember leaving my purse, and it's lying on the coffee table next to the TV remote. I place the keys down next to the purse and walk into the kitchen to eat breakfast. Opening the refrigerator, I realize I probably had nothing that Patrick would eat here. I guess I might want to ask him what he likes for breakfast if I'm going to keep inviting him to spend the night.

Opting for an apple and granola bar, I put them in my purse and get ready to leave. The only thing I don't have is my briefcase, and I don't think I'll need any of the files in there today. The only important file in there is the one for the pending grant.

I go to unlock the doors on the black Mercedes and accidently hit the alarm button instead. Great job, Ems. I finally get the alarm turned off and unlock the doors. Sliding into the driver's seat, I realize my feet are nowhere near the gas pedal.

I feel around the seat looking for the buttons to move the seat forward and after hitting the third button the seat finally moves in the correct direction.

Placing the key in the ignition, I turn it to start the car that's worth more than I make in three years. I'm glad he trusts me to drive his car because I don't. I pull my phone out of my purse, turning on the Bluetooth, and hoping it will sync automatically. Yes, finally a first try victory.

Pulling out of the parking space, I drive to the center with the radio full blast. I hope that no one will mess with the car in the parking lot, and on the drive to the center, I decide I'll park where I can see the car from my office window. I'd feel horrible if something happens to it.

THE DAY HAS GONE BY SO SLOW AND I THOUGHT FOUR WOULD never get here. I only had one client today and the center took the kids on a field trip so I was stuck in the office doing paperwork, and thinking about dinner with Kenneth, Mom, and Patrick.

I hope he doesn't expect me to call him Dad, because I don't know if I'll ever be able to call him that. Maybe after I get to know him and build a relationship with him I'll think differently. Patrick texted me throughout the day, checking on me and making sure the car drove okay for me. I think he worries a lot too, but doesn't let it show. He also reminded me to park in reserve spot number five on the right as soon as I entered the parking garage.

The drive from the center to Patrick's office takes longer than yesterday because everyone is getting off work and trying to get home. Or they are in a rush to get to the casinos. Rushing to get nowhere quickly.

I pull into the garage, parking in the spot he told me, and walk to the building. Stopping by the security desk, I tell them where I'm going and I get a personalized name badge to keep. *Patrick must plan to keep me around*, and I make it to the eighteenth floor.

Walking down the hallway, I admire the pictures again, but don't stop to study them. As I come to the opening, I see Kristin is on the phone, and I stand back, waiting for her to get off but she waves me forward and toward Patrick's office. I walk up to the door, knocking on it before I push it up.

Patrick looks up behind a pair of reading glasses, our eyes meet. He takes them off and comes around the desk, meeting me halfway through the office, pulling me into his arms and kissing me senseless.

"Hey, gorgeous. I missed you. How was your day?"

"Missed you more. Long and boring. Yours?"

"Hectic. The market is crazy right now and I'm making sure that our financials are in good shape because if the market tanks, we could too."

"Oh, wow." I actually don't know what all that means, but I'll ask him to explain one day. "Are you about finished or do I need to go to dinner alone?"

"I'd never let you go alone. I'll be finished in a few minutes. Do you want a drink or anything while you wait?"

"No, I'm good. Kind of nervous actually, because this still feels so surreal."

"I can see how you could feel that way. Did you talk to your mom today?" He looks at me with curiosity.

"Yes, she called when I was on lunch break, telling me she made it safely and the place is enormous and breathtaking," I say with a smile.

"Sounds like she's happy there."

"I think she might be happy to not be alone. I hope he isn't stringing her along."

"I don't see him doing that," I reply honestly.

"I somewhat agree. He did look like he still cared for her a lot."

"Yes, I agree…all finished.?"

"Thanks for letting me drive your car. You'll have to adjust the seat and mirrors." I smirk.

He laughs and says, "I figured as much."

Patrick pulls me into another kiss, lighting my desire on fire. I almost want to say screw dinner and go home, but I can't. My need to know that my mom is somewhere she can heal is greater.

"I put the address in my phone, do you need it?"

"No, he gave it to me as well, so I put it in my phone." He grabs my hand and we make our way down to the garage. He opens the door for me and closes it when I'm in. He's quickly in the driver's seat and we're on our way to dinner. I hope once we're there, my nerves settle down.

I've lived in the Reno area all my life and I can say I've never been to this part of the area. I look down at the address on my phone, Flagstone Road, Reno. I don't think it's too far, but I'm not sure.

Patrick turns on a gravel road, and I'm about to ask him if we're lost when we come to a gate. There's a black box on the left before you come to the gate, and Patrick rolls his window down, punching in the password on the number pad. I don't even have it. The gates swing open slowly, allowing us to pass through them.

"How?"

"He called me earlier today to make sure we were still coming. I guess your mom was nervous that you wouldn't come."

"Seriously?" I asked a little upset.

"Yes, but I assured him we would be here. Your mom's just worried about you, with everything going on."

"Ugh, but I'm not the one who's been in the hospital," I bite out.

"I know, Emily. Everything will get out in the open and worked out."

"You're right," I say because he's right.

"This doesn't look like I thought it would," I say looking at the non-mansion looking home.

"It's really a country house." He looks impressed.

The enormous timber house sets at the base of the mountains, and shrubs and trees line the driveway up to the garage of the home. Large barns set off to the side of the house and no other houses can be seen from here. This house is excluded from everyone, everything.

He parks in the driveway and squeezes my upper thigh gently. "Ready?"

"Yes."

We get out and make our way to the front door and Kenneth meets us before we can knock.

"Glad to see you, come in. Cassie is out on the deck."

"Thanks."

"I'll show you the way. Do you want something to drink? Dinner's almost ready."

"I'm good," Patrick and I answer at the same time.

Kenneth smiles and leads us to where my mom is, and when we make it out to her, we see she's talking to a man. Who is he?

"Emily, Patrick, this is my good friend Mike. Mike, this is Cassie's daughter Emily and her friend Patrick."

Patrick looks like he's been kicked in the gut with that introduction, but the look quickly fades.

"Nice to meet you both," he says as he stands up and shakes both of our hands.

"Please sit wherever you want, I'm going to check on dinner. Anyone need anything?"

We all shake our heads no.

"How are you feeling, Mom?"

"Better now that I'm out of the hospital and I don't plan on going back there anytime soon."

"That's good to hear." She smiles and I return the smile—glad she's realizing that she needs to take better care of herself.

There's an awkward silence and I don't know what to say. I'm trying to think of something when Mike speaks up.

"Emily, I've heard a lot about you today. Sounds like you're doing some amazing things in the nonprofit sector."

"I do what I can with the money I'm given. Thanks to companies like Patrick's, I'm able to help more people than ever."

"Sounds like you enjoy what you do."

"Very much so. Anytime I can help feed someone or make sure they have shelter, I feel like I've spent that grant well."

"I can see why your mom is very proud of you." He takes a sip from his wine glass that was on the table. "What do you do, Patrick?"

"I'm the CFO at CU Gold Company."

"You're doing a lot of business around the world," he says with a cocked eyebrow.

"We are. One of the largest gold companies out there.

"How long have you been there?"

"If you count my internship, over six years. Worked my way up from data entry to where I am now," he says with pride.

"Sounds like you're driven."

"Very much so."

"Hate to interrupt everyone, but dinner is served," Kenneth says as he walks out to the patio.

We all get up and follow everyone in the house, and go to the right into a dining room that overlooks the mountains. The table is a large oval walnut table with enough place settings for everyone. Kenneth helps my mom sit down, and I sit next to her with Patrick's assistance. In the center of the table sets a large pan of lasagna, a huge bowl of mixed greens salad, with various dressings on the side, and platter of garlic bread. My breath is going to be icky after this.

Kenneth helps Mom get her food, and everything is passed around so everyone can fill their plates. This feels normal, and right now, I'll take normal. I just wish Nate were here to enjoy this too.

Patrick

*A*FTER A DELICIOUS MEAL, KENNETH AND I ARE IN THE kitchen cleaning while Cassie lies down for a while. Emily and Mike went out to the deck to talk, and I'm sure he'll have some words of wisdom to help her mom move through the stages of grief and help her as well.

"Thank you for getting Emily here safely," he states in a fatherly tone.

"No thanks needed, but you're welcome."

"So, how long have you and Emily been friends?" Oh great. I haven't had a father interrogation before. This should be interesting.

"Around a month," I say, handing him dishes.

"Oh, I thought it would have been longer, but when it's the right person, you know." He finishes loading the dishwasher, and mumbles to himself, "I wish I would have realized that sooner."

"I agree." He turns around to me trying to figure out if I heard the last part or not.

"I'm not going to sugarcoat this. I fucked up. I know. God, do I ever. I know you can't make Emily do anything she doesn't want to, but please don't let her give up on me."

"I don't know if I'm the best person to be talking to about this because my relationship with my own father is shit."

"I understand. I want you to know I don't plan on going anywhere. I left Cassie once and I'm not leaving her again. I'm going to make it right, like I should have done to begin with."

"Just don't hurt Cassandra. I don't know if Emily would be able to forgive you if you did."

"I don't plan on it."

"Good, then I don't see why Emily would have a problem with getting to know you. You just have to ask. She's a pretty understanding person." I lean against the counter, watching him, trying to get a read on him.

"Thanks, I'll remember that." He half smiles. "I guess I don't need to have the 'hurt my little girl' speech with you, do I?" His tone goes from soft to hard.

"No, not at all." I chuckle.

"Good." He pats me on the back and we head to the deck, and what I thought would be a dick measuring contest was averted. My cell phone vibrates in my pocket as we walk out, I see it's a text from Addison.

> **ADDISON:** *Hey, big bro. Letting you know there is no change in Dad's status, but he is still holding in there. How are things with you, Emily?*
>
> **ME:** *Good about Dad. Emily and I are good. She just found out about a dad she didn't know she had.*
>
> **ADDISON:** *OMG Poor girl. Keep an eye on her. She's good for you. Love you. Talk soon.*
>
> **ME:** *Love you too.*

I put my phone in my pocket, and Mike and Emily's voices roll into the house as we get closer to the deck. They are talking about sports—Mike's passion according to the small talk at dinner, revealing that he has several sports clients.

"Hope we aren't interrupting anything," Kenneth says as he steps out onto the deck.

"Not at all. We were talking about the upcoming football season, and it seems that Emily is quite the Bronco's fan."

"Guilty." She smiles as I take a seat next to her on the loveseat and put my arm around her shoulders. She leans into me and her citrus scent travels to my nose, relaxing me.

"Oh, really? We might just have to catch a game, then," I say, nonchalantly.

"I would love that!" She says as her eyes go wide with excitement.

Conversation between the four of us is light, and her mom joins us a short time later, joining in the conversations. Cassandra looks a lot better than she did at the hospital yesterday, and I think that she's content here. I hope it works out for her and Kenneth because I would hate to pick up the pieces of Kenneth destroying Emily.

As darkness takes over the sky, Emily yawns. I know she gets up early and goes to bed early so I need to get her home.

I lean over and whisper, "Are you ready to go?"

"Yeah, I'm tired."

"Okay." I smile at her. "Kenneth, Mike, Ms. Janes, we're going to get going. It's getting late."

"Oh, okay," Cassandra replies, "I guess I didn't realize how late it was."

"You both are welcome here anytime, please come up whenever you want." Kenneth stands and shakes my hand after I help Emily up.

"Thank you. I'm sure we will visit again," Emily says with a smile. She walks over to Cassandra, hugging her and kissing her on the cheek. "Talk to you tomorrow, okay."

"Yes, night darling, Patrick."

"Nice meeting you, Mike. Take care."

"You too, Patrick and Emily," he says, shaking both of our

hands.

"Night, Emily," Kenneth pulls her into a hug and she doesn't hesitate.

"Night, Kenneth," she says, smiling.

We walk toward the front door and Kenneth follows us, turning on the lights before we need them. I get Emily in the car and walk to my side of the car, waving at Kenneth before I get in and shut the door. We're quickly off the property and onto a state road, taking us wherever she wants to go.

"Where am I taking you; your apartment or my house?"

She looks at me, mischievousness dancing in her eyes. "Your house."

"Do you want to stop by your place to get clothes?"

"Yes, if you don't mind.

"Not at all."

"Thank you. So what did you and Kenneth talk about?"

"That's bro talk."

"Um…"

"I'm messing with you. Just make sure you give him a chance; get to know him. I told him I would encourage you to."

"Maybe you should do the same with your dad." *Ouch.*

"I don't know how good that will do. He's non-communitive and they don't know if he will ever recover."

"He's still alive right?"

"Yes, but I don't know if he can hear me or if he even wants to."

"Remember the letter he wrote? Maybe that's your real dad, Patrick. I know he's hurt you pretty bad, but at least try so you can say you have."

I sigh. I know she's right. "Fine. For you, I will try."

"For yourself."

"I will try for myself, for you."

"That works." She places her hand on my leg, rubbing close to my manhood. "I talked to Dr. Mike about everything. He suggested I write letters to Nate. That way I can get the emotions out I'm feeling and reading them at a later date will help me see how far I've come."

"I can see that. It's a good idea."

"I think so. You know what else is a good idea?"

"What? Watching the stars from your bed," she says as she rubs my cock through my slacks.

"I like the way you're thinking, but you might want to watch your hand. I don't want to have to pull over and fuck you on the side of the road."

Her hand stills. "You wouldn't."

"I've been thinking about you wrapped around me since Sunday, don't tease me."

She moves her hand onto my leg and doesn't move it. "Sorry." She bites her lip like she has something else to say but won't.

I move her hand from my leg and place mine under her dress. The garment is loose and I can move my hand up her leg without restriction. As I get closer to her mound, she wiggles in the seat with want, moving me closer to her. She's wet, very wet and not wearing any panties. I think someone was a little presumptuous.

"Forget something this morning?"

"Umm," she moans as I rub her slowly. This is a lot harder than I thought it would be, but I don't want to be a tease. "I wanted you when I woke up this morning."

"Oh?"

"Mmm, but you left me."

"I'm sorry. I'll make it up to you." I see a side road and I quickly turn down it. I drive a little farther down and see a pull off that looks well hidden. The gravel road I turned down doesn't look traveled.

"What are you doing?"

"I can't wait," I say shutting off the car. "I hope you don't mind quick and rough."

"No, why?"

I get out of the car, hurrying around to her side to get her out. The moon and stars light around us as I lead her to the rear of the car.

"Bend over the trunk, spreading your legs."

"We're doing it here?"

"Yes, I left you unpleased this morning and I'm rectifying the situation."

"In middle of no—"

"Emily, spread your legs," I say sternly as I unzip my pants, pulling them down enough to get my cock out without catching it in the teeth of the zipper. I stroke it a few times, getting it hard enough to roll on the condom I had in my pocket. I flip the blue skirt of the dress over Emily's fine ass and caress her, making sure she's wet enough for me. She stands on the toe of her heels, allowing me to align myself to her. I thrust hard into her, causing her to moan out in pleasure.

"Am I hurting you?"

"No, don't stop. Fuck me…hard."

"I'd planned on it. Hold on tightly."

Emily's moans and our bodies coming together mix in the echoes all around us. She tightens around me, feeling her body preparing to release. As her body trembles with her release, I let go, coming with her, and riding out the orgasm, making sure she's fully satisfied.

I slowly remove myself from her, pull my handkerchief from my back pocket, and clean her up, putting her dress down and helping her off the rear of the car. Using the other side of the kerchief, I remove the condom and clean myself up, tucking myself in and fastening my pants. I help Emily into the car and get myself in as well, quickly turning on the car and turning it around to head to her apartment. I can't wait to get her home.

CHAPTER FIFTEEN

Emily

BRIGHT SUNLIGHT AWAKENS ME AND I ROLL OVER TO SEE Patrick still sleeping. After staying here for the first time almost two weeks ago, I fell in love with this bedroom. Mostly because Patrick was in it, but also because of the amazing view of the mountains the windows face. The negative part of the windows are they face to the east, and there is a valley between the two peaks, and this time of year the sun shines in here early. Or so Patrick said it did.

Today we are sleeping in so I actually get to see the sunrise in here. I'm at the mercy of Patrick after getting my SUV from his office last week, I left it at my apartment, and we still have been riding to work together in the mornings. Which is fine because I normally get to drive his car, except today he's dropping me off at the center before he goes to the office. He'll be in to help me after his meeting. I'm going to work on organizing the food pantry in preparations for our annual food drive.

"I can hear you over there thinking. Why didn't you wake

me up earlier?"

"You need the sleep because you don't sleep much."

"Neither do you because of me."

"I don't mind."

"Good." He pulls me into his body and I feel his erection resting beside my hip.

"I'm going to shower, want to join me?" He licks his lips.

"Yes, showering together saves water."

"Sure it does." I wink at him as I pull away from him and get out of bed. I saunter to the bathroom and turn on the water. I know he'll be in here in a bit. After brushing my teeth, I check the water's temper and get in, getting on with my much needed routine.

"You began without me?" He huffs as he pulls the door open and quickly closes it before all the warmth escapes its glass and stone confines.

"Should have been in here sooner."

"I had trouble getting up." I look down…he's standing before me fully erect.

"Doesn't look like you have any problem getting up."

"Not when it comes to you. Let me show you."

This was tricky the first time we tried this but we got this down, and a lot easier without condoms. I'm on birth control and we've both been tested, and whatever kind of relationship we have going I don't think is going to end anytime soon. The first time we had sex without a condom, was the first time I'd ever gone without and it felt like nothing I'd experienced before.

He sits down on the seat built into the shower, stroking himself, making sure it's hard and ready for me. On a whim, I bend over and take most of him in my mouth. Relaxing, I take all of him, he hits the back of my throat, and I try not to gag.

"Holy hell, Ems. Keep doing that and I'm going to come down your throat." I'm not a swallow kind of chick. I remove my mouth, sucking hard all the way to the tip. "You little tease," he groans out. He reaches for me, grabbing me by the waist and pulls me to him, and rubs his hand down my freshly waxed mound, teasing my skin as he makes his way to my clit. With his thumb pressing on me, his fingers tease my folds, making me wet with desire.

"Babe."

"What's that, Emily?"

"Patrick."

"You know I like it when you talk dirty."

"Fuck me, Patrick, rough and hard!"

"Yes, ma'am." He spins me around, my ass in his face, as he re-situates himself in the seat. I straddle his legs and he places his hands on my hips, guiding me down on him, where he buries himself in me. Placing my hands on his legs, I thrust my hips up and down in a steady rhythm, hitting my G-spot with every downward thrust.

I can feel my orgasm building, and I feel breathless, my body tense from the building pleasure that's consuming me. Patrick takes over, lifting me up and down on his cock, and I moan out his name. As he slams me down, my orgasm crests, and I come all over him. He keeps lifting and slamming me down until he groans out, filling me with his release.

Patrick pulls me into his chest, holding me close until we both catch our breath. I find myself falling in love with this man more and more each day. I know it's only been a few months, but it feels like a few years. He inspires me…but I know it's probably too soon, so I am locking that away in my heart for now.

"I guess we better shower or our employers will think we aren't coming in today." I begrudgingly pull myself from him.

"This is one time I definitely dislike you being right."

I stick my tongue out at him and shower by myself.

*P*ATRICK PULLS UP TO THE CENTER AND DROPS ME OFF AFTER a kiss that won't let me forget that I'm his. I'm wearing one of his Johnny Cash T-shirts, jean shorts, and flip-flops. I wanted to be comfortable because doing inventory is time consuming and dirty.

I walk into my office after unlocking the door and do my normal routine of locking up my purse and briefcase, and check emails. Since nothing is too pressing, I will put it off until tomorrow, and stroll to the pantry.

Normally one of the AmeriCorps workers helps me, but oddly, today we don't have anyone scheduled to be here. Patrick volunteered to help me and should be here within an hour to assist me. He said his meeting should be brief since it's an interview for a new manager since the other one quit.

I turn on the radio we keep locked up in the cabinet to help break the silence of the room and get to work pulling out boxes of food where everything can be seen. I'd made spreadsheets to keep tally of everything and pull them out of the drawer to get a fresh one started.

Humming along to the music, counting jars, cans and boxes seem to fly by. Then I belt out "Until I Wake Up" by J.R. Richards as it plays on the radio. I think this sometimes about Patrick and me. I feel like it's all a dream and it can be gone before I get to fully enjoy what we have.

"Hey, beautiful." His warm breath causes my body to freeze and my heart nearly stops. I will myself to move and it complies, taking a defensive stance.

"Umm. Hi, Victor."

"Hi, yourself," he reaches out, brushing my hair off my face.

"What are you doing here?" I shakenly ask.

"I thought you could use some help since you're in here alone."

"I'm fine, thank you. Actually, I'm almost finished."

"Oh. Well, in that case, how about I do this—" He comes to me; I try to dodge him.

"No, Victor. I have a boyfriend."

"That's news to me," he says as he closes in.

"No, Victor…" I holler out as he puts his icy cold hands on me.

Patrick

*I*M GLAD EMILY REMINDED ME HOW TO GET TO THE PANTRY this morning or I might have forgotten with all of the rooms in this building. Walking closer to the pantry, I hear music coming from the room and know that is where I'll find Emily singing along to the music. I'm outside of the room and I can hear voices coming from the room.

"I do. So no, please, no."

I hear Emily say and I run in the room, wanting to get to Emily as soon as I can. When enter the room, I see Emily's back against a shelving unit with Victor trapping her in, not letting her move.

"I think she said no, Victor," I shout as I push him out of the way, pulling Emily into me. She is visibly shaken and I can feel her body trembling.

"Hey, man. What's your problem?"

"You're my problem. I think my girlfriend said no and no definitely means no," I say as I clinch my fist at my side as he smirks at me.

Emily knows I'm seeing red and I'm about to beat the shit out of this punk. "Patrick, he isn't worth it."

"Are you going to file sexual harassment against him?"

"No, it's all a misunderstanding…"

"Emily?"

"It's not worth it. Victor, as you can see now, I do have a boyfriend."

"Yeah, I see that. Whatever, man." He turns from us and walks out of the room, punching the cinderblock wall. *Idiot.*

"Gorgeous, you really should file a complaint."

"I might be guilty in leading him on."

"I doubt that."

"I don't know. I've never come out and told anyone about our relationship."

"I think we just did."

"True."

"And I think that a lot of people take your compassion and caring as more than that. So please watch yourself with him. I don't trust him."

"I will."

"Good, let me help you get this finished and get out of here. I have a hot date with my girlfriend tonight."

"Oh?"

"Yes, and it's a surprise."

She sticks her tongue out and I go after her, pulling her into a kiss, leaving her breathless. I hope she watches herself around that jackass. There is something about him that is off and I don't like it one bit.

Helping Emily reminds me of my days at the grocery store and she's impressed with my stocking abilities. I try to joke with her, hoping the tension caused from Victor will disappear. We're finished stocking the shelves an hour after I arrive, and I'm able to whisk my gorgeous girlfriend away from the center and to her apartment to get prepared for our date.

I grabbed one of my suits and the bag of clothes I haven't had to use for a while from my closet in my office and brought it with me so I wouldn't have to go to my house to change before dinner. I get dressed after leaving Emily in the bathroom to finish her routine.

Even though she looks like she needs fucked, I don't tease her because I don't want her to think I'm horny twenty-four hours a day, but honestly, she makes me that way. Just thinking about her makes my cock throb...I need to get my mind off her and on dinner.

We are going to a little bistro on the Westside of the city. I made reservations before I left work because I know it's popular and fills up quickly. The menu is of their choosing, and you have to eat what they fix because they use seasonal, local foods. They might have filet one night and salmon the next, which I like because it's offers variety and you never know what you're going to eat. Although I cheated and talked to the owner since he is one of my golfing buddies. Tonight's dinner is filet and I know it's excellent.

"Gorgeous, are you almost ready? Our reservations are in

forty-five minutes, and I don't know what traffic is going to be like."

"Yes, can you zip me, please?" she asks as she walks out in a black fitted, knee length dress that shows off every curve of her body and I don't know if I want her to go out in this. I don't want others to look at her body. She's mine. For me only.

"Um, are you wearing a jacket over this?"

"No, it's 80 degrees out."

"Oh."

"Why? Does it not look good?"

"No, you look amazing. It's other people I'm worried about."

"Mr. Matheson, are you jealous?"

"Not at all."

"Yeah… What was that when you caught me? Oh, that's right. You don't lie very well, babe."

"I might not be able to control myself with you wearing this."

"Like my choice of clothing will change that. You said something similar when I had a T-shirt and boy shorts on."

"What can I say? I find you enchanting and stunning and I want you all to myself."

"You have me all to yourself. Now take me to dinner or I'll have to go alone."

"Never."

"Good, let's go," she says as she kisses me on the nose and walks to the front door, waiting on me to catch up.

She can be so feisty, keeping me on my toes and I love it…

I…I'm falling in love with her.

CHAPTER SIXTEEN

Emily

I DON'T KNOW HOW LONG IT'S GOING TO TAKE TO GET USED TO the fact that I have a father…who happens to be a Hollywood actor. Since the month he's been in my life, I've learned so much about him, about my family that I had no idea about, and I've learned about how life will probably be like once the public finds me. So far we've been under the media's radar and that suits me just fine.

"Emily, I want you to know that your mom and you are my number one concern. When the media gets wind of this, I'll have my publicist release a statement and sugarcoat it. I don't want your mom to look bad."

"That's works for me. I don't want either of you to look bad. We are here together now. Things can't be changed."

"I agree, but I don't want you to think I'm making up for the past either."

"How can you make up for something you didn't know about. Just live for the now." I smile at him.

"That I can do," he says before he goes silent. "I can't wait for *you to meet your grandmother and aunts."*

"That would be amazing. What are they all like?"

"Well, your grandmother looks similar to you, dark hair and brown eyes, and tall. We're not American, you know that right?"

"No…" I'm not?

He laughs. "No, we are Lebanese. I was born in Beirut, but we moved to Canada when I was a small boy. That's where I grew up and started acting. I started traveling, trying to get small parts and that's when I met your mother…"

His eyes light up as he talks about meeting my mom. He continues to tell me about my family and I'm in awe about how much I don't know about myself.

We briefly talked about Nate, and I'm glad because I've been thinking about him like crazy lately. Maybe because it's getting close to our birthday? I've written him over thirty notes so far. The latest one this morning, telling him about my relationship with Patrick and about our mind-blowing dinner at a bistro.

The filet was to die for, it nearly melted in my mouth because it was so tender and cooked to perfection. The appetizer was cheeses and crostini and Patrick was feeding me with his fingers—it was seductive foreplay that lasted all five courses of our meal, and we didn't even attempt to make it to his house. We went to my apartment and made love until the early hours of the morning.

The letter I wrote Nate didn't include that part, but I did tell him about getting to know Kenneth and how I was glad that at least he got to meet him. I just wish that Nate would have known that he was our dad.

I've stayed in my office most of the day because I'm afraid that I will run into Victor. I don't know what to say to him because I am afraid of him. If Patrick hadn't showed up, I don't know what would have happened—I don't even want to think about it.

Work will be slowing down a bit since I'm at a standstill since I still haven't heard about the grant yet. Patrick said not to give up hope; they are probably waiting on second quarter numbers to come out before they make a decision since the market has been so crazy.

I look out my window, thinking of ways I could raise money instead of using my own for the center and my phone chimes with a new text. Patrick is probably texting me. I pick up the phone from my desk and look at the screen to see it's actually from Kenneth.

> **KENNETH:** *Em, would you and Patrick like to come to Montana for a few days and then to LA for a film premiere?*
>
> **ME:** *Are we ready to go public?*
>
> **KENNETH:** *It's better we act first, then them hunt you down I believe.*
>
> **ME:** *True. What does Mom think?*
>
> **KENNETH:** *She'll back you in whatever you decide.*
>
> **ME:** *Let me talk to Patrick, okay?*
>
> **KENNETH:** *Of course. Chat later.*

Me: *Okay.*

This isn't a texting conversation because I have to talk out each part of this. I hope Patrick is available so I text him to ask.

Me: *Hey, babe. Free to talk? I need your opinion.*

I hit send and a few minutes later, my phone is ringing.

"Hey, you."

"I was just thinking about you."

"Oh?"

"Last night was pretty hot. I really liked that position. We might have to try that again, tonight."

"Mmm. We'll see."

"So what's going on?"

"Kenneth wants to go public with our relationship?"

"How public?"

"He's invited us to his ranch in Montana and then to LA for a film premiere."

"Shit. Are you're prepared for that?"

"I don't know if I'll ever be ready." I bit my lip thinking. "I just don't want it to change us."

"Emily, nothing will change the way I feel about you."

"I feel that same way about you."

"Good, so stop worrying."

"I think I just want to get it over with so I don't have to keep it a secret from the people I work with anymore. I don't know how many times I've almost let it slip."

"Then let's go and have a good time."

"Can you get off work?"

"Yes, I haven't used many vacation days since I've been here."

"It shouldn't be a problem for me either."

"Sounds like we're going to Montana and LA, gorgeous."

"I guess so. I can't wait to see you in a fancy tux."

"I can't wait to see you in expensive lingerie."

"You're an animal."

"Only for you, gorgeous."

"I lo—need to go. I'll see you when you pick me up in a few hours."

"Okay, have a good rest of your day."

"You too, bye."

"Bye."

I quickly hang up, I almost told him I loved him, and while I still have my phone in my hand, I send a text to Kenneth.

ME: *Yes, we would love to join you in Montana and LA.*

KENNETH: *I'm overjoyed. I'll get the itinerary to you tonight.*

ME: *Thank you!*

I put the phone down and open my email up, composing an email to my boss requesting time off. I hope she doesn't have a problem with me taking seven days off, because it's not like I take off a lot anyways. Then send a text to Addison to see if she wants to meet for lunch. I love that she goes to school so close to my work.

$\mathcal{T}$HE PAST FORTY-EIGHT HOURS HAVE BEEN A BLUR OF PACKING and traveling, but once we arrived here at Kenneth's ranch in Montana, it's all worth it the stress. Unlike the privacy we experienced in his country house, Kenneth's cattle ranch is a lot different. The ranch is located in western Montana's Sula Basin and houses a full-time culinary team, maids, farm hands, and more job titles than I know about.

As I look out the window of the room Patrick and I are sharing, everyone seems busy, rushing around like they're setting up for a party, but I'm not sure as it could be their normal routine. I return to unpacking the clothes I brought for the next six days here and leave the clothes I brought for LA in my bag. I don't even know if those clothes are good enough for that scene. I'm so nervous about that. Patrick told me I'd fit right in, but I don't know. He looks sexy in anything he wears.

I sit down on the oversize king bed and think about what it's going to be like at the premiere. Patrick told me he has been to a few lower budget premieres and they weren't as bad as he thought they would be, but they weren't A list actors like Kenneth. I need to smile and look as natural as possible on the red carpet and pray that I don't trip.

"Ems," my mom's voice comes through the door as she knocks and opens it slightly.

"Come in, Mom," I say with a smile.

"I didn't know if you were busy or not." She looks like she has something on her mind.

"No, just getting everything organized. Patrick is off with Kenneth doing some male bonding or whatever guys do when they get together." She laughs quietly as she sits down next to me on the bed. "What's going on outside, looks like they are getting organized for a party."

"I'm glad that you've not been one to follow celebrity gossip."

"Um, why?"

"It would have ruined me telling you this."

"What?"

"Kenneth asked me to marry him. I didn't hesitate in telling him yes." My hands cover my mouth in excitement, stopping the holler that wants to come out.

"Seriously? You're getting married? When?" I bounce up and down on the bed like a child.

"Tomorrow." I freeze.

"Mom. I have nothing to wear. Do you even have anything to wear? Why didn't you tell me sooner?" I start to hyperventilate. Nothing is in place. "What are we going to do, what are the plans?"

"Well, calm down. Everything is taken care of because it just happened and we planned the wedding. I picked out dresses for you to look at and I hope you like at least one of them. The seamstress will be here in a bit to make sure it fits, and she will be bringing you several dresses to try on for the premiere."

"How are you so calm about all of this?"

"I've been talking to Mike a lot and that has helped me tremendously. And Ken and I…are whole when we are together. All these years of missing something, someone. As soon as we reconnected, we knew, and he wasn't letting go this time."

"I'm so happy for you, Mom." I hug her, letting the tears of joy run down my face.

"I was worried that you would think we were rushing."

"No, never. I see the way he looks at you. I know he loves you."

"The same look I see in Patrick when he looks at you…"

"I don't know about that… I mean, isn't it too soon?"

"There's no time on love, darling. Your heart knows when you meet someone if you're going to love forever. Your mind might not realize it at that time, but your heart does. I guess what I'm saying is if you feel that way, he probably feels the same way about you."

"Ugh. Why is love so difficult."

"It's only as difficult as you make it, Emily. Stop over analyzing it."

"That's easy for you to say, you're getting married to a man who has professed his love to you."

"But I had to wait almost twenty-five years for him to. There were so many years I wish I would have said 'I love you,' or had told him my feelings. Just don't make the mistake I made. Go with it and be happy." I should listen to her, because she's seems so happy now, like she's found where she exactly needs to be.

"I love you, Mom."

"I love you too." She hugs me tight. "Ready to pick your dress? Ferna should be here shortly."

"Yes!" I say excitedly. We leave the room, holding hands like we did when I was a small child, and it brings me comfort. I take a cleansing breath and realize everything seems to be falling into place perfectly.

Fate…an unwanted fate…is slowly bringing everything together.

When we walk into the den, I see it's now a dress studio with a changing curtain, and several dresses lying about. The scene before me is rather overwhelming. I hope she didn't pick out anything with pink. Mom walks over to the dresses and picks them up one by one, inspecting them. She holds up a baby blue dress, turns around, and hands it to me to try on.

"Please try this one on."

"In here?"

"Yes, no one will disturb us."

"Okay." I step behind the curtain and strip my clothes off, thankful I wore granny undies and a cotton bra. I put the satin material on my body and I instantly don't like the dress. The color doesn't look good on my skin, and I step out from behind the curtain.

"No, don't even zip it up," Mom says before I could even ask to get the dress zipped. She looks through more dresses and holds up an indigo blue dress and I fall in love with it. "Let's try this one."

I take the dress and put it on, the material feels fantastic on my skin, and I zip it up, it's almost a perfect fit.

"That's it. You look stunning. Ferna? I think it needs taken in a little bit."

"Yes, ma'am. I agree."

"Will it be a problem?"

"No, ma'am. I can have it finished in less than an hour." She walks over to me. "Miss, can you hold your arms up so I can mark it, please?"

"Yes, of course." I stand in the middle of the den with my arms up in the air while the little dark haired woman, marks on the dress.

"Thank you, miss. You may take it off now." She smiles big. "Ma'am, are you ready to try on your dress?"

"Yes," Mom says with a smile.

Ferna pulls the dress out of the bag and brings it over to my mom. Mom quickly walks behind another curtain to put the dress on, and I take the dress I had on off carefully and put my clothes back on. As I hang the dress back up, Mom comes around the curtain, and I stop in my tracks.

"Oh, Mom. You look stunning," I say as tears well in my eyes.

"Thank you, darling. Ferna said it was me, and I have to agree."

"Most definitely," I say as she turns in the ivory lace column gown. She looks amazing and even though it has long sleeves, they are lace and she'll be cool in outside. The front and back both have V's but she doesn't look like she's trying to act younger than her age. I'm in awe of my mother's beauty at her age.

"It is you," I say as I wipe the tears from my eyes.

"I'm glad you approve." She walks to me and hugs me. "I think we are ready for tomorrow."

"Patrick! What's he going to wear? He didn't bring a tux!"

"No worries, dear. I made sure that he was taken care of too."

"Oh, you have *everything* planned out."

"That I do."

"I'm so happy for you, Mom."

"Thank you." She hugs me again and goes to get out of the dress. The next time I see her in it, she will be marrying my dad. My dad. Sounds so weird and wonderful at the same time.

"Emily, there are a few of Kenneth's friends coming tonight for the wedding tomorrow. I'm sure they will want to meet and talk with you. So don't you and Patrick go into hiding after dinner."

"Yes, Mom…" I say sarcastically with a huge smile so she knows I'm teasing when she sticks her head around the curtain. "Do you know who is coming?

"I think Charlize Theron and a few of his band members."

"What? Band? He has a band?"

She laughs. "Yes, and he travels around and plays gigs too."

"Is there anything the man doesn't do?"

"He doesn't do negativity. Between then and now, Kenneth

has had a lot tragedy," she says as she sits on the edge of the couch, wringing her hands. "A friend of ours, more a friend of his, died of a drug overdose. It happened around the time you and Nate were born. Then he had a girlfriend, which broke my heart even more when I found out, and they were expecting a baby together. However, a freak accident killed her and the baby. "

"That is horrible."

"I know. It's enough to change a person, but Kenneth is still the same person he was twenty-six years ago even after learning about you and Nate."

"Maybe being back with you will change his path?"

"Perhaps. We are both happy and being together is helping me heal from Nate's death. I tell him stories about Nate and he beams like a proud papa. I hope you give will him a chance…"

"I'm working on it, Mom. It's still new and I'm trying to wrap my head around everything."

"I know, darling. Are you ready to go find the handsome boyfriend of yours? I'm sure the guys are wondering what's holding us up."

"Yes, I'm kind of hungry." She hugs me and we walk out of the den in search of the guys.

CHAPTER SEVENTEEN

Emily

The sun shining in the window awakens me, and I instantly regret drinking too many glasses of Moscato last night. I roll over and see Patrick is still out, and I wonder what time he ended up coming to bed? The guys were in a heated game of poker when I crawled into bed at two.

I lie next to him, placing my head on his chest and listen to his heart beat, *tha-thump, tha-thump*. His chest is exposed and I take the opportunity to play with his blond chest hair. He isn't too hairy, but the perfect amount of hair to run your fingers through. The trail of blond leads down to happiness, and I run my fingers down the trail, hoping to wake him up, in more ways than one, and feel that he's not wearing boxers either.

"I wouldn't do that if I were you," he says with his eyes still closed.

"Why is that?"

"Because, as horny as I am at this moment, I'd be everything but slow and easy."

"Mmm. Maybe that's what I want." Before I get the T on want out, I'm on my back, and he's in between my legs.

"Good morning, gorgeous."

"Was someone feigning sleep?"

"Maybe. Wrap your legs around me, Emily."

"What if I'm not in the mood?"

"Then I'll go shower and relieve myself."

"Nooo. I was teasing. I always want you," I say as I wrap my legs around him.

"This won't be gentle. Hold on, gorgeous," he says, then slams his hard, throbbing cock into me.

"Ahhhh," I moan out in pleasure.

"Like that?" he asks as he slams into me, harder and harder, and I can feel an orgasm building quickly.

"Yes, pound me, Patrick," I moan out.

"Yes, ma'am." He grabs the headboard above me as leverage, and thrusts into me harder and I let go, coming on him as he moans out my name, his own desire releasing. Gently, he falls on top of me, kissing me.

"That's a hell of a way to wake up. Sweating all that alcohol out from last night," he says as he pulls away from me slowly and lies back on the bed.

"I agree," I say looking around for Kleenex and spot them on the nightstand. I reach over and grab a few. Before I can clean up, Patrick takes them out of my hand and cleans me and himself.

"Shower?"

"Yes, please. I need to use the bathroom though."

"Okay."

"I'll start the water while I'm in there."

"Sounds good."

I roll out of bed, walking to the bathroom. I'm in desperate need of a shower.

$\mathcal{T}$wo hours after showering with Patrick, I'm sitting in a chair downstairs getting my hair and makeup done for the wedding. I'm a ball of nerves and excitement. I hope this wedding goes exactly like Mom and Dad have it planned out.

I wish it were Patrick that was standing up with Kenneth, but it's his agent and longtime friend that will be up there with him. Patrick will be sitting in the front row with a few of my mom's friends and the chair with Nate's picture. At least being here, I get to meet some of my family from Canada.

I've learned about my dad in the few months that I've known about him. His childhood was similar to my own as he didn't have a dad either, but had a very supportive mother. When I met her last night, I realize that I look a lot like her, and it makes me thankful I get the chance to learn more about where my family is from.

"Everything okay, darling," my mom asks from the chair across from me.

"Yes, Mom, thinking about everything that has happened in

the past three months. It's so unreal."

"I know. I have to stop and pinch myself to make sure I'm awake. This has been my dream for so long, but with Nate…" She says with tears forming in her eyes.

"None of that today, Mom. Nate's here with us. He's happy for you and Dad. So enjoy your day." I give her a reassuring smile.

"I know…it's…"

"Mom, it's okay."

She nods at me before the makeup artist touches up her makeup, making her look even more beautiful.

"Are you ready to get your gown on?" I ask after I get my dress on and zipped up.

"Yes." She stands up at the same time there's a knock at the door.

I walk over to answer it and find Patrick on the other side of the door.

"Hey, babe."

"Hey yourself, sexy. I came baring a letter and gifts from your dad. Everyone decent?"

"Yes, come in."

He walks through the door and has a couple of boxes.

"Cassandra, this is for you and so is this." He hands her the letter and a rectangular blue jewelry box. Tiffany blue. "Ems, this is for you." He hands me a smaller box.

"Thank you, babe." I give him a kiss and he shuts the door as he leaves the room.

"Well, what are you waiting for, Mom?"

"You go first."

"Okay," I say and slowly remove the lid for the box. A teal bag greets me and I pull it out of the container. Opening the drawstring bag, I turn it upside down in my hand, and out comes a key necklace imprinted with Tiffany & Co. on the pendent.

"I love this," I say as I show my mother. "Your turn. Did you read your letter?"

"No, I will now," she says gently ripping open the envelope. I watch her as she reads the paper and tears start forming in her eyes.

"Mom, everything okay?"

"Yes, darling," she says as she fans herself. "Your father really loves us." She smiles.

"That he does." I walk over to her, hugging her. "I'll hold the letter while you open your box."

"Perfect. Thank you." She takes her time opening the box and when she finally does, a Tiffany Majestic diamond necklace greets her. "Oh, my heavens," she breathes out. "It's stunning."

"Let me help you put it on," I say as I find a place to set everything in my hands.

"Thank you," she says as she hands me the necklace and turns so I can fasten it for her. She turns back around.

"Mom, it's perfect." I say as tears start to well in my own eyes.

"Let me help you with yours," she says, beaming.

I pick up the necklace from the counter and place it around

my neck so she can grasp the clasps. She gently takes a hold and fastens the necklace.

"Beautiful."

"Thank you so much, Mom," I say as I turn around, hugging her tight. "Are you ready to be Mrs. Reed?"

"As ready as I'll ever be. I've been waiting for this day for over two decades."

"I love you, Mom. I am so happy for you."

"For us." She smiles. "I love you too, darling. So very much." She hugs me again and slowly lets go.

I walk over and peek through the fabric on the French patio doors, all the seats are filled, and there are people standing around the chairs. I think more people came than what was expected.

The cover band finishes with their rendition of Beyoncé's "Halo" and I know my entrance song is next. As the first lyrics of "Butterfly Kisses" echo through the ranch, I make my way to where the justice of the peace and my dad are standing with my bouquet of ivory and indigo orchids in my hands.

The walk is longer than most weddings I've been to, but there are a lot of people here. When the singer belts out the last word of the song, I'm kissing my dad on the cheek, then go to stand on my mom's side, and smile at Patrick when our eyes meet.

As the band starts playing "Reign of Love", the audience stands as my mom walks out the doors. Several members of the crowd gasp as my mom walk toward us. She is glowing in her ivory dress, Tiffany diamonds, and a bouquet of indigo orchids.

As she arrives, my dad meets her on the bottom step to help her up the steps.

I take her bouquet from her then watch her and Dad join hands, reciting their vows of commitment to each other. As the justice goes on, he asks for their agreement to honor each other, and they both answer, "I do." The justice asks for any objections and crowd is silent.

"You may kiss your bride." Dad takes Mom around the waist and kisses her dramatically, leaving her breathless. "Ladies and gentle, I would like to introduce you to Mr. and Mrs. Kenneth Reed." Everyone in attendance claps with hoots and hollers coming from every direction. They walk down the aisle back into the house as William Limburger and I follow behind them with the justice of the peace trailing behind us.

"Beautiful wedding, Mom," I say as I step inside the house behind my parents.

"It was perfect." She beams.

"Ken, Cassie, I need you two to sign the paperwork and then Emily and William, I need you two to sign as witnesses," the justice says as he lays a paper down on the island.

Mom signs, then dad, handing me the pen, I sign and then William does. "I'll file this Monday. You're legally married, but not on file until then."

"Okay, thanks, Jim, for marrying us."

"My pleasure. Glad you two found each other again." He shakes Dad's hand and hugs Mom. "Nice meeting you, Emily."

"Thank you, likewise."

"Ready to get this party started," William asks?

"Yes," Mom answers bubbly.

"Let's go," Dad says as he tugs her out the doors, and I look for Patrick.

When they are out of the doorway, I see Patrick standing off to the side looking at his cell phone. I walk up to him, kissing him on the cheek.

"Everything okay?"

"Yes, Addison text giving me an update on my dad, and wanted to see how you were handling everything."

"That is sweet of her."

"You're like the sister she's always wanted."

"Awe. Really?"

"Yes, I don't like to shop or do whatever you two do when you go out together."

I giggle. "You're silly."

"Ready to head to the reception?"

"Yes, round two of drinking?"

"I'm sure of it."

"Please come to bed with me tonight."

"Oh, I will. I can't wait to peel you out of that dress."

"You're insatiable."

"Only when it comes to you."

We walk into the barn and over a hundred round tables with eight chairs fill the thousands of square foot building. Old fashion candelabras hang from the rafters and white twinkling lights line the beams and rafters, giving the space a soft glow. Each table has two white and one indigo orchids in a vase with tea lights around the flower arrangement. The flowers are simple but elegant, just like my mother.

Patrick and I walk to the table in the front of the seating area, with my parents and sit down, and we prepare the next chapter in our lives as one family. I am so excited that I get to share this part of my life with Patrick.

I'm thankful my mom gave my dad a second chance. Here's to love and new beginnings.

CHAPTER EIGHTEEN

Emily

BLACK LIMOS LINE HOLLYWOOD BOULEVARD AS THEY SLOWLY drive down the crowded street that runs in front of the famous Chinese Theater. I look through the dark tinted windows from inside a limo at the hundreds of people screaming and waving as the procession passes by them. The nerves flutter in my stomach, and I feel like I'm going to be sick.

After the wedding, the most stunning contemporary wedding I've ever seen with celebrities involved, everything was calm and under control. Then paparazzi got wind of the wedding and they've been trying to get interviews, exclusive wedding pictures, info on my mom; it's become a circus, and I wonder what my life will be like when I return to Reno.

The car comes to a stop and it's time for me to put on my smile and be polite to the people who want the scoop on my family. Kenneth's bodyguard opens the door, letting him out to assist my mom out of the car. She looks stunning in her Vera Wang gold sheath dress. The designer sent it over with her wedding dress.

After she steps out without incident, Patrick gets out, turns around, and offers me his hand. I take a deep breath, praying I can get out of the car without anyone seeing my goods. I place my black strappy sandal clad foot out the door, while the other foot pushes me outside of the car and into Patrick's awaiting arms. I picked out a Donna Karan black draped V-neck dress to wear and Patrick hasn't been able to keep his hands off me since I put in on in the hotel.

Lights flash all around us, and people are shouting for Kenneth's attention all along the red carpet area. Security dressed in all in black usher us forward, while Kenneth's publicist walks next to him and mom, trying to keep everyone moving without incident.

"Mr. Reeves over here, I have some questions."

"Mr. Reeves, congrats on your marriage!"

"Ms. Janes, how long have you and Mr. Reeves known each other?"

Kenneth holds is hand up and says, "We're here to enjoy the movie and family time. Please contact my publicist for further comments. Have a good night," he responds to the reporters vying for his attention.

"Mr. Reeves can we get a picture of you all?"

"Ken, who's with you tonight?"

Kenneth waves to the fans shouting his name and he takes my mom's hand and quickly poses for a picture before walking into the Chinese theater, a landmark I never thought I'd be in this life time, and Patrick and I follow closely behind.

"Are you okay?" Patrick murmurs in my ear.

"Yeah, that was a little crazy."

"I wouldn't be able to keep my cool if people came at me all the time," he says as he pulls me into his body.

"I know. I hope it's nothing like this when we get home." I cringe at the statement.

"I have a feeling it's going to get crazy, but I've planned for it."

"Wait. You have?" I look up at him, waiting for him to tell me more.

"Yes, I didn't want to have this conversation here, but… Emily, move in with me," he says as he looks me in the eyes.

"Patrick, Emily, the movie's almost beginning, ready to sit down?" Kenneth politely interrupts before I can reply to Patrick.

"Um, yes," I say to him, caught off guard by Patrick's confession.

Patrick takes my hand and pulls it to his lips, kissing the back of my hand. "You don't have to tell me right now, think about it, okay?"

I nod before we follow everyone in the theater and before we sit down, I know my answer—I knew the moment he asked me.

"Yes," I whisper in his ear before I take the seat next to my mother.

Patrick

*M*Y HEART THUMPS IN MY CHEST AND I FEEL LIKE I JUST RAN a marathon. I can't believe I threw that out there and didn't get the typical Emily hash and rehash. She simply said yes before she sat down, leaving me standing up in the middle of the theater gaping like a fool. As the movie rolls, I can't concentrate on the action on the screen; my eyes stay on the gorgeous woman next to me.

As the movie concludes, everyone around us applauds, hooting and hollering as the credits roll. Kenneth bends over asking Emily something that I can't hear and she gives him a look of *I don't know* then she turns to me.

"Do you want to go to the after party with them?"

"Truthfully? No. I want some alone time with you."

"Sounds good to me," she says with a large grin.

She leans over to her mom and Kenneth and tells them what we decided, and I can see her parents' heads nodding while they listen to her talk.

I can't wait to get out of here and to the hotel. As much as I like fine dining and fine women, this is a lifestyle I wouldn't do well in all the time. I value my privacy and my alone time. I'm sure that it will change a little since I'm dating actor Ken Reeves daughter, but we know him as Kenneth Reed, husband to Cassandra, and father of Emily and Nate.

When our limo arrives, Emily and I walk to it alone, photographers flashing with each of our movements. Security opens the limo door and I help Emily into the limo seamlessly, getting in after her. They shut the door forcefully, and we are on our way to our room at The Redbury. The drive that should be only five minutes is turning into going nowhere fast, but I can think of a way to pass the time.

I press the button to talk to the driver. "Yes, sir."

"Take the extra long way to the hotel." Emily looks at me with curiosity.

"Yes, sir," the driver says through the intercom.

I make sure to close the curtain before I remove my jacket and tie, and I throw them on the adjacent bench seat and unbutton the top two buttons of my shirt. Then I pounce on my prey, pulling her on my lap.

"What are you doing?" She acts surprised, but it turns her on. I can see it in her eyes.

"I've always wanted to have sex in a limo. Here you are in a limo and we are stuck in traffic. So the timing is perfect."

"It's going to be a little hard with you in that tux and me being in this dress. I have to return it, I think."

"Don't worry. I'll buy if I have to."

"Okay."

I stand her up and push the skirt of the dress up over her hips, exposing me to her lacy panties. Sitting her down on my lap, I reach behind her, unzipping her dress, and pull the soft material off her arms and over her breasts, revealing pert nipples behind her lacy black bra.

"Panties?" I smirk.

"No! I'll get them off." She moves quickly and removes the thin scraps of lace from her body, and I grab the panties and place them in my pants pocket. I don't want them left behind. She straddles me again, her knees resting in the seat on either side of my thighs. I make quick work of unfastening my pants and remove my hard cock from its restraints, and stroke it while I tease Emily with my other hand.

"Mmm, gorgeous. I think someone's a little excited."

"Always when it comes to you."

I grab her around the waist, trying to figure out an angle and the way we are isn't going to work. "Gorgeous, this way isn't going to work. I'm going to move so you can lay your back on the seat."

"Alright." She gets up, without thinking, and hits her head on the ceiling of the limo.

"Are you okay?" I look at her concerned.

She laughs. "Oh my, I'm so embarrassed."

"Don't be. Are you okay?"

"Yes, I'm fine," she says as she lays down.

"Good. Wrap your legs around my waist," I say as I place myself between her legs. "Comfortable?"

"As much as I can be in a limo." She beams.

I bend down and kiss her as I roughly enter her, wrapping

her arms around my neck, holding onto me tightly. She moans into my mouth and I deepen our kiss as the passion escalates, and she meets me thrust for thrust, giving it to me as much as I give it to her.

I push up from her, sweat beads on my brow, and drips down her neck, mixing with hers.

"Come, Patrick," she moans out. Oh shit, that's hot. "I'm… about to…" she moans out and thrusts her hips into me and doesn't move them as she comes on my cock while I pound into her, filling her with my own release.

I nearly collapse on her, but I catch myself and push myself off her and onto my knees. Digging my handkerchief out of my tux pocket, I carefully clean us both up before helping Emily into her dress and me into my pants. Once we are put back together, looking thoroughly pleased, I push the button to let the driver know it's okay to take us to the hotel.

AFTER LYING IN THE HOTEL BED MOST OF THE NIGHT TALKING, we decided to skip checking out LA because it doesn't appeal to either of us and head home to Reno a couple days early. LA is a nice place and all, but we enjoy being able to see the real stars at night.

Kenneth said he completely understood and was happy that we came out here with him as a family, and he pulled some strings, getting us tickets home tonight. They are going on a honeymoon after they leave LA on Sunday. He has a few promos he has to do for the movie and will be free of work until he decides to take a new part in a film.

The drive to the airport is thankfully uneventful, but as soon as we walk into the airport, I notice a few paparazzi types following and snapping pictures of us. I move myself in between them and Emily, trying to block their shot. We make our way to check in and an employee leads us to the VIP lounge. This is a perk I do like. As we get on the plane, a few people stare, but don't take pictures or ask questions. I'm thankful for that.

Flying from LA to Reno is a little over an hour flight and it feels like you're landing right after taking off. We exit the plane and no one seems to be worried with who we are, and I breathe a sigh of relief. Maybe they will give up trying to find out who she is.

We make our way to where we left the car last Thursday and I load our luggage after getting Emily in the car. As we leave the airport, I think about all the work we have to do over the next few days. I need to make room for Emily's things…making me wonder how much of her stuff she is actually going to bring.

"Gorgeous, are we going to be able to get all your stuff moved in a few days?"

"I'd hope so. All the appliances and furniture except the bedroom suit came with the apartment. It's a furnished apartment. So it shouldn't take long for me to pack up everything to get organized to move."

"I like the sound of that."

"I thought you would." She bites her lip, in thought. "Patrick, I have to confess something."

"Are rethinking moving in with me?"

"No, not at all. I just want you to know I'm probably going to be a mess until I get comfortable in your house. It's nothing like I've lived in, and even though you don't act like it, flaunt it, you have a lot more money than I do. I don't hold that against you at all, but where you might just go out and buy something, I will have to think about it and rethink about it, and organize my finances. I don't even want to start to think about how messed up my routine—"

"Gorgeous, I know. I understand. If you didn't freak out a little, I'd be worried. I know this is a big change for you."

"I love you," she says, putting her face down so she can't see my reaction. I pull off on the side of the road, and I lift her chin so she can look me in the eyes.

"I love you too, Emily." She smiles, tears welling in her eyes. I lean over and kiss her, giving her everything I feel for her. We release to catch our breath, placing our foreheads together, not letting go.

"Ready to go home?"

"Yes, I am. I've missed the stars."

"Me too." I pull the car onto the interstate, driving a little faster than what I should to get us home.

CHAPTER NINETEEN

Emily

$\mathcal{A}$FTER ENJOYING VACATION FOR THE PAST ELEVEN DAYS, I don't want to get up and go to work. I think I'd like being my own boss and working from home. Like that'd ever happen. I open my eyes and look at Patrick's side of the bed, I notice he isn't there, and I feel the bed to see if it's still warm. Luckily, it is, or we would discuss him leaving me.

He walks in the room, looking at me, smiling, and with a tray of food in his hands. "I was trying to surprise you with breakfast in bed."

"I'm totally surprised. Although at first, I thought you left without me."

"No way."

"Good." I frown a little. Now I have to drive myself.

"Do you not like what I made?"

"No! I love it. Thank you. I was thinking I can drive myself to work now since my SUV is here."

"That makes you sad?"

"Yeah, I enjoy having you to talk to before and after work. It's like my time to decompress."

"I can still drive you."

"Are you sure?"

"Gorgeous, if it was an issue, we wouldn't have done it over the past month and a half."

"True. I love you, handsome."

"I love you too, gorgeous," he says, kissing the top of my head.

He takes a piece of the toast off my plate and eats it. Good thing he's sexy in his shorts and bare feet or we'd have issues.

"I'm going to take a shower. If I keep standing here looking at you dressed like you are, we won't get out of here on time."

"Um… I'm not wearing anything."

"Exactly."

He walks out of the room as I stick my tongue out at him. I hear the shower turn on and shortly after, I hear him warbling "Woman Woman" by AWOLNATION. He's a train wreck. I place the empty plate on the tray and set it on his side of the bed. Getting out of bed, I run to the hallway restroom to relieve myself and back in the bedroom to the en suite bathroom.

I prop myself up again the door jam, watching him sing into his shampoo bottle and getting down with his sexy self.

"I wouldn't quit your day job," I deadpan.

"But I'm a good singer. I can sing real good." He looks hurt, but he can't keep the serious face and laughs. "In my dreams. Get in here with me, gorgeous. I'm lonely in here all by myself."

"I thought you'd never ask," I say as I get in as he shuts the door behind me. "Keep your hands to yourself, mister. We have to make it to work on time since we've been off."

"I know. Luckily I had Kristin keep me up to date on everything, and you…"

"I'm my own assistant. Maybe there will be good news when we return. Maybe we'll have an update on the grant."

"Perhaps. The quarterly numbers that I saw last week looked excellent and they were finalized Thursday. So today we should definitely hear something."

"Fantastic. Move out of the way, mister. I need to wash my hair." I bump him with my booty and he swats at it.

"Yes, ma'am. Kiss me, I'm finished showering and I'll get out of your way." I pull him into me, kissing him like a lovesick fool.

"I love you."

"Love you too, gorgeous." He gets out, grabbing a towel, and dries off his body. The things that man's body does to my desire are enough to make me crazy with need. I have to look away or I'd have to please myself before finishing my shower.

I hurry up and finish with my shower, getting through my routine in record time. Even though I didn't want to get up when I first woke up, I do miss seeing the kids. Something good is going to happen today. I feel it.

Unlike usual, Patrick walks me into the building, walking with me as we were inside the doors of the entrance. He gives a kiss on the cheek, and I continue my way farther into the building. I notice several of the parents dropping off their children staring at me. I get to the main office and all of the office staff is here. Did I forget the monthly meeting? Once Kelly sees me she screams, "Emily!"

They all run over to me, all talking at once and I don't even understand what they are saying, even Victor's in the office, but he's hanging in the background.

"Okay, one at a time. What's going on?" I ask, trying to figure out what is happening.

"How could you not tell us you're Ken Reeves daughter?" Kelly semi shouts.

I knew this was coming. These ladies are on their celebrity gossip.

"Short story. I've only known for a little over two months. Some things happened between my parents and now, they are together, married and we are getting used to being a family."

"Awe. That's amazing. We saw you on the red carpet. The celebrity rags are trying to figure out all about you. We had a few sketchy looking people come in looking for you, but we kindly said no comment and they left after the realized we weren't giving them any info."

"Ugh. I'm sorry. I was hoping that my family life wouldn't affect work."

"It's okay. We had some signs made to protect everyone. *Photography in this area is strictly prohibited*, since there are kids here. We not only need to protect their privacy, but yours as well."

"I agree. If you realize that this becomes a huge issue, I'll take a leave—"

"You will do no such thing. You're an asset to the center. Don't let a few nosy people ruin what you do here," Kelly's assistant, Cheyenne, speaks ups.

"I agree," Kelly chimes in.

"Thank you, that means a lot to me, because I love working here, with you, the children, and everyone we are able to help." Kelly hugs me, knowing how much I love being here.

"Okay, now that we got all that out of the way… How was your vacation?"

"Fantastic. Ate too much, drank too much, and didn't sleep enough."

"Sounds like the perfect vacation," Kelly says with a laugh.

"It was." I smile.

"Well, it's time to get to work, the other staff is probably wondering what the holdup is.

Have a good day everyone," Kelly dismisses everyone with a wave.

I turn to head to my office and stop when I hear my name called out, and turn around.

"Hey, I…um… Can we talk in your office?" Victor asks, picking at his nails.

"Sure." I turn and go to my office, unlocking the door, and walking in the room, trying to place the desk between him and me. He doesn't come in all the way; maybe he can tell I'm hesitant about being alone with him.

"Thanks for talking with me, I wanted to apologize for my behavior a few weeks ago. I'm really sorry and I wanted to thank you for not holding it against me."

"You're welcome. I'm sorry if I lead you on in any way."

"You didn't, I just wasn't thinking straight…I thought you were playing hard to get… Well, you have a good day."

"You too," I call out after him as he walks out of my office.

I sit down at my desk, trying to figure out if I can trust Victor or not. I think he was being honest… I'll just keep an eye on him. I get going about my morning routine I've missed and check my voicemail, sixty-four new messages, and I put the phone down, deciding I'll need a cup of coffee to get through all of those messages. I can't wait to see what my email looks like.

An hour later, I'm frustrated because most of those messages were from people trying to get a hold of me for a statement or an interview. I'm afraid to answer my office phone now, and my cell phone rings with an unknown or blocked number. I never thought that this would be how it would be.

I grab my phone and text Patrick, I hope he's free to talk.

Me: *Hey, babe. How's your day?*

I wait for a few moments before I set my phone down and work on paperwork for a new grant lead I have. Fifteen minutes later, my phone chimes with an incoming text.

Patrick: *Crazy. Has the media been bothering you?*

ME: *A little. They are blowing up my phone and email. You?*

PATRICK: *I'm going to have to give Kristin a raise.*

ME: *That bad?*

PATRICK: *Yes, but I think after the newness wears off, they will go away.*

ME: *I hope so too.*

PATRICK: *Remember not to believe a word that is in the gossip mags or from someone else besides your parents or me. These people print anything for a dollar.*

ME: *I know. That was one thing Kenneth made sure was stuck in my head.*

PATRICK: *Good. I have to go into a meeting now. Call if you need anything. I love you.*

ME: *I love you more.*

His comment has me curious to what's in the celebrity rags, but I don't tempt myself to look at the unconfirmed news sources. I have more things to worry about than what someone thinks about a celebrity they don't even know.

I sent a few quick texts off to my parents, telling them I miss them and I hope they are enjoying themselves. I have no idea where they are, and that is fine with me—not knowing is sometimes the best. Putting my phone on my desk, I resume filling out the twelve page grant document. Every bit of money will help and I hope I'll be able to get this for the center.

Patrick

J BROWSE THE CELEBRITY GOSSIP PAGE BECAUSE I KNOW somewhere along the line, I was mentioned being linked to Kenneth. Which caused an influx of calls and emails for Kristin to be handled. Being linked to someone famous isn't a huge deal, but when it's new and people think they have a story, they will try any angle to get the first story out to the masses.

"Ken Reeves finally gets the girl and weds longtime love over the weekend."

"Ken Reeves reveals he has two children with longtime love."

"Actor Ken Reeves' daughter Emily Janes with the CFO of CU Gold Company, Patrick Matheson, do we hear wedding bells for them too?"

These headlines have a spin of the truth, but the articles are complete nonsense. Emily isn't pregnant, Cassandra wasn't in a mental institution…I hope Emily doesn't read this garbage. I close my browser and prepare for my meeting with the board, and I hope I find out something about the grant for the center.

My phone notifies me of a new text, probably Emily's reply to my last message, and I see I also have a new message from Addison. I really need to call her.

ADDISON: *I'm mad at you, Patrick Harrold! I had to find out that you're dating Ken Reeves' daughter from a gossip rag! SERIOUSLY! Dad is making slow* *improvements.*

ME: *I'm sorry. You have the right to be mad. I should have called and told you. Good on Dad. I'll be in to see him. I told Emily I would try to forgive him.*

ADDISON: *Whoa. I need to thank her. Actually, she told me at lunch a few weeks ago about her dad and asked me to keep it hush. I knew you knew so I didn't say anything. I need to get to class. Love you.*

ME: *Love you too.*

I stand up, putting my phone in my suit pocket, and walk out my office to see Kristin on the phone talking to someone who obviously isn't listening. I stop, waiting on her to finish the call and she politely hangs up on them.

"The media?"

"Yes, these people are ruthless."

"I'm sorry. Damn vultures."

"We'll get through it, Patrick."

"Thanks. Board meeting in ten minutes. Call me if you need anything."

"Will do."

"Oh, can you pick up lunch for us, you and me?"

"Of course. The deli on the corner?"

"Yes, my normal, ham and cheddar on wheat."

"Got it."

"Thanks." I walk to the staircase and double step it up to the boardroom. As I enter, I feel all eyes are on me, but no one says anything and the meeting commences. I'm glad to be in a room of professionals who don't give a shit who you know or who you're in bed with as long you represent the company in a good way, and I try my damnedest to do just that.

The meeting goes longer than I expected, but we go over the profit and lost for the second quarter and the numbers look on track for a record year. All donations and grants are approved for this quarter and that makes me excited to know that we are able to help the center again. I can get the check for the center before I leave today and drop it off when I pick up Emily, this should make her day.

THE REST OF THE DAY FLIES BY WITH CALLS ABOUT ADJUSTED budgets and getting expenditures approved. I think some of the calls were just to talk to me for the hell of it. I turn off my computer a little before four; I'm done looking at numbers and spreadsheets for the day. I want to stop and pick up flowers for Emily on my way to pick her up. The grant check was inter-officed to me so I have that in my inner suit pocket, ready to give to the center.

I pull into a parking place in front of the center, and I look around a see a few people in cars who look like they might be media people but I'm not sure. Get out of the car, juggling the flowers and my keys in my hand, and shut the door. I walk to the entrance with a vase of cream tulips in hand. When I saw them, they reminded me of Emily, stunning without the fuss.

The center is full of activity when I walk through the doors. Children are running and yelling in the hallway, parents pulling their children who don't want to go home, and children quietly sitting along the wall reading. I open the door to the main office, and the chaos from the hallway quiets when the door closes. I see the assistant and wave at her. She waves as I go to Emily's office. Her door is open when I get there, and she looks in deep thought.

I knock on the door, startling her. She looks up and smiles a big smile of happiness.

"Hey, handsome. You're early." She stands up, stretching and walks over to me, kissing me on the cheek. "Are these for me?" She eyes the flowers.

"Yes, they are for you and I have something else for you and the center, so I thought I could come a little early." Her eyes widen, she takes the flowers and sets them on her desk.

"We got the grant?"

"Yes."

"Ahh. Yes. Thank you so much. So when should I expect the check so I can tell Kelly?"

"How about now?"

"Fantastic! Let me get Kelly." She rushes pass me and I can hear her heels quickly clicking on the concrete floor all the way to Kelly's office, where she stops and I hear a loud, "Yes!" Then two sets of heels rapidly clicking toward me.

"Mr. Matheson! Great to see you again," the older woman cheerfully boasts as she enters the room. She takes my hand and shakes it excitedly.

"Mrs. Lui, likewise," I say, smiling. "I have something for your center. I'm glad that CUGC could help you." I pull the check out and hand it to her.

"Thank you so much, this will allow us to reach out to a lot more people. Thank you, thank you."

"You're welcome."

"I appreciate you dropping this off. Oh, I hope you will be joining us at the Gala on Thursday, Mr. Matheson. CUGC will be mentioned as one of our supporters."

"I think I saw the invitation on my desk. If Emily is attending, I'm sure I'll be there." I look at her, questioning if we are going.

"Um. Yes, I forgot to say something." She begins to bite her nails.

"Perfect! I think you'll enjoy yourselves, but I'd better let you two get going. See you tomorrow, Emily. Mr. Matheson, stop in anytime."

"Thank you, Mrs. Lui." She turns and leaves the office with a little skip in her step.

"You made her day, Patrick," Emily says as she snuggles up to me.

"Good, I hope I made yours too."

"Everyday, babe." She hugs and kisses me quickly on the lips.

"So what is this Gala?"

"Basically, all of our donors and other supporters are invited to the event to raise more money for the Greater Centers of Reno via donations or through the auction. Also, they recognize people's work in the community, companies' donations, and give a basic run down of where the money raised is used. Most of the time the event is stuffy—I kind of feel out of place."

"Why?"

"Because I'm taking their money to do the work I do... I mean I love my job, but wouldn't you love to be able to take your money and know firsthand where that money is going. Physically hand someone food that you know is going to keep them from going hungry."

"I can see your point, but I guess I get to be that person for CUGC. I've seen what the grant has purchased and I've seen who that money has helped."

"Maybe I'm being crazy. Anyways, let me save my work and get everything turned off, and I'll be set to go," she says a little frustrated.

"Alright."

She quickly clicks buttons on the keyboard and then turns off her computer, desk lamp, and unlocking drawers to get things out and locking them. She looks up at me with a smile and I know that she's ready to get out here.

"Finished?"

"I am," she answers excitedly.

"Let's get out of here." I walk out behind her and I step out of the way so she can lock the door behind me. "What sounds good for dinner?"

"Anything. I'm famished."

"Chinese?" Sesame chicken sounds good.

"Yes, please."

I get her in the car and look around, trying to see what cars are in the parking lot. I get in the car and take the long way to the restaurant, looking behind me frequently to see if anyone is following us. There's no one suspicious around, and I hope the calls and emails are as far as these people go.

CHAPTER TWENTY
Emily

$\mathcal{T}$EARS RUN DOWN MY FACE AS I WRITE ANOTHER ENTRY INTO my letters to Nate journal.

> *Thursday, July 21*st
>
> *Nate,*
>
> *I miss you everyday, but even more today, our birthday. How I wish I could celebrate twenty-four years with you. I'm thankful I got to spend as many years with you as I did. I'm thankful that you were my brother. I couldn't have asked for anyone better to grow up with.*
>
> *I hope you're looking down on us, keeping us safe. Everything is a little crazy since the media is finding out that Dad had us and no one knew about it until recently. I don't understand why they think our personal lives are any of their business anyways.*
>
> *Mom is doing great and she's so happy. I know she was happy when you were here, but Dad makes her*

radiate. I honestly believe love can heal a broken heart.

I'm sure you know Patrick is amazing. I love him so much, and I honestly believe you two would have been the best of friends. He loves me, takes very good care of me, and makes sure I'm protected, safe, and sound. We are going to the Gala for the center tonight. You remember how I begged you to go with me last year since you were home? Thank you so much for making me laugh and have fun that night. I'll never forget the feather lady... I hope I don't run into her tonight. Ahh.

I better let you go so you can party it up wherever you choose to.

I love you always,

Ems

Closing the leather bound journal, I hold it to my chest, and let the tears flow down my face, dripping on the top of the pages. The days that tears fall for my brother's loss are less and less as each day goes by, but there is still a crack in my heart that I don't know if it will ever heal. I place the journal on top of the nightstand next to the bed and get out of bed to get dressed for work.

Wonder what Patrick is up to since I haven't seen or heard him since he got out of bed almost an hour ago. Walking into the bathroom, I stop in place when I get in there. White rose petals lie on the surface of the double sink, the garden tub, and all over the floor. Candles placed sporadically throughout the room, on the counter, ledge of the tub, in the shower, and in the window, twinkling in the semi-darkness. How did he prepare all of this without me noticing?

I turn around to go find him and almost run right into him.

"Happy birthday, gorgeous," he says, kissing me on the lips with a huge bouquet of white roses.

"Thank you, babe. This," I sweep my arms around, "is amazing and beautiful."

"You're welcome. Where would you like your flowers? They're in a vase."

"On the table in front of the window?"

"Okay." He kisses me again and walks into our bedroom, placing the flowers on the table, and comes into the bathroom pulling something out of his pocket.

"This is a little something I picked up. You have another gift coming later."

"Um, okay." He slides open the dark blue square Alex and Ani box and in the box lies a silver Queen's Crown Charm bangle bracelet. "For my gorgeous queen, this reminds me of your kindness, your compassing, and your grace when helping those around you. I love you, Emily Kenae. Happy birthday." Tears of happiness run down my face as I jump into his arms, hugging and kissing him.

"I love it so much. I'll wear it today! Too bad I can't thank you properly."

"You wearing it is all the thanks I need, gorgeous."

"I love you," I say kissing him again.

"I love you too, birthday girl. We probably should get going since we are leaving early today to prepare for the gala." He hesitantly stands me up.

"True. I don't want to ruin everything you've done," I say looking at everything covered by the petals.

"I can redo it later. I have more petals." He winks as he walks over to the shower, turning it on so it gets hot and steamy.

"Outstanding. You spoil me," I say as I grab our towels and lay them on the ledge next to the shower.

"I love spoiling you. Ready? The water's hot," he says, holding the door slightly ajar.

"Yes." He holds the door open for me and when I walk in, he swats my ass.

"One of twenty-four. This could be fun," he says, pulling me into his chest and grabbing my bottom with both hands.

"Tease!"

"There's eighteen hours left in this day. I might have to do them when we get home," he says kneading my cheeks.

"Is that a threat?" I look at him curiously.

"No, it's a promise." He releases me, but swats my backside again.

"Two of twenty-four."

"Patrick!"

"Sorry, gorgeous. I'll stop." He kisses my forehead, then showers while I try to tame my raging hormones. When we get home tonight, it's so on.

I quickly shower and get dressed for work and I opt for semi casual today. I have a feeling I will be spending a lot of time with the kids in the summer program today, and I get thinking if Patrick has time to stop by the grocery to pick up a fun snack for the kids. "Do we have time to stop by the grocery and get mini cupcakes and ice cream cups?" I look over to Patrick as he adjusts his tie in the mirror.

"Of course. So we need to go to the grocery store?" He looks at me in the mirror's reflection.

"Yes. Is the cooler in the garage?"

"Um. Yeah, I'll get it and meet you in the car."

"Alright, I love you."

"I love you too, gorgeous." He kisses me softly, not messing up my lipstick.

He walks out of our room and down the stairs, and I know I need to hurry because he'll be ready to leave in less than ten minutes. I hope he has coffee on because I need a dose of caffeine. I hurry downstairs and grab a travel mug to fill with coffee and cream. I give it a quick taste and I would gulp the mixture if it weren't so hot. I grab my purse and briefcase off the table next to the garage door and head to the car. Patrick is waiting for me and we are quickly off as he gets my door shut and gets in.

Patrick decides to go to the grocery close to the center so we don't have to worry too much about the ice cream melting. I bought all the mini cupcakes and ice cream they had in stock. I hope this will be a nice surprise for the kids at the center.

When we pull up to the center, there is a huge banner in the doorway that says, *Happy birthday, Ms. Emily!* Tears spring to my eyes because I didn't expect the kids and staff to do anything like this. Patrick pops the trunk, opens the door for me, and gets the cooler out of the trunk to take into the center. I shut the door and trunk so we can lock the doors.

"I think they are happy to celebrate your birthday with you." Patrick smiles as I open the door for him to let him in the center.

"I never thought they would do anything like this. I'm kind of embarrassed."

"Don't be. You know how kids love birthdays."

"True."

"Where am I taking this?" He holds up the cooler.

"The kitchen, follow me." I guide him through the hallway, around kids running up to me and giving me hugs and saying, "Happy birthday, Ms. E.!" Not one time did Patrick get aggravated with the kids that were holding up our progress to the kitchen.

"We'll set the whole cooler in the walk-in freezer," I say as I open the door for him.

"Okay," he says placing the cooler on the floor.

"Thank you so much. Sorry I've made you late."

"I'm not late, so don't worry about it."

"Thank you. I'll walk you out."

Children who didn't hug me or give me birthday wishes yet, greeted me on the way back through and Patrick was smiling and laughing with the kids. We finally make it to the front door.

"I'll see you around two, gorgeous. Have a great day."

"Will do. You too, babe."

I kiss him quickly on the cheek and watch him walk out to the car, get in, and drive away. I turn around and go straight to the office. When I open the door, the room is full of balloons and handmade *Happy birthday!* signs, and on my office door are pictures and birthday wishes from the children. I love my job. I unlock my door carefully, trying not to rip down any of the decorations.

"Happy birthday, Emily," the voice says behind me. I turn around and glad to be in the main office and not mine.

"Thank you, Victor."

"I got you a little something. I hope you enjoy it."

"You didn't have to get me anything, but thank you very much. Is it okay that I open it later?"

"Yeah. Well, I need to get to the gym. I'll see you later. Have a good one."

"Thank you. You too. Oh, Victor?"

"Yeah? I brought in cupcakes and ice cream for the kids later. Thought we could do that around twelve thirty?"

"That should work. I'll let the rest of the staff know and plan for then."

"Perfect. Thank you." I hold up the gift so he knows I was thanking him for that too.

I make sure he's gone and get my door unlocked. Walking

around my desk, fall into my office chair, letting my purse and briefcase fall on the floor. Even though it's only seven thirty, I feel like I've been here hours. I unlock my drawers with the keys that are still in my hand, and pick everything off the floor and put it all in the drawer and lock it. Then I remember my cellphone is in my purse, so I have to get back in the drawer.

I place my phone and keys on my desk and get to my usual morning routine, but stop to look at the envelope that Victor gave me. Deciding to open the slightly thick envelope, I gently rip open, and pull the card out. On the front of the card is a cute little dog with a party hat on with a *Happy birthday* sign hanging from his mouth. I open the card and on the inside is a gift card for Starbucks. I remove the card and see that Victor had the children sign the inside of the card all around the simple statement of *Have a great birthday*. The card has me smiling and I'm elated that Victor took the time to have the children do this for me. I smile and place the gift card in my drawer and set the card on my desk.

Since I've put off my work, I pick up my phone to listen to voicemails, some media people are still trying to get an inside scoop, but I'm old news. Dad and Mom, on the other hand, not so much. I move on to my emails and there are a few *Happy birthday's* from co-workers and acquaintances I've met along the way, and even Kristin sent me a birthday wish via an e-card. She's such a sweet lady.

I'm so enthralled in my emails I don't notice a knock on my

office door.

"Emily?" I look up and Kelly is standing at the threshold of my office.

"Good morning, Kelly. How are you?

"I'm good. Happy birthday."

"Thank you. So, are you prepared for tonight?"

"Yes, they are projecting a larger than normal turnout since the economy has started to bounce back."

"Outstanding."

"Besides wishing you a happy birthday, I wanted to give you a heads up you might want to prepare a speech."

"Um. Why?"

"I nominated you for an award. I hope you get it, kiddo. You're pretty special to me and this community."

"I don't know what to say...thank you."

"You're welcome. I don't know how else to tell you I value all your hard work. The Community Centers of Reno value your hard work. You're a phenomenal person, I hope you know that." Tears pool in my eyes.

"Thank you, Kelly. You don't know how much that means to me. I do what I do because I love it. I love helping people."

"It shows. Thank you for being part of the team here." I get up and walk over to Kelly, hugging her.

"Thank you."

"Now that I've made both of us an emotional mess, I guess I better get some work done. You're leaving at two today?"

"Yes, and I brought in cupcakes and ice cream for the kids. Victor and I talked about serving it around twelve thirty."

"The kids will love that. If I don't see you before then, I'll see you in the cafeteria."

"Alright." She waves as she leaves my office.

Shortly after she left, my first client of the morning arrived, and I hope that the other three show up as prepared as her.

"*B*APPY BIRTHDAY, MS. EMILY…" THE CHILDREN SING OUT before they eat their cupcakes and ice cream. The kids are going to be hyper after all this sugar, but I thought about it because they have gym time after they eat. I hope they don't eat too much and get sick from getting excessively hot.

I'm sitting at the table with several of the first graders I helped teach play basketball and they say, "Ooh, Ms. E." I have no clue what's going on until they point behind me. I turn around in my seat and see Patrick walking toward me with another bouquet of roses. He has a thing for white. I stand up, meeting him half way.

"Hey, I thought you were getting off at two?"

"No, you're getting off at two. I'm here because I wanted to give you another birthday present."

"Babe, you've given me enough."

"I have some more."

I'm about to say something else and Kelly interrupts me, "Boys, girls, and staff, Mr. Matheson is here for a small presentation. Mr. Matheson, the floor is yours."

He winks at me and walks to where Kelly's standing, and I walk slowly over to him before he talks.

"As you know, today is Ms. Emily's birthday, and I didn't exactly know what to get her for her birthday—"

"Patrick—"

"Ms. Emily, that's not polite." He winks again. "As I was saying... I didn't know what to get her so I thought I would do something for her that I know that she would be proud of. I'm here to donate one hundred thousand dollars to the center in the honor of Emily Janes." What the...no freaking way. "And these flowers are for her."

He hands me the flowers and kisses me on the cheek. The children are hooting and hollering, not only for the funding, but for the kiss as well.

"I don't know what to say besides thank you. Thank you so much, Patrick."

"You're welcome. You still have another gift too," he murmurs.

"This is all too much." I feel overjoyed and overwhelmed.

"Nothing is too much when it comes to you," he whispers in my ears, causing a shiver to run through my body

"I'm a very lucky girl." I beam.

"No, I'm the lucky one. I love you, gorgeous." His breath tickles my ear and another shiver racks my body.

"I love you too," I whisper.

Patrick hands Kelly the check, tears stream down her face and I know that Patrick overwhelms her as much as he does me. Patrick's compassion is showing, and I hope that it's enough to get him to see his dad—one step at a time.

WHEN WE ARRIVE HOME FROM WORK, PATRICK POUNCES ON me and makes sure that I get the rest of my birthday spankings. Then, with the extra rose petals and candles, Patrick decorates the bedroom and bathroom again, making me feel special all over again. When he finishes, he picks me up, and gently lays me on the bed, slowly making love to me until we're both moaning each other's name out in pleasure.

He makes me feel like no other man has before. His actions and words reach deep inside my soul, making me feel everything he says and does. I love him…and I want to be with him the rest of my life, he is my forever.

As much as I enjoy lying in Patrick's arms after making love, I know that it's time to get dressed for the gala. Last year when I attended, I felt so out of place next to millionaires, CEOs, and investment brokers. I felt like I was trying to fit in even though I was the one that was doing the "dirty" work for these people, but I don't mind. I love what I do.

This year, I feel like I belong because I *am* the one that is one on one with the people the center's service. Being on Patrick's arm doesn't hurt either because he makes me feel like I am priceless.

"Babe, I'm going to get showered and dressed. You know it's going to take me forever."

"Okay. I'll be in there to shower with you in a few," he says kissing me on the temple.

I reluctantly get out of bed, making my way to the shower and turn it on. As I wait for it to warm, my mind drifts to our trip to the dress shop to pick out the dress Tuesday night.

"Welcome to Bella Bella Couture, how may I assist you?" the sales consultant asks Patrick as we enter the store, completely overlooking me. Not a good move. Patrick notices and winks at me.

"Hello, we are looking for a dress for my gorgeous girlfriend for a gala we are attending Thursday. She would look stunning in a paper sack, but we need something a little more upscale." Her cheeks flush with embarrassment and she gives me a half smile.

"We have designs that would be perfect for a gala. Please follow me, miss. Sir, you can have a seat in the waiting area." She points at an area with oversized, comfy looking chairs. "I'm Ginni by the way." She offers me her hand and I give it a small shake.

"Emily."

"Any color you prefer over another, Ms. Emily?"

"Blue, she looks indescribable in blue," Patrick offers from the waiting area.

My heart beats double-time with his confession to Ginni and she smiles at me with a slight hint of jealousy on her face.

"Any particular shade?"

"No, I like all blues, so let's see what you have. I would like

something classic, not really form fitting but not layers of bulky fabric." She nods at my requirements and gets to work looking through the rows and rows of dresses in the showroom.

I feel like I'm prepping to go to prom all over again. She hangs dress after dress on the rack for to me look at and decide if I want to try it on, but before I decide if I want to put it on my body, I look at the price tag. Sticker shock. No way am I going to be able to afford a few of these on the rack so far.

"Emily, stop looking at the tags. You're to get a dress that fits you and your personality. My treat." I look at him. I don't want to yell at him across the store, so I go with it.

"Thank you." I blow him a kiss.

I try on dresses from Prada, Gucci, Vera Wang, Donna Karen, Ralph Lauren, and other brands that I've never heard of before. When I put on the Ralph Lauren dress, I know I've found my dress. The way it fits my body and makes me feel in it, screams to me buy this dress. I walk out to show Patrick and he has to adjust his position in the chair when I seductively sway out of the fitting area. The floor length, sweeping airport blue jersey dress—embellished with delicate ruching and an elaborate crystal brooch at the shoulder and slit up the left side to mid-thigh— makes me feel like a queen going to a ball.

"We'll take this dress," Patrick says after clearing his throat.

"You look stunning, Ms. Emily, and the fit looks as if it doesn't need to have any adjustments made. It's like the dress was made specifically for you."

"*I have to agree.*" *I carefully take off the dress and give it to Ginni to remove all of the tags and steam the garment, so it's perfect for the gala. I eye a pair of strappy black Michael Kors sandals and I have to touch them.*

"*Try them on, if you like them, get them.*" *I look around to make sure Ginni is nowhere close.*

"*Patrick, I can't ask you to buy these for me too. I'm going to feel like I owe you.*"

"*This is where you need to justify spending, I understand. Please don't. If I were worried that you were using me for my money, we wouldn't be here. I want to take care of you and treat you. I enjoy doing these for you because you aren't materialist and don't ask for much. This is something you want and I'll happy obliged and buy it for you.*"

I stand in shock, unable to say anything for a few moments. "Thank you." I hug him tightly, not wanting to ever let him go.

"Hey, I thought you would be in the shower," Patrick says in my ear as he comes up behind me, hugs me, and caresses my breasts.

"I was thinking about our shopping trip Tuesday. You really do spoil me, you know that?" I turn in his arms, placing my hands on his firm chest.

"I do, and I enjoy every moment of it too." He kisses my nose, teasing me.

"I love you, Patrick Matheson."

"I love you more, Emily Janes." Sigh, this man makes me

melt into a gooey mess.

Patrick

𝒯HIS WOMAN…I WANT TO GIVE HER THE WORLD AND I AM going to try my damnedest to do just that. Funny she brought up our shopping trip to the dress shop. The sales consultant was so jealous of Ems and I might have been a bit of an asshole to rub my need to spoil Emily in her face. She pissed me off when she over looked Emily and looked straight at me when we walked in the door.

"Gorgeous, I hate to rush you, but we need to get going. The traffic will be hectic around the museum at this time of day."

"I'm almost finished," she yells from the bathroom.

I stand before the floor length mirror, adjusting the blue tie that matches Emily's dress and my three piece black Hugo Boss suit. Even though most of these guys will be in tuxedos, I feel more in charge in a suit, and this suit fits me impeccably well. I see Emily walk out of the bathroom in the mirror's reflection, so I turn to take her in and feel weak at the knees. She looks like a goddess. My goddess; I notice she's wearing her queen bracelet she received for her birthday.

"You're breathtaking, Emily. I don't know if I want to share you with anyone else."

"You better, especially after all the time I took to get dolled up. I really don't think you have any room to talk, Mr. Sexypants. That suit." She bites her lip. "Fits you perfectly in all the right places and I better not see any old ladies pinching your ass."

"This ass is for your hands only."

"Good. I'm ready to go if you are."

"I am." I let her walk in front of me so I can stare at her fine ass as it sways, causing me to have to stop and adjust myself. She makes me completely unsustainable when it comes to her and her body.

We get to the garage and I help her in the car, making sure her gown is in without catching it in the door. Before I get in, I take off my jacket and hang it up in the backseat. I don't want it to wrinkle on the drive nor do I want to sweat since it's hotter than hell outside.

The drive to the museum is uneventful, but as we pull in front of the museum to valet the car, the line is a lot longer that I thought it would be. I debate on parking the car myself, but I don't want to make Ems walk in this heat. Fifteen minutes later, the keys are in the hand of the valet and we are walking in the building, her hand in the crook of my arm.

"Wow. This looks astounding."

I look at her and say, "That's only because you're here, making it gorgeous." Our eyes meet and she looks at me stunned that I would say something like that. I don't know how she isn't used to my praises of her, and they are the truth. I see no other woman as mind blowing as her.

"Thank you." She kisses me on the cheek.

The gala is taking place in the Skyroom and we eventually make our way there after making small talk with people I know from business dealings and golf. I made sure to introduce Emily to everyone I talked to so she doesn't feel left out or out of place. She has an amazing way with people, and it floored me when she told me she felt out of place last year. I'm making sure that she doesn't feel that way this year.

The Skyroom in decorated in tons of silver and white, and the décor reminds me of something I saw from the *Great Gatsby*. I'm waiting for Leo to jump out in full costume. We walk around the room, and Emily introduces me to the executives at the Community Centers of Reno. After talking, the CEO and I realize that we play golf at the same time every Sunday. How we haven't connected before now is beyond me.

The emcee of the gala takes the stage and thanks everyone for attending, and then asks everyone to take their seats because dinner service would soon commence. We finish our small talk and head to our seats. The table happens to be close to the stage and I hope this placement means good news for Emily.

Kelly and her husband Scott, two of the center's AmeriCorps volunteers and their dates join us at the table. The conversation is light and amusing throughout the meal. I notice that Emily isn't eating as much as she normally does and I wonder if she's nervous.

"Feeling okay, gorgeous?"

"I have butterflies. We are so close to the stage. What if I am chosen? What do I say? I'm afraid I'll look like a fool."

"Ems, if you win, you'll win with grace and will know what to say when you get up there."

"I'm glad someone has confidence in me."

"Always." I kiss her on the temple and she sighs.

The waiters remove dishes from tables as people excuse themselves from the table to go smoke or to go to the restroom. Emily excuses herself and I help her up from her seat. I watch her as she disappears around the corner with a smile on my face.

"She's going to freak out, isn't she?" Kelly asks as she sits down next to me.

"I think she will after the fact. She'll tell them how she feels, and those words will leave them speechless. Then they will get their checkbooks out."

"I hope you're right. I wanted to thank you again too."

"It's my pleasure. I met Emily because of the center. I want to make sure that you have enough to provide for all."

"Thank you. Here she comes. We'll talk soon." She pats me on the arm and goes to sit next to her husband. I stand up, helping Emily in her seat and sits down.

"What was that about?"

"She was thanking me again for my donation." She smiles.

"Kelly is going to thank you every time she sees you."

I chuckle. "That isn't necessary."

"That's how she is."

The emcee returns to the stage, stopping our conversation.

"I hope everyone enjoyed dinner. I wanted to extend my thanks again to everyone here tonight. You in some way have touched the lives of the individuals that the Community Centers of Reno service. Without you, the centers are nothing." She claps and the room joins in the round of applause.

"Before we get underway with the honors part of the program, I want to remind you we have silent auction items waiting for your bids in the outer hallway. Items include one of a kind artwork to all exclusive weekend getaways. The description of what's included in the auction is on the bidding sheet. May the highest bid be in your favor." Laughs echoes throughout the room.

"The honors of the night go to our top five corporate donors and personal donors. It's rare to see someone's name on both lists and I actually asked if it was a typo and learned it wasn't. Now I'm curious. Patrick Matheson, CFO of CU Gold Company, please come up and accept the platinum donor award for CU Gold Company and the platinum donor award for your personal donation." The room erupts in applause. I didn't think I'd have to go up there.

I stand up, buttoning my jacket as I walk up on the stage. The emcee shakes my hand and presents me with the awards, I stand on stage for photos and I turn away to take my seat and she stops me.

"Mr. Matheson, not so quick, we're curious to know why

you pick the Community Centers for your donation." She smiles, offering me the podium. *Well, shit.*

I clear my throat and talk. "I didn't know much about the Community Centers of Reno until the day I presented Project Hope with CU Gold's donation. Instead of leaving after the check presentation, I stayed and interacted with the people that make up the Project Hope community. The caring and compassion I saw in the couple of hours there touched me and made me personally want to help more, and when I met the Project Hope's Outreach Coordinator." I look at Emily and our eyes meet.

"I instantly knew why that center was so successful and served as many individuals as it does. Because of her and the center's dedication to make a change in the community is why I personally donated. I encourage everyone in here that donates go to your local center and volunteer. Not only will the center appreciate your help, but you can also see your donation at work. I thank you for recognizing CU Gold and myself. I know CU Gold will stand behind me when I say it's an honor to be a community partner with the Community Centers of Reno. Thank you." I smile and the applause is deafening.

I walk down the stage and as I sit down I notice Emily is patting her eyes dry.

"Your speech was exceptional."

"Just the truth. If it weren't for you, I wouldn't be here." She kisses my cheek and we turn our attention to the rest of the honorees.

I feel a tap on my shoulder during a pause in the program and turn to see a person holding a camera. "Mr. Matheson, can I get your picture for the gala website?"

"Of course. Here or elsewhere?"

"Here is fine."

I stand from my seat and ask Emily stand up with me. I wrap my arm around her, pulling her into my body for the picture.

"On three. One, two, three." The flash is bright and I see little orbs in my vision after the flash. "Perfect. You're a stunning couple. Thank you, Mr. Matheson, Ms. Janes."

"Thank you." I nod and we return to our seats.

"I'm going to have to see if I can get a copy of that." Emily smiles at me. "We have very few pictures together."

I pull my phone out of my pocket and click on the camera app. "I think we can fix that." I wrap my arm around her and snap several pictures of us smiling. The last picture I take is of me kissing her on the cheek. Emily is a natural beauty and I'm thankful she's mine.

"Please send those to me."

I hand her my phone. "It probably would be better to email them to yourself. I'll let you do it so you have the ones you want and like." She looks at me shocked that I handed her my phone. I have no secrets.

"Alright," she says as she takes the phone and looks at the pictures. A few moments go by and she smiles, and I look down and see she's looking at the pictures of her that I've taken since we've been together. She looks up at me, curious.

"I had no idea you had pictures of me."

"I wanted something to look at when I was in long, boring meetings."

"Oh, I see."

"You're gorgeous; I always want to stare at you."

"Your sweet talk will get you everywhere, Mr. Matheson," she sasses.

"I hope so." I wink.

"Testing," the emcee's voice echoes through the room. "We will get to the next round of recognitions in five minutes, thank you."

"Gorgeous, I'll be right back."

"Okay, I love you."

"Love you too." I kiss her cheek and get up to use the restroom and to find the emcee to see if I can get in a birthday wish for Emily.

CHAPTER TWENTY-ONE

Emily

𝒯HE EMCEE TAKES HER PLACE BEHIND THE PODIUM AND Patrick hasn't returned. My palms sweat as anxiety builds in my chest. I hope in the chance that I am honored he's here to see it. I look around for him and I don't see him anywhere. This is not like him. I hear hushed gasps and whispers behind me, and I turn to look around again. That's when I see Patrick coming with a cake, topped with a silver sparkler in the center of it. Oh my.

Our eyes meet and his smile warms me instantly. When he's almost to the table, the emcee talks, "We have someone celebrating a birthday today. If everyone could join in and sing *Happy Birthday* to Emily Janes from Project Hope, I'm sure she'll be honored. Begin at three. One, two, three..." The lyrics of *Happy Birthday* belt out around me.

I feel my face flush with embarrassment as Patrick sets down the cake in front of me. When the song is over, everyone hoots and hollers. I politely nod to the emcee to let her know I appreciate her kindness, and in return, she smiles and waves.

"Why do I have a feeling you set all of that up?" I whisper in Patrick's ear.

"Guilty."

"That was kind of embarrassing."

"I'm sorry, gorgeous. That wasn't my intention."

"I know. Thank you and the cake is beautiful."

"They have a box to put it in if you don't want to eat it."

"Mmm. I think I want to eat it in bed tonight.

"Oh?"

"Yes."

"Ladies and gentlemen, the second portion of our evening is beginning. The time has come to recognize the employees that make our centers thrive."

The emcee lists all the employees with years severed at the centers, employees of the month, and the AmeriCorps volunteer's awards, and followed by awards given to employees by their center's directors. The last award of the evening should be coming up, and I'm positive I'm not in the running for it so I take a relaxing breath to let the nerves out that I was holding.

"For our last recognition of the night, the Humanitarian of the Year is the highest honor from the Community Centers of Reno. This individual puts in more hours than what is required of her. She's often in the center at seven and doesn't leave until five. In her day at Project Hope…" My ears begin to ring and I feel Patrick squeeze my thigh. Did I actually win this award?

"…she's a friend to the youth, teaching them basketball or

listening to their problems. Those in need, reach out to her help to keep a roof over their heads or food on their tables. She goes beyond the call of duty to help those who need our help. On the behalf of the Community Centers of Reno, I would like to present Emily Janes, Outreach Coordinator at Project Hope with the Humanitarian of the Year award. Ms. Janes, please come up and accept your award."

I'm in shock, because I'm sure someone else is more deserving.

"Gorgeous, that's you…" He kisses my cheek. My mind finally gets my legs to work and I stand up, making my way up on stage amid the round of applause.

The emcee hands me the award after shaking my hand and I know I have to give a speech. I inhale deeply and let it out before I reach the mike.

"Thank you. To receive this recognition is humbling. When Kelly told me she had nominated me for an award, I didn't think it would ever be for the Humanitarian of the Year honors. I wish I had prepared a better speech." The audience chuckles at my admission.

"First, I would like to thank the staff I have the honor of working with every day at Project Hope. Their compassion and drive to help the community encourages me daily to do the same. I would like to thank our donors also. Without them, we wouldn't be able to open our doors to those in need." I pause, collecting my thoughts for before I proceed.

"Working for Project Hope has opened my eyes up to the suffering we have in our very own community. Children going hungry, without proper shelter, or without the necessities that we take for granted. That needs to change. I've made it my mission to serve everyone that comes through our doors; I try to make sure they have what they need when they leave. I love being hands on with the children and with the community. Having that one on one contact allows me to know what's happening within the community, our community. Because I took the time to listen, I quickly learned there needed to be a change in how those in need of services are assisted, and being at Project Hope has allowed me to be that change. We all are that change, and couldn't be more honored to be part of the Community Centers of Reno than I am this very moment. Thank you." I look to Patrick and he stands up clapping along with the rest of the room.

When I return to my seat, everyone is still clapping and I do a half bow to thank them all again, and the room is still applauding.

"Thank you, ladies and gentlemen. That concludes our honors ceremony. If you bid in our silent auction, please check in to see if you won. Thank you again for coming and supporting the Community Centers of Reno. Enjoy the rest of your evening," the emcee says before she walks off the stage.

"Well, that was surprising," I say to Patrick before I'm tackled behind from Kelly.

"Emily, I had no doubt you would win," she says as I turn to face her.

"Thank you, I'm honored you think that much of me."

"Without you, we wouldn't serve half the people we do. You're the first person I've had in that position that has loved that job."

"I do very much."

She hugs me again. "Congratulations, both of you."

"Thank you," Patrick says, smiling.

"I'll see you around. If I don't see you before you leave, have a good evening and I'll see you tomorrow."

"Bye, Kelly," I say hugging her again.

"Let's go see if we won anything," Patrick says to me as we pick up our awards.

"I didn't bid on anything."

"I did." He winks at me as he grabs my hand and we walk out to the hallway.

Tables flank both sides of the hallway with assorted gifts spread out evenly among them. I hesitate, looking at the baskets and items sitting on the tables, and Patrick gently tugs me to catch up with him. He knows exactly where he wants to go. At the end of the table, I notice there's a large framed piece of art. As we get closer, I notice it's a picture of Petah Coyne's *Untitled #1205, (Virgil)*. He looks down at the sheet and smiles.

"Looks like I need to pay."

"You won this?"

"Yes."

"I didn't know you liked Petah Coyne."

"Oh, is that who created it?"

"Yes, why did you bid on it if you didn't know anything about it?"

"It's where I found you." I look at him. "The day I came to the museum, this is the piece of art I found you in front of. It's my reminder to keep looking and I'll find exactly what I need. That day was the day I realized I needed you." I'm shocked he remembered. Love fills my heart.

"I love you, Patrick."

"I love you too, Emily." I place my award in front of him, putting my arms around his waist, and hug him. His arms close around me, enclosing me in his warm hug.

"I'm going to get this paid for and we can get out of here if you're ready."

"Sounds good to me."

He gets the attention of the attendant behind the table and fills out the paperwork that has to be completed in order to pay for the artwork. While he finishes up, I look at the other items that were available and the few pieces of art that are on display, and I get a chill down my spine. I slowly turn around and see Victor staring at me, *How did I not notice him before?*

I stand still and he stalks toward me. "Emily, congratulations on your honor. You're very deserving of it."

"Thank you, Victor. I didn't know you were here. I thought you would have been sitting at our table."

"I came in late and set with a few other people I knew from the center on the Southside of the city."

"Oh. I see. Well, it was good seeing you, but I need to get going."

"See you tomorrow," he says and walks off.

I look up and notice Patrick walking toward me. I shake off the odd encounter with Victor and smile at Patrick's sexiness as he gets closer to me, and I'm glad that we decided to head home because I can't wait to eat my cake in bed with him.

I wonder what cake on Patrick's abs would taste like? I think I'm going to find out.

CAKE ALA PATRICK WAS FANTASTIC AND VERY STICKY LAST night, leading to hyper sex from all the sugar. As I get out of bed, I find crumbs of cake I missed cleaning. Before I head to the shower, I grab my phone and text my mom, letting her know about my award from last night and checking to see if we are still on for dinner tonight. I know I won't get a reply until later in the morning.

Patrick and I go through our morning routines a little draggy this morning. Being out late then cake tasting lasting until one, only gave us four hours of sleep. I hope that today isn't a long day. After we finish upstairs, I make sure to grab a thermos of coffee to take with me. I know I'll need several cups to make it through the day.

When we arrive at the center, everything is normal and prepared to begin a new day. Patrick helps me out of the car and walks me to the entrance, kissing me on the cheek before I go in.

"Have a great day, gorgeous."

"You too, sexy."

He winks at me before I walk into the building. I hope this day goes smoothly.

CHAPTER TWENTY-TWO
Patrick

$\mathcal{E}$MILY'S BIRTHDAY CELEBRATION TAKE TWO IS A GO. EMILY'S parents had planned to take her out on her actual birthday, but since the gala was the same day, they decided to do it the next day. With Friday being the kick off to the weekend, Cassie and Kenneth went a little crazy with planning. Well, Kenneth did. I think he's trying to make up for all the years lost.

What makes all of the plans so great is that she's in the dark. She knows that we are going to dinner with her parents, but she doesn't know that my sister coming too. I guess she will when she walks out to the car in five, four, three, two, one...the door in the front of the center and Emily's beautiful smiling face greets me as I get out of the car to open the door.

She squints her eyes, trying to figure out who is in the backseat of the car. As she gets in, she turns around and smiles even bigger.

"Addison. How are you?" she asks excitedly.

"I'm well, you?" Addison smiles, largely.

"Great! Thank you. Are you going to dinner with us?" Emily

asks, confused.

"I am. Patrick invited me. I hope you don't mind."

"Not at all. It's nice to see you." Emily gives her a big smile.

"Ready to go," I ask Emily.

"Yes, are we going straight to the restaurant?"

"We are meeting your parents first."

"Oh, okay. Mom said you know the plans and they'll see me when we arrive."

"Yes, Kenneth texted me this morning."

"Why do I have a feeling that this isn't going to be a quiet dinner?"

"I'm sure it's going to be a quiet dinner." I wink at her.

I turn the car to head southeast to the Reno-Tahoe International Airport. When I take the exit for the airport instead of staying on 580 to go to our house, she looks at me trying to figure out what's going on.

"Babe, where are we going?"

"Meeting your parents."

"At the airport? I thought they were at their country home."

"I'm not sure. I was told this is where I need to go."

"Okay." She looks around outside of the car, trying to figure out what's going on.

I drive around to the Atlantic Aviation building and park in front of the building.

"Patrick. I don't see my parents."

"Hmm. I wonder if they're inside."

"I'll call my mom." She pulls her phone out of her purse and calls. "Hi, Mom. We're where you told Patrick to meet… Alright. We'll be in. Love you." She hangs up. "She said they are inside."

"Okay. Well, let's go in."

I get out of the car and get the doors for Addison and Emily, and I take Emily's hand as we walk to the building. As we enter, I see her parents sitting in chairs waiting for our arrival.

"Emily, darling. It's so good to see you. Sounds like you had a wonderful birthday yesterday." Her mom stands and hugs her tightly.

"I did, missed you though."

"I missed you too."

"Happy birthday, Emily," Kenneth says as he hugs her after.

"Thank you so much. All ready?"

Her parents laugh at her question. "I think we should be asking you that." Her mom smiles.

"Um, why?"

"Patrick, you didn't tell her?"

"No, ma'am. You told me to keep it a secret so I did."

"Wise man," Mom says, patting me on the arm.

She places her arm around Emily's shoulders. "Darling, we are taking you and everyone here to Vegas for the weekend. Our plane leaves in thirty minutes."

"Holy cow! I haven't packed. I only have the clothes that I'm wear—"

"I packed for you. Our luggage is in the trunk." I smile at her.

"I can't believe this. Is this really happening?" She looks at all of us in disbelief.

"Yes, Emily. You have a busy weekend ahead. Ready to celebrate your birthday?"

"As I'll ever be."

"I'll get the luggage."

"Wait, I'll help you. Let's get a trolley," Kenneth offers.

"Thank you," I say, smiling at him.

We head out to my car and get the suitcases that I had packed in the trunk. I hope I included everything that she'll need, but it's not like we can't pick up something I missed. We meet up with the ladies inside and take our luggage to the baggage service.

Kenneth and Cassandra lead everyone to the private plane that will be taking us to Vegas. Emily looks overwhelmed with everything but once the shock wears off, she will enjoy herself. Once we are on the plane, Emily asks to sit next to the window and I let her, remembering she loves to look at everything we fly over.

After the captain's instructions, the plane goes down the runway and lifts into the sky. Emily's enamored with the view out the window, unable to pull herself away from all the twinkling lights below. I can't wait to see her reaction when we fly over Vegas with all the twinkling and flashing lights.

The plane hits a pocket of turbulence, and she grabs my leg, trying to steady herself.

"It's okay, gorgeous. Just a little turbulence."

"Sorry, I wasn't expecting it because I was so engrossed in the earth below."

"I'm right here. Squeeze me all you need."

She runs her hand up my thigh and grazes my cock through my pants.

"Except there. Your parents and my sister are sitting around us," I whisper in her ear.

"You said…"

"My leg and my hand are both fine."

"Oh." She giggles.

The rest of the flight is smooth and we're landing before I realize how long we've been in the air. Emily oohs and aahs as we fly over the heart of Las Vegas before landing at Atlantic Aviation in Las Vegas.

"Vegas looks so different up in the air than on the ground."

"That it does."

We exit the plane and I see a black SUV waiting close at the tarmac for us to get into. Our luggage is loaded into the rear as we get into the front of the vehicle.

"Are you telling me where you're taking me or do I have to wait until we get there?"

"Darling, you'll find out in fifteen or so minutes," her mom says as she places her hand on Emily's.

"You're killing me with the secrecy."

"It's all part of the surprise."

"If you say," Emily says, trying to act mad but you can tell that she barely able to contain her excitement.

The SUV pulls in front of the Caesar's Palace and comes to a stop, and Emily freaks out from all the unknowns, from the lack her not planning everything.

"We are staying here?" Kenneth nods at her. "Oh my God. Thank you."

"I notice some cameras around, just be polite and smile," he reminds everyone.

The valet opens the doors for everyone and Kenneth helps Cassandra exit the SUV, and I walk around to help Emily and Addison, letting the ladies walk in front of me as we enter the white stone ancient Roman architecture style building.

As we make our way in the glass doors, Kenneth speaks with the concierge and comes back to hand us our room key and Addison one as well. We walk to the elevators to take us to our rooms.

"This is way too much," Emily murmurs to herself as the doors close to the elevator.

"Gorgeous, nothing is too much for you."

"I'm still trying to come to terms with everything you gave me and did in my name, but all of this… I don't know if I'm ever going to get used to being Kenneth's daughter."

"That is what makes you different from all the other rich and famous' children. You don't expect this every single day. You're humble. Just say thank you and be yourself."

"Easier said than done," she says as we get off the elevator and make our way to the room. Addison's room is in the opposite direction, which is good. I don't have to worry about Addison hearing Emily moan out my name when I have her tangled up in the sheets later on.

"I know. You like to work for what you have and I'm sure you're feeling like it's a handout."

"That's exactly how I feel. I felt that way with you at first, but you squelched that feeling when you told me you loved me."

"I do love you, very much. I understand where you're coming from. I felt the same when the Carlino's helped me, but I realized they weren't doing it to just because they felt bad for me, they did it because they loved me and wanted me to better myself."

"They sound like amazing people."

"They are. I need to take you to meet them.

"You do." She smiles at me.

"I'll put that on my list to do." I smile at her as I slide the key card in the reader and open the door.

"Wow… This room is unlike anything I've been in before…" she trails off while looking around and walks to the window that overlooks the magnificent pool.

I watch her as she turns back around, walking around the room, taking in everything around her. The white and gold décor, the multiple rooms, especially the large king size bed with satin sheets, and the large tub in the bathroom.

She looks gorgeous, even after working all day and flying. I can't wait to see what she looks like in what I picked for her to wear to bed tonight. Even though she looks stunning in nothing, a little satin and lace would be a bow on her gorgeousness.

Emily's phone ringing pulls me from my thoughts and I look at her as she talks to her mom while she walks around the room. She puts the phone down, and looks at me in incredulity.

"Dinner at Nobu in thirty minutes with everyone."

"Sounds good."

"Please tell me I'm not dreaming." She looks overwhelmed

"You're not gorgeous." I pull her into my arms and kiss her forehead, and she rests her head on my chest.

"I love you Patrick."

"I love you too, Emily." She lets out a soft sigh.

"I'd better go clean up. Where's our luggage?"

"Umm. I thought it would be here by—"

"Luggage," accompanies a knock on the door.

"Your luggage is right there," I smirk and open the door.

I pull out a fifty to tip the bellhop and he doesn't take it. "Mr. Reeves took care of everything, sir. Thank you and enjoy your stay at Caesars Palace," the bellhop says as he shuts the door behind him.

Two can play at this game, Kenneth.

Emily

PATRICK PLACES OUR SUITCASES ON THE BED AND I LOOK through what he'd packed. I come across a pale yellow satin and lace negligee and wonder where it came from. I hold the provocative garment up to show him.

"I don't remember owning anything that looks like this."

"You didn't. I bought it today." He grins mischievously.

"Hmm. What makes you think I'd wear something like this?" I try to look appalled.

"I'm sure if I ask nicely you will." Patrick stands beside me, looking sweet and innocent.

"You're probably right. Thank you, it's very sexy." I almost blush.

"No, thank you. I can't wait to see it on you." He pulls me in, kissing me, leaving me weak at the knees.

"I need to freshen up," I say as I step out of his hold. I pick up the clothes I laid on the bed, walk to the bathroom, and get ready.

Twenty minutes later, I walk out of the bathroom and into the bedroom and notice that Patrick has changed into a casual suit, sans a tie. He has the top buttons open, giving a hint of what's hidden behind his suit.

"Mmm. You look spectacular."

"You look pretty handsome yourself." I walk up to him and kiss him on the cheek.

"Addison should be here—" *Knock, knock, knock.* "There she is."

He walks over to the door and Addison's standing there in a red dress that fits her perfectly. She walks in after Patrick moves out of the way.

"Wow, big bro, you clean up nicely." She smiles, teasing. "Ems, I love that dress on you. Blue is your color."

"Thank you. I love your dress. Isn't that the one we got when we went out at lunch a few weeks ago?"

"Yes. I'm glad I finally had somewhere I could wear it without feeling overdressed."

"Are you ready, Emily?" Patrick interrupts our conversation, politely.

"Yes," Addison and I say in unison.

"Good. Your parents are waiting for us." He opens the door and waves us out.

We meet my parents down in the lobby and walk to the restaurant. We are led to a private dining area in Nobu restaurant, which I am glad. I felt as if everyone's eyes were on us as we walked through the restaurant to the semi private area close to the bar, and I would hate to have people watch me while we ate. I'm normal like them, and I wish people would realize that celebrities are people just like them.

"Is this okay, Emily?" Mom asks.

"Yes, it's perfect," I say as Patrick pulls out a chair for me to sit in. Everyone else sits down around me, Mom and Kenneth to my right and Patrick and Addison to my left.

Since everyone likes sushi, we order several different flavors to share. We make small talk as we watch the sushi chef create the dishes we ordered. One by one, the dishes are placed in front of us to eat. The flavors of the sushi are like nothing I've had before. I eat a lot of sushi at home, but these flavors and textures will make me a sushi snob.

After our quiet dinner conversation, our drinks are refilled when they remove our empty plates. I honestly think this is almost the best birthday I've had, but my heart feels a little heavy that Nate can't be here to enjoy this too. I know he's here, though. I can feel him, and earlier I thought I smelled his cologne when we walked into the elevator.

A man comes to the table to talk to Kenneth privately. The man leaves and comes back a few minutes later carrying a box and bags. Another man is following behind him and he pulls a chair up to the table so the first man can set down everything in his hands.

"Thank you, Lee," Kenneth says as he shakes the man's hand, tipping him. "What's a birthday celebration without gifts?"

My eyes go wide. "I wasn't expecting anything."

"That's what makes this fun," my mom says. "Patrick, darling, do you want to go first?"

"Sure. As you know, I donated to the center in your name. Additionally, I'm donating to Veterans Homebound Inc. in honor of your brother." My jaw drops open and I hug Patrick tightly.

"We are also matching the donation," Kenneth says across the table, grabbing my mom's hand.

"I...I don't even know what to say." The tears spill from my eyes. "This will help so many soldiers and their families. Thank you, all of you." I smile.

"Happy birthday, Emily," Addison says as she picks up a box wrapped in blue and white striped paper.

"Thank you." I smile. Carefully, I unwrap the gift, and underneath the wrapping paper is a box. I lift the lid off the box and pull the tissue paper off the gift, a beautiful wooden photo frame. "This is exquisite! I love it, thank you."

"I thought you needed something that would make my brother look a little better." She winks.

"You're funny tonight, Addison."

"Payback, Patrick." She smirks at him.

"Kenneth, darling, can you hand me the bags, please." He nods and hands her the bags. "You know how I am with wrapping, Emily. Happy birthday, dear," she says as she hands me three gift bags.

I set them on the table in front of me and proceed to remove the tissue paper from the big bag. Looking in, I see a larger blue box. Grabbing the box, I slowly open it and sitting in the black velvet is a breathtaking ruby and diamond necklace. I love it. I move to the other bags and find the matching earrings and bracelet. I'm so spoiled.

"Mom, I love the set. Thank you," I say as I reach over and

hug her.

"You're so welcome, darling," she says as she hugs me back.

"I guess I'm up next," Kenneth says as he pulls out an envelope from his inside jacket pocket and hands it to me. "You may open it now."

I carefully open the envelope and pull out the tri-folded piece of paper.

Ms. Emily Kenae Reed Janes,

This notification is to inform you that a trust has been set up in your name for the amount of five (5) million dollars. The full amount is available at your disposal immediately.

If you have any questions, please contact the bank.

Sincerely,

Herbert Dull

President, Reno Bank and Trust

What the hell?

"Um. I don't understand." What the hell does this mean?

"I set up a trust fund for you. You can use the money however you wish," Kenneth bluntly states.

"I don't know what so say. I can't take *five million* from you," I whisper-yell.

"You're not taking it, I gave it to you."

"You worked for the money, I didn't."

"Emily, you're my daughter. Even if I had been around if you were younger, you would have still received the trust. Take it and use it as you wish."

"I can't wrap my head around this," say as I get out of my seat. Dad and Patrick get up too, thinking I'm bolting, but I'm not. I walk around the table to Kenneth and hug him. "Thank you."

"You're welcome, Emily. So very welcome," he says and kisses the top of my head.

"So I can use it in any way?"

"Yes, why?"

"I think I'm going to set up a charity. Patrick and I were talking about it a few weeks ago," I rush out.

"Are you sure that's what you want to do?"

"Yes, absolutely," I say as I walk back to my seat, Patrick assisting me.

"Well, if you're serious, let me talk to my lawyer and accountant. Then we will talk more about setting up a charity in Nate's honor and you can run it how you see fit and hold on to your money."

"You'd do that for me?" I ask in shock.

"Yes, of course. Emily, you are so caring and compassionate. I'm proud that you're my daughter." I know he loves me; my dad loves me.

"Thank you, Kenneth…Dad. That means a lot to me."

"You're welcome." He beams.

"Thank you everyone, I love each and every one of you. This birthday is so special. I thought I would be sad without Nate, but we are honoring his memory in so many ways. For that, I can't thank you enough." I smile at everyone place my hands in Mom's and Patrick's hands, squeezing them gently.

"Happy birthday," they all say in unison and tears spill down my face again. This will be a birthday I'll never forget.

CHAPTER TWENTY-THREE

Emily

I ENJOY TRAVELING, BUT I LOVE SLEEPING IN MY OWN BED... well, Patrick's bed. When I woke up Saturday, I had to ask Patrick if I dreamed everything from dinner. He just chuckled at me and proceeded to make sweet, slow love to me before I showered to spend the day at the spa with Mom and Addison. Then we had room service for dinner. I had no idea what Patrick and Dad did while we were at the spa.

Sunday, we ate brunch and packed up to return to Reno. The flight was fast and I slept the entire ride home. When we got home, even though it was in the middle of the afternoon, I fell back asleep and didn't wake up until Monday morning. The weekend was fun, but exhausting.

Before we came home, we made plans with Addison to visit Mr. Matheson tonight since Addison was going to be there. I kind of know why Patrick won't go by himself, but I'm hoping that by some miracle tonight that everything can be let go. I know it's a long shot, but I'm staying positive.

Work has been slow today since two of my appointments canceled, and I've been watching the clock, hoping it's time for Patrick to pick me up. Another thirty minutes and I'll be out of here. My mind drifts to my plans for the charity if it's something Dad can do. I'll be able to help organizations as well as individuals. I'm excited to hear something back.

A gentle tap at on my door pulls me from my thoughts.

"Hey, gorgeous. Ready?"

"Hey, you. I didn't even realize it was time."

"I'm early. I should have text."

"You're fine. Let me get everything put away and I'll be ready to leave."

"Okay." I hurry up and get everything put away and locked up, and then we walk out the door to the car.

Patrick pulls into the semi empty parking lot that belongs to the rehabilitation center and parks the car in a spot close to the door. I look at the door and see Addison standing by the entrance, waiting on us. Patrick gets out of the car, walking around it to open my door.

"Are you sure you want to do this?" he asks, nervously.

"Yes, thank you for bringing me to meet your dad." I give him a small smile.

"Might as well get it over and done with," he says as he takes my hand.

"Patrick."

"Well, it's how I feel, Ems. I can't control myself when I'm around him. He makes me so mad. I want to punch something or drink until I'm numb," he rushes out, upset.

"I'm here with you; I'll help you get through. Okay? Try to relax a little. Remember Addison will be here too."

"Okay…you're right. Thank you for coming with me," he says and he pulls me into him and kisses the top of my head.

"Cut it out, you two lovebirds."

"Hey, Addison. How are you?" I ask as we get up to her.

"Good, still tired from the weekend though. Thanks for inviting me."

"Anytime."

"Ready to go in?"

"Yes," I say as I smile.

As we step in front of the doors, they automatically open. Addison takes the lead and walks us to their father's room. When we arrive to the room, an older gentleman is dressed and sitting in a chair. Addison knocks on the door and his eyes move to the door.

"Hi, Daddy. You have company today. Patrick is visiting and he brought his girlfriend to meet you." The man doesn't move as Addison speaks, but his eyes do. "Ugh. I forgot my purse in the car. I'll be right back. Patrick, stop being rude."

He shuffles his feet and moves into the room. "Hi, Father. This is my girlfriend, Emily Janes. Emily, this is my father, Harrold."

"Nice to meet you, Mr. Matheson." I smile because I know

he can see me since his eyes moved earlier.

"Emily, go ahead and sit in this chair. I'm going to see if a nurse can bring in another chair so everyone can sit down."

"Okay." I smile at him and he walks out of the room. "Mr. Matheson, I'm going to talk with you for a moment, because I'm sure you can hear and understand me. I know a little about the relationship you have with Patrick. I'm sorry that it hasn't been the best, but I'm sure there are reasons for your actions." I take a deep breath and continue.

"But that's not what I'm going to talk to you about. I wanted you to know I'm not going to judge you. I'm going to tell you how wonderful a man Patrick is. I met him at my community center. His company gave us a donation to help with our programs, and our friendship started there. He came to the community center and spent time with the kids we help and even gave the center a personal donation." I lick my lips, getting moisture back in them.

"He's very compassionate, caring, and very respectable to not only me but everyone around him. I wanted you to know what kind of man you raised. You should be proud of him. He is an astonishing person to know and be around." A tear streams down the man's face. He's heard me and he understands what I'm telling him.

"I look forward to getting to know you. The real you that wrote the letter to Patrick." I smile at him.

His cheek starts to twitch, like he's trying to smile. Patrick walks in the door and notices.

"Emily, did you say something to my father?" Mixed emotions play across his face.

"I did. I gave him my opinions of you."

"Paaa…" Mr. Matheson mumbles out.

"Dad?" Patrick sounds shocked

"Paaa…"

Addison walks into the room and hears.

"Dad! He's trying to talk. I'm going to get the nurse." She runs out the door and comes back with a nurse in tow.

"What happened?" the concerned nurse asks me.

"I sat with him and talked with him while Addison and Patrick were out. I think he was trying to smile too."

"Oh my heavens. Mr. Matheson, I've been praying for you. Looks like God is working on you. Let me get the doctor that's on rounds. I'm sure he'll want to look at you," she says before she walks out of the room

Tears are running down Mr. Matheson's face. He's trying to reach out and Patrick walks over to take his hand.

"Dad, I'm so sorry for the words I've said to you over the years. So, so, sorry," he says as the tears run down his face.

I can't help but to start crying myself. Addison walks over to her brother and father and hugs them both. I hope this a step in the right direction they need to be a family again.

"Hello, I'm Dr. Grace, and I would like to check Mr. Matheson out, if everyone could step outside."

"Of course, Dad, Emily and I are going to go for now. I'll be back to see you tomorrow, okay?" Mr. Matheson tries to smile again and shakes his head. "Addison, I'll call you," he says as he hugs her.

"Bye, Mr. M. It was nice meeting you and I'm sure I'll see you soon." I smile widely at him. "Addison, I'll text you later," I say as Patrick grabs my hand.

We walk to the door, with Addison following us.

"Sounds good. Patrick, I'll text you with what the doctor says."

"Thanks. Love you, sis."

"Love you too."

We walk down the hall, out the building to the car. Once Patrick gets in the car, he loses all control and beings to sob, letting out all the years of anger and pain caused by the lack of relationship with his father. I place my hand on his leg, touching him so he knows he's not alone. He needs this time to purge his body of the emotions he's feeling.

Ten minutes go by and he sits up, pulling a handkerchief out of his back pocket, and wipes his face then blows his nose.

"I'm sorry. I don't even know what came over me. I felt the urge to cry, I needed to cry."

"I understand. Do you feel better?"

"I do. It's hard to explain, but I feel…hopeful. I feel like it's possible to have a healthy relationship with my father," he says with a smile on his face and tears in his eyes.

"That makes me really happy to hear you say that," I say as

I move my arm from his thigh to his shoulder and pull him into a hug.

"Thank you, Emily, for supporting me and not pushing me to go."

"You're welcome. I knew it had to be on your terms."

"I love you, gorgeous."

"I love you too."

Patrick

THIS WEEK HAS BEEN ENLIGHTENING IN SO MANY WAYS. I'VE been spending time with my dad before picking up Emily from work. After Emily gets off in a few moments, we are going to VHI to deliver the donation and to volunteer. To say I'm a little nervous is an understatement. These men and woman sacrificed their lives for their country and I'll never do anything that courageous. I'm in awe that their honor never waned.

I look up and see her walking out of the building with a little extra pep in her step, and I get out of the car, walking to the other side.

"Hey, gorgeous. You look happy."

"Dad just called. He has all the paperwork for me to look at for the charity. It's a go if I want to take control of it!"

"Congratulations," I say as I hug her tightly.

"I'm so excited, but I want to talk it over with you first since

I won't be making money."

"Emily. What have I said?"

"Not to worry about finances," she says as she gets into the car. I shut the door and walk to the driver's side, getting in.

"I make more than enough for us to live comfortably without you working."

"I know. I guess I have the trust fund too."

"You're to only use that on yourself."

"I can use it however I want." She scowls at me.

"I'm serious, Emily. That is *your* money. Please do not spend any of it on me," I say sternly.

"Ugh. Fine." I knew she would see it my way.

"Are we eating before we go to VHI?"

"No. I thought we could eat with everyone there."

"Sounds like a plan."

I put the car in drive and go to the building that houses VHI. The building reminds me of the rehabilitation center Dad is in, and I guess it is the same thing but for the military. I pull into a parking space a little ways from the door so the family members have closer access.

"Ready to meet some amazing people?" Emily asks from the passenger seat.

"Yes, I sure am." I get out and walk around the car, getting the door for her.

We walk into the building and Emily leads me to the office that oversees the operations of the organization.

"Hey, Amy, how are you?" Emily asks as we walk in.

"Emily! Oh, sweetie. It's good to see you. We've missed seeing you around here."

"I know. I've been meaning to come in and volunteer, but everything has been crazy."

"Your mom was in earlier this week with your dad. We had no idea."

"You and everyone else. I'm sorry I'm being rude, Amy, this is my boyfriend Patrick Matheson. Patrick, this is Amy Patton. She's COO of Veterans Homebound Inc."

"Nice to meet you, ma'am."

"Likewise. So are you guys here to volunteer?"

"Yes, and something else," Patrick answers as he pulls out an envelope out of his pocket. "This is being made in the honor of Nathan Janes."

Amy takes the envelope and opens it and her eyes widen as she reads the amount. "Oh, Patrick. Thank you." She walks around the desk and hugs us both. "This will touch the lives of so many people."

"You're so welcome."

"If you don't mind, I'm going to run this to my office and I'll show you where we need help tonight." Tears well in her eyes as she smiles at us.

"Thanks," Emily says before Amy turns around and heads to the back of the room, walking through a door into an office.

"Um, babe, you donated a hundred thousand right?"

"At least. Yes."

"Patrick?"

"Five hundred thousand." Emily's eyes widen.

"Oh my. No wonder she's acted like she did."

"All for a good cause."

"That is so true."

"Okay, Emily and Patrick. I hope you don't mind assisting our soldiers eating dinner."

"Not at all, Amy. It would be an honor," I say.

"You can bring him anytime," Amy whispers to Emily.

"Follow me and I'll get you set up with everything you need." She leads us to the dining room where several people sit at the tables by themselves. "Sit and talk with whomever. Several people in here need assistance with holding utensils or getting their drink. I hope to have enough volunteers and staff to help everyone. Treat them like an adult even though they might not be able to eat like one," she says, then shows us where the special utensils and extra napkins are located.

"I'll be back before dinner starts. Enjoy yourself. Some of these guys have amazing, bone chilling stories to tell."

"Thank you, Amy," Emily says before she walks away. "You ready to try this?"

"Yes, I think so."

"You'll be fine."

She squeezes my hand and walks off to sit with a woman at a table. I notice an older gentleman at the table off to the side where Emily went and I go to him.

"Hello, sir. May I join you?"

"Yes, young feller. What's your name?"

"Patrick. Yours?"

"They call me One-eyed-Charlie, but you can call me Charles."

"Nice to meet you, sir."

"Likewise. Ever been in the military?"

"No, but my father was in Vietnam."

"Ah, yes. I was there too," he starts off. Then continues with a story that I don't know if I'm going to be able to fully understand…

O N THE RIDE HOME, ALL I CAN THINK ABOUT IS THE STORY that Charles told me during dinner. I understand why so many men came back with PSTD from that war. The conditions were deplorable. Today's wars are similar but it seems like we are desensitized to women and children being forced to wear bombs to kill our soldiers.

"Well, what did you think about volunteering?" Emily asks after a period of silence.

"It was eye opening and I feel like it's not enough."

"I know what you mean. The first time I volunteered, I didn't want to leave. There was so much that needed to be done still."

"I agree. I need to decompress after listening to Charles's

recollection of Vietnam."

"Listening to their stories, it's so hard to imagine living like that for even five minutes."

"I know."

"Do you think we can talk about the charity for a little bit after we get home and get out of these clothes?"

"Yes, of course, but I thought it was pretty much decided?"

"You know me. I need to analyze it all."

"True, but I don't want you to even put our finances or anything in the equation. This is all the charity."

"I know. You made that clear the first time."

"Good," I say as I push the button to open the garage door.

"I can't wait to get out of these clothes and into a T-shirt."

"Mmm. I can wait to see you in nothing but my T-shirt on," I say as I help her out of the car.

"Maybe I should put pants on so you're not distracted."

"I'll be good."

"Sure?" she says as she opens the door to the kitchen and hits the button to close the garage door.

"Yes, you need to talk. Sex is on the backburner." I smirk.

"Funny. Help get everything figured out, then I'll make sure you go to bed, pleased."

"Deal."

She sets her purse by the door, walks over to the fridge to get a bottle of water out, and carries it up the stairs. I follow behind her, watching her ass sway in the tight gray skirt she has on. She walks in our bedroom and places the water on her nightstand, then heads to the bathroom to change clothes. A few moments later, she walks out in one of my Johnny Cash T-shirts. While she was changing, I stripped down to my boxers and got into bed.

"I'll be right back. I left my phone in my purse."

"Okay."

She walks out of the room and I can hear her run down the stairs. A few minutes later, I can hear her running back up the stairs and she walks into the bedroom.

"Dad emailed me all the paperwork. Can you please look through it and make sure that it looks like it's a sound plan?"

"Yes."

She hands me the phone and I start reading through the documents. From everything I can see it looks like Kenneth has everything covered. Working with an appointed board is ideal so you can have people from different sectors helping with ideas. The governing of the charity is set up so no one can get money and run with it. If this is what Emily wants to do, it's set up to be very reputable charity.

"Gorgeous, I don't see anything wrong with anything here. If this is what you want to do, do it. Go with it. You'll do great things."

"Thank you, babe. I'm going to put my three weeks in tomorrow, if that's okay with you."

"Yes, of course."

"Fantastic. I'm so excited. Three Friday's and I'll be my own boss."

"That you will be, congrats, gorgeous."

"Thank you for being so supportive of me."

"Always."

"Now to make you happy," she says as she goes under the sheet.

"Oh…"

Her hands pull the fabric covering my cock and her lips replace it. This will definitely leave me pleased.

CHAPTER TWENTY-FOUR

Emily

This day...a day I never imagined would come...my last day at Project Hope. The past three weeks have been a rush of emotions, good and bad. Although I'll no longer be an employee after today, I'm positive it won't be the last time I'll be here. I vowed to make sure that the people of the Project Hope community are provided the services they need.

After training my replacement, Hannah Lancaster, I know she will carry on the same compassion and drive that I did when I was in the Community Outreach Director. For once, I'm grabbing the opportunity in front of me and I'm going to use it to help others.

"Emily, do you need help with anything?" Kelly calls out from inside her office.

"No, I have everything handled. Patrick should be here shortly."

"Just let me know if I need to take you to the tavern."

"Will do."

I get my phone out of my purse and hit send. The phone rings three times and goes to voicemail. *That's odd.* Before I can put my phone back in my purse, it rings.

"Hello?"

"Hey, gorgeous. I ran into a little problem I have two flats on my car. I have Triple A on the way to tow, and I'll meet you at the tavern in less than two hours."

"Alright. I'll have Kelly take me there."

"Sorry, Ems."

"I know, babe. Be careful and I'll see you soon."

"I love you."

"I love you too." He hangs up.

My stomach rolls and feeling of unease comes over me, but I blame it on nerves. I walk to Kelly's office and knock on the doorframe. She looks up.

"Do you mind if I ride with you? Patrick will be late."

"Of course not. I'll be ready to leave here within thirty minutes."

"Sounds good," I say and turn from her doorway, and walk to the gym to say good-bye to a few of the kids I got really close to. I notice Tasha is missing. She's always here from open to close since her mom works at a restaurant.

"Have you seen Tasha," I ask Victor as I walk farther into the gym.

He looks around then at me. "Now that you mention it, I haven't."

"Did her mom call to say she was sick or anything?"

"I'm sure she did since Tasha isn't here. I bet the front office forgot to say something."

"Perhaps. I think I might pull her record and call just in case."

"I'll do it," he offers quickly. "I have the numbers back here. Can you keep an eye out on the gym while I call?"

"Sure." He nods and jogs to his office. I glance and see him on the computer, and I focus back on the gym full of children. A few minutes later, I look back in his office and I see him on the phone talking to someone. I look away, watching the kids, and look back to see him walking toward me.

"I talked to her grandma. Tasha is home with a stomach bug. She should be back Monday."

"Thanks for calling. I was hoping to see her. I guess I will use her as my excuse to visit."

"She is pretty special young woman."

"Are you coming to the tavern tonight?"

"Yes, I'll be there as soon as everyone is picked up." He looks down at his watch. "I need to get them rounded up. Parents will start coming in shortly."

"Okay. See you later."

"Talk to you later," he says before he blows his whistle at the kids.

My eyes prickle with tears as I walk down the hallway, running my fingers along the wall as I walk. I'll never forget this center and the children and staff who make it what it is. I know I made the right choice to leave, but Project Hope will always hold a special place in my heart.

I go to the staff restroom and freshen up. I'm positive I'll be teary eyed at the tavern, but it will be too dark to see my messy face. As I exit the restroom, Kelly passes me.

"I'll be ready in a few."

"Okay. I'll be waiting."

I mentally and physically say good-bye to Project Hope.

KELLY PULLS HER BLUE TOYOTA IN FRONT OF WORKING MAN'S Tavern, and we get out of her car and walk into the bar to my former co-workers yelling, "We'll miss you!" as the smell of fried foods and beer hit my nose.

"Oh my goodness! I'll miss you too." I hug as many people I can.

"Here you go, first drink is on me," Victor comes up beside me with Margarita—one of my favorite drinks.

"Thank you, Victor." I smile at his kindness, then take a sip of the salty sweet mixture.

I walk around the bar, stopping to talk to people as I make my way to sit down at one of the booths that we designated as ours. As I sit down, Victor comes beside the table and brings me another drink.

"I noticed you were getting low."

"Oh, thank you," I say, giggling.

"You're welcome," he says as he walks away, talking to a guy who works at another center.

"Emily! Are you having a good time?" Kelly asks as she occupies the place Victor just was.

"Yes, thank you so much for this."

"You're welcome. Enjoy!" She shuffles off with a drink in hand to talk to other staff members, and Victor comes back to sit down.

"So, are you all set to start your charity?"

"Yes, I believe so. My dad's lawyer helped me get all the legal parts all squared away. We are finishing up writing the procedures and hopefully I can hire a few staff members next week."

"Sounds like you're on it." He smiles, but it looks almost like it's fake.

"I'm trying to be and I hope to be big enough one day to be partners with Project Hope," I say before taking a sip of the fresh Margarita.

"That is very ambitious."

"No." Yawn. "Oh goodness that was rude. As I was saying before I yawned, I want to help everyone. The centers need help too." I take another sip of my drink, hoping the saltiness will awaken my senses.

"You're correct about that." He takes a sip of his beer, keeping his eyes on me as he does.

"Wow, I'm feeling kind of out it. The bartender must have

made this a double." I feel a little dizzy from that last sip.

"Very possible." He smirks as if he knows something. A shiver runs down my spine from the look.

"I hope Patrick arrives soon. I might have to leave my own party early," I say, slightly pouting.

"Want me to take you home?" His eyes light up with the statement.

"Naw, thanks though. I'll be right back, I'm going to freshen up." I stand up and stumble away from the table.

Damn, I'm drunk off two drinks. I look around, not remembering where the restroom is until I see the big neon sign. I clumsily walk in and relieve myself, and wash my hands. Looking in the mirror, I laugh at myself because I'm so toasted.

Pushing on the restroom door, I fall out the door and almost hit the floor, but strong hands catch me. Patrick? I close my eyes because I can't hold them open anymore. He'll make sure I get home. He's trying to talk to me, but I don't understand what he is saying so I just nod my head. I'm lifted off the ground and put into a vehicle that doesn't smell familiar, but I can't open my eyes. I'm so sleepy I must sleep. I can't wait to be home in our bed.

Patrick

FUCK. I HATE BEING LATE. MY NERVES ARE RAW AND EVERY little thing is setting me off—I need Emily—something doesn't feel right. I need to hold her, kiss her, and smell her citrus scent. I look out the glass window in the garage bay and watch as the mechanic tightens the last lug nut on my car. The shop manger calls out my name, letting me know my car was almost ready. I walk to the desk quickly and I pay with a swipe of my card to get me out of this dirty place.

When the mechanic pulls my car around the front of the building, I hop in, and push the gas pedal down to the floor. I need to get to the tavern as fast as I can, screw the police. Weaving in and out of traffic, I make it there in fifteen minutes.

I pull into a parking spot half a block down from the bar, and I walk in the front to see the party is well under way. I look for Emily, but I don't see her, and set my eyes out for Kelly. I find Kelly by the bar, chatting it up with a big man that I'm sure is a regular at the bar.

"Hey, Kelly."

"Patrick! Have you come to steal our girl away already?" she asks with a look of disappointment.

"No, I'm just looking for her. Have you seen her?" I say as I look around the bar again.

"She's over there at the table chatting with Victor." She points over to an empty booth. "Oh, I guess they aren't there now."

"Do you know how long it's been since you've seen her?"

"Twenty-thirty minutes. I'm not sure. I've been chatting and drinking. If she's not in there, I'm sure she's probably powdering her nose."

"Thank you, Kelly."

"No problem," she says before she turns back to the man she was talking to.

I march over to the restroom and wait casually outside the door, waiting to see if she comes out. After fifteen minutes, I know she's not in there, so I return to the bar area and start asking a few people I've seen at the center before.

"Hello, Josh?" He's an AmeriCorps worker that sat at the table with us at the gala.

"Hey, Patrick. How are you?"

"Well, I'm looking for Emily. Have you seen her?"

"Oh, yeah, man. She went out the back door with Victor. People normally go back there to smoke," he says as he points to the back of the building.

"Do you know how long ago?" I rush out.

He closes his eyes briefly in thought. "About thirty minutes ago."

"Thanks, man," I say before I bolt.

I hurry to the hallway where the back entrance is located and slam the door open, running outside in full force. There's no one here, but I see something lying in the middle of the alley. As I get closer, I see that it's Emily's purse.

Fuck.

"Hold on, Emily, I'll find you. Even if it's the last God damn thing I do, I will find you," I yell out in the shaded alley.

My knees give out from under me and I fall down on

pavement. The rough surface bites at my knees and palms as they slam on the weathered pavement. Anger flows through my body, causing violent shivers to take over. I gasp for air, trying to fill my burning lungs. Tears cloud my vision as my mind spins out of control. Taking deep, uneven breaths, air fills my lungs with the oxygen I need and I let it out slowly to regain control of my head and body. I need to focus so I can find Emily.

I wipe my eyes with the back of my hand before standing up, and I pick up Emily's purse from the ground. My gut is telling me that Victor has a part in Emily missing from the tavern. I run back inside the bar, looking for Kelly again. She's not at the bar and I frantically walk around trying to find her. I spot her at the table that Emily was supposed to be at and rush over to her.

"Hey. Do you know where Victor lives?" I say breathlessly.

"Yeah, but I can't give out that information," she slurs out.

"I think Emily is with him. I can't call her because she left her purse." I hold it up to show her.

"Oh. Well, let's do it this way. You know the road the center faces?" I nod. "Go east one block. Turn left and go three blocks. Turn right at the stop sign and his house is in the middle of the block on the right," she says slowly.

"One, three, middle?"

"Yes. Let me know what you find out. I have her belongings in my car," she says as she pats my hand that I placed on the table to steady myself.

"Will do, thanks, Kelly."

Hastily, I make my way out of the tavern and get into my car to the center. As I pass it, I go one block to the east and turn left, and slowly drive three blocks down. I look to the right before turning, I don't see anything, and I turn right and pull in the driveway in front of the house. Getting out of the car, I take the steps two at a time to get to the front door, and I pound on the door and get nothing.

I walk around the house to see if I can hear or see anything and there's nothing, no sound, no people, it's empty. Jogging to my car, I open the passenger door to pick my phone off the seat, and it rings with a text from a number I don't know. Shutting the door, I lean against the car and open the message.

UNKNOWN NUMBER: *I believe I have something you want…and I know you have something I want.*

All the air leaves my lungs. My hands start to shake as I type back a reply.

ME: *Who is this?*

UNKNOWN NUMBER: *Not important. 10 million in non-sequential, unmarked bills. Tomorrow. If not, Emily will make someone a nice sex slave.*

Sex slave? My vision turns red, anger fills my veins.

ME: *You hurt her and I'll kill you myself.*

UNKNOWN NUMBER: *Tsk. Tsk. You can't touch me if you can't find me. You will have until 6 pm tomorrow to contact me to arrange the exchange. If I don't hear from you, she will be sold to the highest bidder at 8 pm.*

Goodbye, Mr. Matheson.

Fuck. My heart hammers in my chest as the blood rushes through my ears; the swooshing of the blood is all I'm able to hear. A few moments pass as reclaim control over my body. I pull my arm to throw my phone, but stop mid motion, realizing it's the only form of communication I have with Emily's abductor. I pound my fist on the roof of my car, instead of trying to figure out what to do next.

Damn it. Who the fuck has her?

As I go through all the options, I have been going through my mind, but I decide my first move needs to be calling Kenneth before I try anything else. I need someone that can think clearly, and I'm positive he will know what we need to do.

"Hey, Patrick? How's it going?" he says in a jovial tone.

"Kenneth, it's Emily. Someone has her. I got a text saying they want ten million or they are going to sell her," I rush out.

"Slow down. What about Emily?" he asks, confused.

"Someone has abducted her," I say, trying to slow down my racing heart.

"What?" he yells into the phone.

"Yes, and they want ten million for her." I try not to stutter out.

"I have that much in the bank; do I need to get it?" His voice is calm.

"I don't know. Let's meet up so we can discuss what needs to be done."

"Okay, where?" I can hear him talking to someone in the background.

"Meet me in the parking garage at CU Gold and we will go from there. That way we are close to the police if we want to get them involved."

"See you there in twenty minutes," he rushes out.

"Later." The phone line goes dead.

I get into my car and drive straight to the office. No one should be there at this time of night, except the cleaning crew. I park in my normal parking spot in the garage, and ten minutes later, Kenneth comes pulling in with his SUV.

"I got here as quick as I could," he says as soon as his window is down.

"You're fine. Here are the texts I received." I hand him my phone so he can read them for himself.

"So whoever has her, knows you well?" He looks at me for answers.

"Possibly. I think it's Victor, the guy she worked with at the center with. I got a bad vibe about him, and I told her she needed to stay away from him."

"If it's him, do you think he would hurt her?" Mixed emotions flashes in his eyes, but he quickly recovers and puts his calm and collected façade back into place.

"I don't know, honestly. This isn't sitting well with me," I answer honestly. "I think he will hurt her if we don't find her soon."

"Let's go to the cops. I hope that they can do this without getting the media involved. Get in my vehicle and I'll drive."

" Okay." I'm numb that this is happening.

I lock up my car and get in. The drive to the police station seems like it takes hours when it's only minutes. Kenneth pulls into spot down from the station. He reaches into the backseat to grab a baseball hat and puts it on.

"Ready?"

"Yeah."

We get out of the SUV and walk into the police station. The inside is busy with activity.

"Can I help you, gentlemen," an older officer calls out behind the wall that separates us.

"Yes, ma'am. I'd like to report a crime," Kenneth calmly tells the officer.

"Okay, sir. Give a few moments and I'll get someone for you," she says before she picks up the phone. After a few moments, she hangs up. "Gentlemen, a detective will be with you shortly."

"Thank you," Kenneth says. "We might want to take a seat."

"I'm good. I can't sit thinking about her being out there somewhere."

I begin to pace around the small waiting room, waiting for the detective to come out and talk to us. After fifteen minutes of pacing, a short, stocky man comes to the counter.

"Gentlemen, follow me please," he says as he unlatches the door for us to come in. He leads us to a room off the waiting area.

"I'm Detective Trees. How can I help you?"

"We are fairly certain that my daughter, Emily Janes, has been abducted. He received several text messages from someone who claims to have her and wants to exchange money for her," he states, pointing at me.

"You are?" The detective looks up at him after writing notes on his notepad.

"Kenneth Reed, her father."

"Wait, you look familiar. Aren't you Ken Reeves?" the detective asks a little sidetracked.

"Yes, I am, but I'm not here as him. I'm here as Emily's father," he straightforwardly states.

A little embarrassed, the detective gets back to his questions. "Does this guy who possible has Emily know who you are?"

"Yes, I'm pretty sure he does. They worked together," I say, making my presence known in this conversation.

"And you are?" Detective Trees smugly asks.

"Patrick Matheson, her boyfriend," I bluntly answer.

"You're the one who received the messages?"

"Yes, sir," I say then slide the phone over to him.

"Mind if I take that?"

"No, do whatever you need to with it."

"Thanks. What time did you notice she was missing?" He holds up the phone, examine the messages.

"Around six thirty. I went to meet her at a tavern because her co-workers were having a going away party for her. Today was her last day with the company. I was late meeting her because my car had two flat tires and I had to call to get it towed to the tire shop."

"About what time was that?"

"Around four. Everything is in my call log, just look at it. I called Emily as well. I wanted to let her know that I was going to be late."

"It's now eight. What took you so long to come in?"

"I went to see if she was at Victor's house but she wasn't. Before leaving there, I received these texts. I called Kenneth to see what we should do because I didn't want to get his name in the news unless he knew about it. Together, we decided to come here."

"Sir, are you sure Ms. Janes and you weren't having problems?" Rage fills me. *You're worthless.* I force the voice out of my head and will myself not to slam my fists onto the table in anger.

"Detective, Emily and I are very happy. We aren't having problems. Please, listen to what we are saying; some psychopath has my girlfriend against her will. Please find her before it's too late." My tone and gruffness take him back a little.

"Hold tight, gentlemen. I'm going to run everything by my chief," he says as he picks my phone up and his notepad.

"Thank you," Kenneth says.

Time goes by slowly and Cassandra texts Kenneth, she doesn't know what is going on yet. As soon as we know something, he is going to call her. I get up from the worn table and pace around the room, thinking of any possible lead or piece of evidence that might give the police a direction to go.

Almost an hour later, there's knock on the door and a younger gentleman comes in the room.

"Hello, gentlemen. I'm Chief Lauer. I went over everything that you gave the detective, and pulled up a few files that have similarities. With that said, this is what I can tell you; there is a known human trafficking ring in the area you believe where Emily is. I have a couple uniforms checking out the houses from previous cases. I'm waiting on a report on the phone number you received text messages from. Mr. Matheson, here's your phone back."

"Should we text him to offer him the money to lure him out of hiding?"

"No, because he could send someone else and not even have Emily with him."

"What can we do?" I ask, wanting to get out of here and find Emily.

"Sit tight, we are working on it."

"Please just find her," I beg.

"We will try our damnedest."

"Thank you, sir," Kenneth says.

The chief leaves the room, and Kenneth calls Cassandra. When he tells her, I can hear her sob through the phone.

"Kenneth, if you need to go be with her, go," I say as I

continue to pace.

"Mike's there with her, and they'll come here when we have more information."

"Okay. I'm not leaving here until they know where she is," I bluntly state as I stand next to him.

"I'll be right here with you," he says as he places his hand on my arm.

I grab my phone off the table and send Addison a quick text.

ME: *Hey. What are you doing?*

I hit send and impatiently wait for her reply.

ADDISON: *Getting ready to go home, why?*

I take a deep breath and hit the phone icon next to her name to call her.

"Hey, what's up? Everything okay?"

"No. Can you come to the police station?"

"Patrick! Are you okay? Is Emily okay? What aren't you telling me?" she rushes out.

"She's…" I take another breath. "Someone has Emily."

"Oh, Patrick. I'll be there in ten, fifteen minutes tops. I love you."

"I love you too." She hangs up.

I go to close my phone, but instead open the photo folder and look at Emily's pictures. She's so beautiful, inside and out. I don't know what I'll do if they can't find her. With each swipe of my finger, the tightness wells up in my throat and I can't stop the tears from falling from my eyes. I need to find her…before it's too late.

CHAPTER TWENTY-FIVE

Emily

*M*Y EYES ARE UNABLE TO FOCUS IN THE DARKNESS OF THE room; my mind is blank and unable to remember how I got here as the smell of decay and urine assault my nose. The last thing I remember is having a few drinks at the bar and talking with Victor, but after that, everything is black.

Muffled crying beside me tells me I'm not alone, but I don't know who else is here or how many, wherever here is. I try moving my hands, but they're bound in front of my body, as well as my legs. I close my eyes, trying to remember something about how I got here and my mind fades to Victor. Did Victor bring me here?

A loud scuffling noise in another part of the building alerts me that someone is coming. I don't know if I should pretend to be asleep or I should say something in case it's someone, Patrick, looking for me.

I stay quiet because I have a gut feeling I'm not going to like who this is. A blinding light from a flashlight hits my face before

I have the chance to close my eyes.

"Good, you're awake," the voice says behind the light. "I was wondering when you'd come to."

He flashes the light away from me, shining it on the shivering bodies around me. I gasp before I can stop myself, and he shines the light back on me.

"Yes, I knew where Tasha was all along, but I wasn't going to tell you that. She's worth a lot of money. Not as much as you, though," he says as he moves the light off me and onto a table with candles on it.

"Why are you doing this, Victor," I say as my voice shakes.

He takes something out of his pocket and walks over to the table, lighting the candles. The soft glow of the candles dimly lights the room, and my eyes slowly adjust to my surroundings.

"Because I know that Patrick will come through with the money, or your father will if he doesn't. I figure one of them has ten million at their disposal."

"I don't even know what to think or say because that's crazy!" I rush out.

"Not at all. An actor worth hundreds of millions and a CFO worth tens of millions and I have something they love and want to protect. So I'm sure I'll get the money later today."

"This behavior isn't like you. What did they do you to make you this way?" He sneers with disgust at my question.

"If it wasn't for Patrick, Emily, you would have been with me. But Patrick had to whip his money and dick out and you were all over him. Now, I'm taking something of his, money or you. Either way, I'll get paid."

"Victor, I don't know how you came up with all of that. You're a nice guy and all, but I didn't feel the same way you did. Patrick isn't like that at all…and I never date co-workers…"

"It doesn't matter now, does it? You're here, and if something happens and the two men you depend on in your life don't come through, I have a few bidders that would love a piece of you, and will pay top dollar."

"What do you mean?"

"Sex slave, Emily. You will be theirs to fuck whenever they want. Mmm, what a fine lay you'll make with your firm breasts and tight little ass."

"Noooo! You can't do this, Victor? Why are you punishing me?"

"You shouldn't have turned me down, we could have been really good together," he says as he runs his finger along my jaw and down my neck to my cleavage.

"So you're selling all of us into sexual slavery? We aren't yours to sell!" I yell out.

"Ah, but other countries don't care about that. What these men care about is fresh meat. Virgin meat," he says as he licks his lips.

"I'm not a virgin. How can you even sell me?" I glare at him, looking for answers.

"Beauty. I have a couple buyers who like your looks, and a

couple of others fuck anything with a tight hole..." he trails off.

"What can I do to make you change your mind?" I plead for answers.

"End it with Patrick," he coldly states.

I freeze in place. Not having Patrick in my life would be devastating.

"How could you even ask that of me?"

"I want him to feel the pain that I feel," he spits out as he kneels down in front of me.

"I'm so confused. Why don't you just keep me for yourself, then?" My head is unable to process his words, his hatred for Patrick.

"Money...that's all you're worth to me, now," he sneers.

"Even if I did end it with Patrick, you still would sell me?" I question, trying to make sense of everything.

"Yes," he says as his cold brown eyes stare at me.

He takes his hand and runs his fingers down my face to my collarbone. His fingers play with the lace on my blouse and dips behind it, fondling my breasts. "Mmm. Maybe I'll just have to have a taste of you before I let you go for good."

"Please, no, Victor," I beseech, squirming away from him

He yanks me up by arm and kisses me hard. I feel nothing as bile threatens to come up, and he pulls away angrily. Backhanding me with his right hand, he throws me back on the floor.

"You're such a cocktease. Always teasing me with those stares and touches."

"I promise you, I wasn't. I'm sorry it looked like that." A faint ring of a cell phone stops him from answering. Victor digs around in his pants pocket and pulls out a cell phone and smiles.

"Looks like your daddy and boyfriend went to the police and they are sniffing on the wrong trail. So I'm sure they will be texting me soon with the money delivery," he says, laughing. Chills run down my sore spine because I know this isn't going to end well for someone.

"I'll be back in a bit, my little bitch. I have some errands to run before tonight's bidding starts." He blows out the candle and darkness surrounds me once more.

My only hope is that someone finds us soon…

Patrick

I SENT ADDISON HOME FROM THE STATION A FEW HOURS AGO to shower and get some rest, and she said she'd return if new leads come in. She's upset that I wasn't going home and doing the same, but I refuse to leave. I don't care if I haven't showered or changed clothes in almost two days, neither has Emily, and I won't rest until I can do so with her in my arms.

Twenty hours after reporting Emily missing, the police might have a possible lead on where she is, but they have to go through the proper chains of command to get a warrant to investigate the lead. We don't have time, because it's getting close to 6 pm. Ken and I overheard where the house is located. From what I can gather, it's a known house for human trafficking, but has been vacant in the past months.

The house is located on the Southside of the city. Ken and I tell the detectives that check in on us often that we are going out for some fresh air and decide that we are going to check this place out on our own. The heat outside leaves me almost breathless as we exit the police station, and the unrelenting sun is beating down. I hope it's a sign that we are going to find Ems. We get in his SUV and head to the closest home repair store for a few supplies.

Ken buys a few things in the store; crowbar, hammer, baseball bat, and he had a Taser in his vehicle already, which will come in handy if we do need to break in. I'm positive that Victor that has her, but I don't have any hard evidence.

We leave the store without drawing attention to ourselves, get in Ken's SUV, and drive south. The area isn't far from where we are, maybe a fifteen minute drive, and it's close to the interstate. He drives onto the interstate and speeds to the exit, signaling to quickly exit the interstate five minutes later.

As we turn onto a side road, the area looks run down with old houses that have boarded up windows and roofs that are missing or caving in. After twenty minutes of slowly driving up and down the side roads, Ken takes another right. He drives slowly down the road and a house that looks like it's had someone in it recently sticks out.

"Ken, I think that's the house on the right. Look how the weeds are trampled down around the garage and the brush is flattened by the porch."

"Yeah, none of the others have noticeable signs that someone's been around the property."

"I wonder if we can find some way to look in without being seen," I ask, looking at the house for any other signs of activity.

"Possibly. Let's look at the other houses down this street," he states as he continues driving down the street at a slow rate of speed.

"Yeah. Then we can go down the block to the right and park, then come around from the backside of the house."

"Okay. Sounds like a plan," he says as he slowly drives down the road, looking at the houses meticulously as he drives by.

He turns the corner and parks his SUV on the right side of the road. From where he parked, you can't see the house in question, but from the alley that runs behind this house, you can. We get out quietly and Ken manually flips the lock button before shutting his door.

As we slowly walk onto the property, the brush and weeds snap under foot as we walk around the vacant house, and I hope that they can't hear the snapping stems echoing around us. Pausing to listen, I don't hear movement inside of the house, so I try to find a window or something open to look into the house.

There's a crack in the side window panels, but I'm not able to see inside of the house. The crack is big enough I can hear someone inside talking. A few minutes of silence go by and I hear her voice. Emily. She's in there, and I can tell she is scared. I need to get Kenneth, and I walk to where he's at on the other side of the house, thinking of a plan in my head before I make it to him.

"She's in there and I'm positive that Victor is in there with her," I whisper to him.

"Do you think he has a gun?" he murmurs back.

"More than likely. He's probably expecting the cops or even us."

"How do you want to do this?"

"I'm not sure, because I don't know if there's anyone else in there with Victor."

"Maybe we should call the police and wait for them?" he asks, worried.

"I don't think we have the time." I look down at my watch. "It's almost five thirty, and he wanted a call by six."

"Okay. Let's go back to the SUV, call the cops, and grab the weapons. We need to rush the house. I think that's the only way we are going to be able to do it."

"That works for me." We jog back to the SUV and I grab the baseball bat while he calls the police, letting them know that we've found her.

"They said they dispatched some officers to the location and not to enter on our own."

"I can't promise that. If I hear something going on, I'm going in."

"I'll be right there with you."

"Let's go," he says as we run back to the house.

CHAPTER TWENTY-SIX

Emily

THE STEADY TAP OF VICTOR'S FINGERS ON THE WOOD TABLE TOP is frazzling my nerves. He's antsy and what nerves I have left are quickly zapping away with his unease. I have no idea what's going to happen to me or the others that are being held captive in this shack. The soft cries of the girls break me more and more with each passing minute, I wish I could comfort them, but the bindings on my arms and legs prevent me from moving.

A silence takes over the room, like the calmness before a storm, and I refuse to let myself believe this is the end of my freedom, my life…our lives. I take a deep breath, trying to remain as calm as I can.

"Fuck this. Come on, little slut. Let me show you what you'll need to get used to taking whenever your master requires it."

All the air rushes out of my chest.

"No! She's a child. Don't take her, take me," I breathlessly yell as he pulls a young girl lying by Tasha up by her ponytail.

"Trying to be their savior, Emily? I think it's a little too late for that, but since you're willing now—"

Splintering wood echoes through the room as pieces of the door come flying into the room, allowing sunlight to filter into the room, and I see Patrick rushing through the door with a baseball bat in his hand. Victor is stunned for a moment and scrambles for the gun on the table beside the candles. Before he can fully clutch the gun, Patrick knocks him to the floor with the bat under his jaw, choking him. The gun falls out of reach of Victor's hands

Behind Patrick, my dad enters the door, carrying a crowbar, and looks around the room before he spots me. He rushes over me and tries to get the bindings off my hands and arms. He frees my hands; I look to Patrick and think everything is under control…until he screams out in agony.

Everything goes to slow motion; Victor is wielding a knife and he stabs Patrick repeatedly until the hold on the bat slips from his hands. The wooden bat falls to the ground with a reverberating thud. Dad turns around quickly, swings the crowbar, and hits Victor in the head with a sickening crunch as Patrick slumps down on him, leaving him incapacitated.

"Patrick?" I scream. "Patrick!" I yell as Dad rolls him onto his back. Using the bloody crowbar, he moves the knife from Victor's reach and ties his hands together with the bindings that were on my wrists.

"Emily, put pressure on his wounds," he says as he helps me with the ties on my legs.

"I can't see where the bleeding is coming from," I say as I frantically look for the wounds. The faint sounds of sirens are in the distance and I pray there's an ambulance with the police that are on their way.

"Just press where you think they are."

I nod and press down where I can. Patrick hasn't moved since Victor stabbed him and I don't even know if he's alive. I watch his chest, watching for his breathing and I see the slow rise and fall. He's still with me.

"Patrick, stay with me, babe. Help will be here shortly." Tears run down my face, and everything around me starts to blur.

"Police! Hands up," shouts a male officer as he enters the room. I refuse to move.

"Ma'am, I said hands up," he yells at me.

"Sir, she was the one that was held captive and he was stabbed while trying to get her out. Please get multiple ambulances here. There are other girls here and I don't know if they are hurt or not. This guy over here is the one that had them…" His words fade out and all I concentrate on is the slow rise and fall of Patrick's chest, which gets slower and slower and stops.

"Nooo! Patrick, please don't leave me."

"Ma'am, can you please move. I'm a Medic," a guy says as he comes in from nowhere. I look at him, not understanding. "Ma'am, you need to move." Dad places his arms around me and picks me up, and pulls me away from Patrick.

"No, put me down. I need to cover his wounds," I yell out,

trying to kick out of my dad's hold."

"Emily, the medics are helping him now. You need to get looked at."

"He's coding," the medic yells at the woman with him.

"What does that mean?" I run over to them after getting free of my dad.

"Ma'am, please get back so we can save him." They rip his shirt off and one medic starts doing compressions while the other places pads on his chest and hooks him up to a machine.

"Clear!" The machine goes through all these prompts and I hear, "Shock is advisable." The medic presses the button. "Shocking now." His body jolts up, and the medics start doing CPR again.

"I got a pulse, let's load him up." I look at Patrick with a tube in his mouth and wires on his chest.

"I'm going with him," I yell as they put him on a stretcher and wheel him.

"Ma'am, I have questions for you. We'll get you to the hospital once we get things figured out here," the officer says as he grabs my arm. My dad comes up beside me and puts his arms around me.

"Ems, we will get there as fast as we can. We would only be in the way right now and we need to help the girls that are here."

I lean into him, as everything around me starts to spin... Dad gently places me on the floor. I hear a little voice call out my name.

"Ms. E…"

I lift my head up and turn around.

"Tasha, come here sweet girl."

"Ms. E., it is you. You're okay," she rasps out as she runs over to me as the police let her go. "I was so afraid, Ms. E. Somehow I knew you would save me. I love you."

"I love you too, Tasha." I hold the frightened child in my arms tightly as I pray that Patrick doesn't leave me behind, too.

CHAPTER TWENTY-SEVEN

Emily

*T*HE RAIN GENTLY TAPS AGAINST THE WINDOW IN MY OFFICE, creating a haze over the mountains it falls upon. I start thinking about how much my life has changed in the past year, especially the past six months. I've taken so many things and people, for granted, and I ended up losing those things that meant the most to me. I have so many emotions rolling through my mind today. I go back and re-read what I wrote today.

> *Life without you is harder than I'd ever imagined. Our special moments together have helped me through the past few weeks without completely breaking down. I think you'd be proud of how I'm doing. There are so many things that I miss about you today. Our phone calls, our texts, our stupid jokes I'm sure no one got but us. I'm positive you are looking down on me and keeping me safe, as you always did.*
>
> *The clouds seem to be crying along with me today, they miss your smiling face as well. What I'd do to hear*

your voice one more time…one more time to tell you how much I love you, how proud I am of you. I guess that day will come when it's supposed to.

I never thought I would be here without you, to live life without you, but I'm trying to make the best of it I can.

I miss you today and every day.

Love—

"Ems?"

"Yeah, in here," I holler out as I finish writing the last bit of my journal entry.

"Oh, sorry, gorgeous, I didn't know you were writing." He's scent invades my space as he enters the room with the cup of coffee in the cup he bought me on our first date in his hand, and he places it on my desk.

"You're fine. I was reflecting for a few moments before I start reading through the grant applications that we've received so far." I take a sip of the rich dark roast he has perfected making. "I can't believe it's been six months since he's been gone. It seems like yesterday," I say as I look at the picture of Nate and me on my desk.

"Is writing to him still helping you through the process?" Patrick asks as he sits down in his office chair. I love that this office is big enough for both of us.

"Yes, very much and I think being part of the Nathan Jane's Foundation will help too." I smile as I turn my chair to face him.

"Sounds like you and your parents will do some amazing things for very deserving people."

"You too, right," I ask before I take a sip of my coffee, because I want him to be a part of the foundation too.

"Um…" Puzzlement fills his face.

"I need a numbers guy and I know of an extremely talented, well educated, hardworking CFO I would love to have my way with at this very moment," I say, licking my lips.

"Oh, you do?" He smirks.

"Yes. Please, Patrick, please say yes," I beg, slightly pouting.

He looks at me for a few moments, debating on his answer. Our eyes meet, and I know his answer.

"Yes."

"I love you, Patrick," I say as I jump out of my chair and sit on his lap, hugging him.

"I love you too, gorgeous." He pulls my face down to his and kisses me with the same passion of our very first kiss, leaving me breathless. "As much as I don't want to, I need to get ready to go into work and I guess put my notice in." He slightly winces as he adjusts his still healing body in the chair.

"Are you sure you've had enough time to recuperate?" I ask as I get off his lap.

"Yes, I'm fine as long as I don't overdo it, and I won't. Kristin won't let me."

"You know her heart is going to break when you resign," I say as he stands up.

"No, I think she'll finally retire. She's been there for thirty plus years," he states as he walks out of the office, with me following closely behind him.

"She could always come to work for us if she doesn't want to retire yet."

"Now that's an excellent idea. I'll work on that while I'm there too." He smiles.

"She would be a huge asset to the foundation. Thank you."

"For what?" he questions me.

"Being amazing." I put my arms around his neck, gently snuggling up to him.

"You're the one that's amazing," he says as he lifts my chin, kissing me again. "I need to get going." I pout.

"I know. I'll drive you when you're ready to leave."

"Sounds good." He kisses my forehead. "Want to join me in the shower?"

"I thought you'd never ask…"

"Funny. I'll try to behave." He winks.

"You have to, mister."

"I know." He pouts, knowing he has to restrain from sexual activity until his next doctor's appointment, and he grabs my hand, leading me to the shower.

I turn the water on, brushing my teeth as it warms up. We both get in the shower; washing each other's bodies, teasing each other as we do. Quickly, our time in the shower runs out and we rinse off so we can get out and dress.

"Hey, baby, are you okay?" I ask Patrick as I put my clothes on. He looks in deep thought.

"Yeah, trying to decide if I want to wear a tie or not."

"Go without."

"Okay." He smirks as he finishes buttoning his white dress shirt.

"Are you ready then?" I ask as I slip on my flip-flops in the closet.

"Almost. I need to put my shoes on."

"Black loafers?" I hold them up for him to decide.

"Those work. I won't have to bend over a tie them."

"I know. That's why I suggested them." I beam.

"Brains and beauty…" he says and kisses me on the nose.

"I can say the same about you too, handsome. Let's go. I'll treat you to Starbucks."

"We can go to Starbucks but I'm buying."

"Deal."

"I love you, Emily."

"I love you too, Patrick."

He grabs my hand and we walk downstairs together. WE get into my SUV as it's easier for him to get in and out of right now, and I put the vehicle in reverse and start our journey to his office. I hope that everything goes smoothly with his resignation.

My eyes focus on the road before me, but my thoughts drift to all the amazing things that the foundation is going to accomplish, and I'm going to have the complete support of my family behind me…including Patrick.

I know that Nate is with us every step of the way too.

Thank you so much, Nate, for watching over us… I love you.

Patrick

$\mathcal{T}$WO WEEKS AND TWO DAYS AGO, I DIDN'T KNOW IF I WOULD ever see Emily's face again, or even this office. To live after being stabbed in the lung, multiple times and being millimeters from hitting my heart… it will be an interesting story for my children, our children, one day.

My mind goes to the events of that Saturday in that hell hole. I can feel the pain of Victor stabbing me and everything around me slowly goes dark, and then I wake up in the hospital, unable to move. I was scared, but once I saw Emily, her family, and my sister, I knew I had the support to get through whatever lay ahead of me, us.

I ended up only spending a few days in the hospital. Once I became fully aware of where I was and what had happened, the shock wore off and I was able to move my body. Victor was able to stab me three times before Kenneth hit him with the crowbar, and luckily for Kenneth, he didn't kill him. I don't think he could have lived with himself if he did. He's not that kind man.

While searching Victors' place, the police found that all the girls that were from Project Hope that had ran away weren't actual runaways. They were victims of kidnapping by Victor. So far four of the eight girls have been located and reunited with their families. Emily and I have vowed to assist the police in any way that helps them find the remaining missing girls.

According to the doctors, Victor should make a full recovery. He will be standing trial for the thirteen counts of kidnapping and human trafficking and one count of abduction, and I will be in that courtroom every single moment of that trial to make sure that he gets everything he deserves. I hope by the time they're finished with him, he wishes he were dead.

That's cold hearted of me, but what he did to Emily and all of those other girls is beyond fucked up and he needs to pay. I'm sure he's someone's bitch in prison when he gets there.

"Are you sure you're ready to be here?" Emily asks as she pulls me back to the present.

I pull Emily into me before she leaves, to do whatever she's doing today, and I inhale her citrus scent, letting it consume me, calm me.

"Yes, I feel pretty good and I need to finish a few pending projects so I can leave the company on good terms. They've been good to me for the past six and half years, so I want them to know I appreciate them giving me a chance when they did."

"You're an honorable man, Mr. Matheson."

"Thank you, I will take that as a huge compliment coming from you."

"Oh, it is." She smiles and I kiss her. "I'll see you at four. If you need to come home before then, call me."

"I'm sure I'll be fine, Ems, Kristin will make sure."

"I love you, babe."

"I love you too," I say as I kiss her again before she leaves my office.

I sit down and start flipping through all the papers Kristin has placed on my desk for me to go through, and I chuckle because I'm going to miss her organization. Emily is in no way this organized with my stuff, her stuff, yes, crazy organized. I turn on my computer monitor and pick up my phone to listen to voicemails while my login screen on my computer pops up.

There's nothing important in my voicemails, and login to my computer and wait for the startup screen to load. There's a soft knock at the door and I look up to see Kristin entering the room.

"Patrick, it's so good to see you back to work. You're looking a lot better since I saw you at home last week," Kristin says as she smiles warmly at me.

"Thank you. It feels good to be back, but before I make anything official, I would like to speak to you…off record."

"Oh? Let me shut the door."

"Thank you." I stand up and sit down in a chair in front of my desk, waiting for Kristin to sit beside me. "Emily has asked me to be the CFO at the foundation…and I have accepted. I'm putting in my resignation today."

She gasps and covers her mouth, not saying anything.

"Do you think it's a good move? I'm asking you not as my assistant, but as the woman who basically has been a mother figure to me for the past four years."

She looks at me, tears welling in her eyes. "I think it's the perfect move I knew the moment that I saw you and Emily together that she's your forever, Patrick. Take the opportunity and make it amazing like you did here."

I place my hand on hers and squeeze it. "Thank you, that means a lot to me." I clear my throat. "What would it take to convince you to come and work for us at the foundation?"

This time she can't even move, she's shocked I'd even ask.

"Well?"

She takes a deep breath and a smile adorns her face. "I'd be honored. I would love to work for you… I was thinking maybe it's time to retire, but I'm not ready to. I guess it's on to our next adventure." She smiles.

"You are so correct. Well, I guess I better get busy and get everything in order for our departures. Give me your letter whenever you're ready. I'm turning mine in later today."

"Will do, Patrick. Thank you for thinking of me."

"You're the only person I thought of. You're amazing at what you do and you keep me in line."

"I try." She gets up, and I get up with her and pull her into a hug. "Thank you for everything you do."

She blushes slightly. "You're welcome. If you need anything, please let me know. Make sure you don't overdo it, or Emily will be mad at us both."

"I know. I got the same lecture before she left."

"I'll let you get to work and will talk to you around lunch time if not before."

"Sounds good. Thank you, Kristin."

She smiles and nods before she shuts my office door.

I click on the email icon and browse the hundreds of new emails that are sitting in my inbox. One title piques my interest and I click on the email to expand the whole message.

> *Hey Patrick,*
>
> *Everything is a go with CUGC's donation to Veterans Homebound Inc. The check is ready to be processed, so please reply when you would like Kane to ink it so you can deliver to the center. A few of the board members would like to be present when you present the check.*
>
> *Thanks,*
>
> *Christopher Jules*
>
> *VP, Accounting*

That couldn't have come at a better time, one less thing I'll have to worry about tying up before I leave. I reply quickly to Christopher.

> *Good morning, Christopher.*
>
> *Let's schedule a presentation for next Thursday.*
>
> *I'll get with Amy and make sure that works for VHI.*
>
> *I'll let you know if plans change.*

Thanks,

Patrick

I click send and sit back in my chair, thinking about all the changes that have happened in this year. This time last year, I would have never guessed that I would be in a committed relationship with an amazing woman, working on a stable relationship with my father, and leaving the company I've loved working at for the past six years.

The tormenting voice of my father no longer provokes me, fills me with rage, as that's all in the past and will stay in the past. Thinking of the past, I realize that I need to take Ems to meet the Carlino's. They gave me a chance when I had given up on myself, and I know they would love Emily and the work we are going to do for people.

I'm so thankful to be alive, to be able to give back. Kristin summed it up perfectly; it's time for our next adventure. I smile as I think about my next adventure with Emily and I know might be rushing things, but when I see something I want, I go for it. I want Emily for the rest of my life, it's time to make her mine… forever, and on to the next chapter in our lives, together.

Who knows what will happen next, fate has a crazy way of popping into your life when you least expect it…

Unwanted or not.

EPILOGUE
Addison

THE LOVE THAT PATRICK AND EMILY HAVE IS ENOUGH TO MAKE a person gag, seriously. Always touching each other, kissing… get a room you two. Kidding. I couldn't be happier for the two of them. I'm so glad that Emily is in Patrick's life…all of our lives. She's the sister I've always wanted, and I know she's the reason my family is together.

Dad's doing wonderful and the doctors are even talking about putting a plan in place that includes him returning home within the next four to eight weeks. I can't be more excited for him. Patrick has been visiting him regularly in hospice and it makes my heart swell with happiness that their relationship is growing.

Patrick and Dad agreed that it's time for the house to have some improvements, and together they redesigned the house so it will accommodate Dad with a wheelchair or a walker. I've been staying with Patrick and Emily at their house while the construction is underway, and I don't know if I ever want to leave… Well, except for hearing them bump uglies part makes me want to run for the mountains. Yuck.

Nineteen almost twenty is too young to be an aunt... Emily and I need to have a lot more fun before she becomes a mom. Thankfully, she spares me the details. Speaking of Emily, she just text me. I gotta go. Time for lunch before I head to class. Geniuses can't learn on an empty stomach.

Later gators.

ACKNOWLEDGEMENTS

I WANT TO THANK THE PEOPLE IN MY LIFE WHO ALLOW ME TO do this for a living: My husband, **Adam**, thank you for not throwing me out on the days I forget where the shower is located and how to cook dinner. I appreciate you more thank you'll ever know. My children, **Hunter** and **Dane**, no, you cannot read this… Not until you're 30.

Delisa Lynn, I swear we are related… My sister from another mister, you rock. <3

Donna Dull, thank you for getting my weirdness with covers and blurbs—you are amazing.

Victoria Escobar, thank you, thank you for not killing me. I know I wait until the last moment to send you my files.

Connie Gorman, Christina Concus, and **Marnie Warren**, without you…my words would a jumbled up mess on the pages.

My personal assistant, **Samantha Maren Carpenter**, thank you for your undying support, shares, pimping…the list goes on and on. Thank you so much for not giving up on me and my crazy ways.

This story wouldn't be what it is without my **beta readers**: T.J. Loveless, Dulice Currier, Delisa Lynn, Christina Concus,

Tanna Britt, Kelsey Fischer, and Andrea Collier. I appreciate all your help and insight to make *Unwanted Fate* what it is today. Thank you for your kind words and the brutal truth.

And the most important thank you goes to my **readers**, thank you.

ABOUT THE AUTHOR

a. Gorman was born and raised in a small community in Central Indiana. She left the slow moving life of the country for the fast-paced city life. After spending twelve years in the city and becoming a mother to two wild and crazy kids, she chose to move back to the peace and quiet of the country after marrying the man of her dreams and gaining three more children.

As an avid reader, A. never set out to be an author since she's a full-time editor for several incredible authors. However, after editing one day, a voice started talking to her and talking and talking. She decided to sit down and write what she had to say, and it turned out she had a lot to say. Then that one voice turned to two, and another story came to life. Not believing that anything she was writing was publishable, she asked a few friends to critique her manuscript…and now she's the proud author of the Their Sins series, with several more series and standalones planned.

When she's not corralling their five kids and two dogs or out in their garden, you can find her at her desk editing or writing her next novel with a cup of coffee and classical music cranked up on her iPad. While she loves reading, A. is addicted to all things British, coffee, and gummy bears—in no particular order.

Social Media

Twitter: https://twitter.com/AuthorAGorman
Facebook: https://www.facebook.com/AGormanAuthor
Goodreads: https://www.goodreads.com/annagcoy
Website: http://authoragorman.com

Made in the USA
Columbia, SC
20 April 2024

34672840R00196